CW00865099

The Cloud Palace

Copyright © 2017 Orlando Cubitt

All rights reserved.

Cover Image by Orlando Cubitt

THE CLOUD PALACE

by

Orlando Cubitt

CONTENTS

PROLOGUE

On the back of a postcard I wrote:

Dear ---
If this seems flippant, if this reads as fiction, if this seems like a lie: know that this is true. This happened last year, and, although some of the names have been changed most haven't. This is heartfelt and true. This is fact and all of this happened. And I need to tell you. Because I can't tell anyone else. And I miss you. This all started with you.
   Sort of.

   In my messy scrawl I'd run out of space to explain anymore; it was badly written and it reeked of desperation. I looked at the young shoeless hawker, perhaps six or seven years old, trying to sell postcard packs of twelve sunsets and called him back over. I had a lot more to write yet. I paid the boy for all that he had left in his basket, I tore up my first attempt and started to write...

CHAPTER ONE - THE MISSING

I received the first call at about 7:30 that evening.

-

A couple of hours earlier I'd tried cutting the greys out of my hair. I had cut a patch down to the scalp so ended up taking the clippers to my hair and buzzed in an undercut. In the mirror I concluded that I looked moronic but less grey. Then I'd hurriedly dried a shirt and washed for the third time that day. It was humid in autumn. Under the cold water I had felt alright, but towelling off I had known that a fourth wash still wouldn't have been enough, whatever it was had been burnt in with time. I made a wish that I owned some better hair, and perhaps some nicer clothes. The grunge era was the only time I'd gotten away with my appearance. I was facing exhaustion.

-

That evening I took the bus instead of cycling.

We'd had some time out for the last couple of weeks, so I

stopped at the off license and bought some wine for her to say sorry and out of nerves bought a can of Polish for the walk. There were some flowers that looked perky growing on the edge of her road, I picked them and wrapped them in the paper bag from the wine – they looked nice – I'd made a real effort.

I put the beer can down half finished at the bottom of her block. Someone would drink it. I popped some gum in and chewed for the best.

She buzzed me up and I'd just got to her door when my phone started ringing. No one calls anyone anymore, and it was a number I didn't recognised, so I left it.

She opened the door as it was still ringing and I made a scene of turning it on to mute and putting it in my pocket so she knew all my attention was on her.

Her teeth were a little bit crooked, and she had a fine scar that ran from her ear to her neck, her face told her own story in a way that meant she was beautiful. Truly beautiful you know, instead of just pretty. Real beauty is always a bit scarred.

Her flat was small but she'd made it her own. I felt special there. You could look out over the London as the city fizzed with people getting buzzed-up into their lovers flats on this balmy night.

Her place was once ex-council but now an example classical modern. Music was playing on her laptop – I hadn't heard it before but it was good. I liked everything about this girl. Every new thing she introduced me to I found to be amazing. I'd fallen and I knew it, and I think she knew it too. We kissed.

How was your day?" I ask her as she turns away from me and leaves me at the doorstep.

"Good, you?" she is on tiptoes as she walks away, no socks on. She isn't ready.

"Yeah good" I say.

"I'm going to have a bath, you can open the bottle." And she disappears into the bathroom.

Her bath must already have been run. I could hear her slip into it. Her clothes hanging off the back of the door meant I could half see into it. She gasps as she goes under. I hear the water fall on her, her breath as she comes back up. I imagine being in there, distract myself by screwing the bottle open and I poor myself a big glass and neck half of it, I'll sip the rest I tell myself , don't get too drunk before she's out of the bath.

The phone goes again. I mute the call. Then it rings again. The music from her laptop is still playing, I pick out a lyric "I love, love you like the first time baby". Singing it back now it sounds shit but I remember it – an earnest torch song with a house beat.

A fourth time. I answer it.

"Hello?" I say, never very good on the phone.

"Hello is that Matthew? Matthew Nagel?" A very polite woman, upper class accent, British.

"Yeah, hi? Who's this sorry?" I ask whilst I'm thinking about her in the bath.

"Hello, this is Diana, Johno's mother." The voice is more familiar now she gives me her name. But she sounds older and her voice more formal and reserved than when I would last have spoken to her a long, long time ago. But instead of saying anything meaningful I just come out with:

"Oh , er, hi." I say.

"You remember me, you were sick on our dog at Johno's birthday." Says Diana.

Johno's birthday was 20 years ago, one of the two last times I'd seen him. His parents had hired a village hall. A lot of us drank for the first time that night. Most of the boys had been sick, someone was sick on the dog that had walked into the toilets to eat the sick off the floor. Sick on sick on sick.

"Yes, I remember, I'm sorry about that. Look I'm kind of in the middle of things right now."

There's another gasp from the bathroom. She sounds half

in ecstasy, could I ever move her like this water does. I get nervous how I'll perform that night. What if the sex isn't perfect?

"Look this isn't about the dog." Says Diana.

"Can you call me back tomorrow." I ask

"Johno and you were close..." starts Diana. I go to hang up. I want to get back to the room, to listen to her splash in the bath.

"Yes, look..."

"I'm sorry Matthew, let me finish." She says.

"Sorry of course."

"Johno always talked fondly of you." She says .

"Yes...."

"Otherwise I'd have asked his university friends, but we never really met them." She suddenly sounds sad. Her voice begins to break.

"He's married. I wasn't invited to the wedding." I say.

"And we can't speak to his wife's friends." She says.

"Right?" I say.

I move the phone away from my face. Because there she is: she pops out of the bathroom wrapped in a towel. She smells good and clean. I can start to smell myself against her cleanliness. I wish I were a little cleaner for her. I think about my dick, I threw some water on it. I can always wash it in the sink before sex I reassure myself. She hasn't mentioned the hair cut – maybe she likes it?

I'm done with the phone call I press the screen to hang up. If it was important Diana should've just come out with it. I look over at her, away from me she lowers the towel and I see the small of her back, then the dimples above her bottom. She pulls some knickers on, turned away from me still for a fake privacy. She turns back to me and I see her breasts. Her stomach. I'm obsessed, its taken me half my life to find someone I love.

5

I hadn't hung up, I'd put it on speaker - Diana barks out of the iphone "Matthew, Johno went to India after some troubles in his marriage. He's been gone a year. We need someone to go and bring him back." But I'm not listening because the girl I'm in love with walks towards me and drops the towel. She takes the phone from my hand and hangs up, and then she leaves me hanging as she goes to dry off. The truth was I didn't remember that last bit of the call but I've pieced it together since, sort of.

-

From the moment she'd gotten out of the bath I'd been transfixed. She grinned at me, her cracked tooth poking fun at me.

"Hey!" I say with a smile.

"Hey," she replies and turns back to her clothes rail.

"You smell good" She pulls on a t-shirt, jeans and shoes.

"Let's go somewhere we can talk." She says to me, still facing the clothes rail.

"Sure!" I'm still beaming; this is her effect on me, most of the time.

I'm excited. I want to talk. I want to get to know her. She's had a few tragedies, a few setbacks, but she's strong, she's beautiful, her parents are dying like mine are dying, she likes pretentious art and is spiritual but not religious which although having neither I'm coming round to.

"Let's go to the coffee shop." She said, still not looking at me. I put down my drink.

"Okay." I say.

"And what's with the hair – you in a band now or something?" she teases.

"I, er...well." I mumble.

"You got all your stuff?" she asks.

"Er. Yeah." I say. I pat my pockets down to check my keys. A new pack of condoms are in there too. She walks away to get something.

"Are you breaking up with me?" I ask,. She doesn't reply, maybe she can't hear me?

She walks back into her room and I pour another big glass of wine. I neck it in one. Then I pour another glass. She appears with a cigarette in her hand and lights it. I finish a third glass.

"You're breaking up with me?" I ask her.

"I realised that I'm not ready for a boyfriend yet." She says, but we've been dating for the best part of a year I want to say.

"Is there something I can change?" I ask, and I tug nervously at my hair, and a grey comes loose and drops into my wine.

"No, look, let's go talk." She walks to the front door.

On the way out I pause at the bathroom door, her clothes heaped over it, the grouting is greying too. There is dirt in the corners, hair trapped in the plughole. Take it all in, remember it. The life you could have had I tell myself. She's beautiful. She's shaking the lighter; her cigarette is gone out.

"Shit, hold on. I need a lighter" she says from the open door.

She goes back inside and I hear her routing through drawers.

I close the door and walk away from her.

I take my phone out and erase her number, then try and stop my phone deleting it but it's too late.

I get down the steps and pick up the beer can still there waiting for me. I take a big swig, it goes down in one, then I call Diana back.

"Hi Diana, its Matthew. Sorry about that. Tell me again…"

CHAPTER TWO - JOHNO

I had seen Johno just once since we'd both left home for university. It was at one of those awkward meet ups that everyone with a girlfriend, wife, good job or newly born baby insists on. Often these events would happen at houses halfway between London and the villages we'd all grown up in. Half a step back towards the womby comfort of the Home Counties. The place you can be both glad and embarrassed you were born in.

It was at one of those reunion afternoons in a Richmond riverside function room that we had met up again after about eight years. He was there with his fiancé and seemed happy if more reserved. Gone was the jazz prodigy and the prankster and here was a husband-to-be. They were dressed almost identically and hung on to one another. I think there must have been a couple of dozen of us there that day. Half were the awful "better halves" sucked in to the black hole that is school days nostalgia.

We'd spent most of secondary school fighting and trying to escape one another and now here we all were praising one another's successes at work, successes in marriage, haven't you got great children and so on. Johno seemed happy that day, the two of them very much in love – Isabella I think she was. He did marry her soon after. I hadn't been invited but had seen various photos over the years.

Of those twenty-four in that room that day all but I had attended the wedding. I'd spiralled out of control shortly after that and having lost a grip on reality I also lost my then girlfriend and been fired my job. I'd ironically found a peace that year cleaning plates at lunch and supper services for weekend weddings in Kew gardens. I spent my days scraping plate after plate of cold smoked fish and soggy meringues into slops bins that I would later drive back across London to dispose of at the catering depot. I suspected the other side of the wall that separated porters from front of house there had been more than one old schoolmate getting married. And hearing familiar voices singing to wedding bands' karaoke I'd come to accept we all lived in different circles.

And I'd heard nothing really from any of them since that meet up so the call from Diana intrigued me.

Diana and I had briefly chatted on the phone but she wanted to see me in person. I still couldn't entirely get my head around it but the rough facts were...

Johno had gotten engaged in his mid twenties, been married for five years and then seemingly on a whim gone to India for three weeks after a work stopover in Qatar. He said he'd be three weeks then four. Then he didn't show for Christmas and then he stopped contact. But they knew he was alive for at least six months as his bank kept a trace on him and he and Isabella had a joint account. Isabella had closed that account and then they'd lost the trace. He could be dead. He could be alive. Isabella had moved back in with her parents. Diana had been out to Delhi to search for him but hadn't counted on the heat. The British consul had put out a notice but informed Diana that India was a big country.

I arrived at the station, one stop before that of my parents' nearest. It was all very familiar. It was still humid and hot for the time of year. I couldn't afford a car any longer. I was hoping to save up for one with the current job. After another six months I might have enough credit to get something small on finance. But for the moment I walked or cycled everywhere.

From the station to Johno's old place was about fifteen minutes walk. I'd started to sweat so took off my sweatshirt and brushed the sweat on my forehead into my hair and swept it back behind my ears. I spat into my hands and swept it back some more. Maybe it was smarter that way. The lane to their house was fragrant with something like wild garlic but it was the wrong time of year. Birds, and flowers, and trees. All very calm. All very beautiful. I rarely left London anymore except for the very occasional funeral or holiday. And all those Home Counties weddings I'd still managed to avoid so this was a treat in a way.

Going up the final hill towards their driveway I felt a bit puffed. I sat on the mushroomy things at the end of their drive and took it all in. I loved it and hated it – it was where I was from but I'd rejected all this shit years ago. Comfortable and ridiculous. Actually a croquet set left abandoned on the lawn running up to their house.

I walked up to the house. Didn't even ring the bell before Diana appeared form the side of the house and let me in to their back garden.

Out the back lawn gave way to a tennis pitch and then fields and woods. There was a table ready for me with some jugs of something and sandwiches. I was thirsty after the walk and hadn't eaten yet that day. She poured me a glass and I knocked it back. It was a gin and tonic. Pre-mixed. Strong. She smiled. She sipped at hers.

"Thanks for coming." Says Diana

"Thanks for the gin and tonic"

"Yes!"

"Oh. Well it's a weekend." I say smiling.

"Yes, yes it is."

I didn't really care; I drank most days at lunch anyway but airs and graces.

"Johno always spoke very highly of you." She says, growing more serious.

"Oh? We'd lost contact really."

"I know. But you were really friends. Not like these berks he's met since. Can't trust each other with their wives. Money people you know, like Johno's dad. Pricks the lot of them." Diana says, and she shuffles a little closer to me, and then lifts her drink and she takes a bigger sip.

"I see...."

"Isabella and Johno had some problems, now clearly he's done a runner and left her in the lurch. Now her brother went with her for a few days but he hates him, and Isabella's all but given up. I only want him back selfishly, and also, because I'm not sure he's alive anymore." Confessional tones from Diana. And I see the shame on her face, the shame has aged her, she looks exhausted by this shame, and relieved to have confessed it to me. Her son has failed.

I take another big glug of the tonic mix. I halve a sandwich and start eating. I know there's more she wants to say.

"We were angry with him. He'd gone off the rails a bit. Not much mind but just enough. Isabella is from a good family. Izzy for short, she's coming down this afternoon – you can meet her then. Johno made a promise to her you see." I nod.

"A wedding, that's all it is – it isn't an I love you, you know that don't you." She says. I nod again but I have no idea what she means having never been to one.

"A wedding is a man and a woman telling each other that no matter what that they will look after each other. In sickness and in health. Now in these times Matthew that means not turning into a fuck up? Not losing your job and not running away from trying to have a future with the woman you love."

"You're asking me though to leave my job and go find your son." I add.

"But you aren't married, and you told me you hate your job!" She says and her tone grows ever more serious, she's my friends mum telling me off, I may as well be a kid, I'm still her boys friend, I can still be told what to do, and told off.

"We all make mistakes." I say.

"You can afford to, you haven't the commitments that Johno does. Izzy has a baby. She was a few months pregnant when he left." Says Diana, tearing up a little. Hiding her wet eyes behind the fizz of the tonic bubbles.

"Oh."

"You didn't know?" asks Diana, and at that moment we both realise Johno wasn't that much of a friend to me, or me to him.

I shake my head and eat more of the sandwich.

"We think it might have been the reason he left. He couldn't cope." And she stares at me, as if she's a recruiter working out, faced with a few bad candidates, whether or not I could do the job.

"I only met her briefly but she seemed like a lovely person, they seemed very well suited." I say but don't really mean it.

"They were when they met, but people change Matthew." She says

"That's true"

"Except for you, you're still the same. Aren't you?" she says and sips more of her drink, a few tears drop into the glass. I look away as she starts sobbing properly. And I cry too for her, for me, because she might be right, because my friend had a kid but didn't tell me, because I'll never have a kid with you.

I indulge myself in a sob, sip the gin and tonic and stand and walk away from the table towards the flowerbed. There are rhododendron bushes twice my height, flowering in pinks, I walk to the edge of the bed and almost into the bush and force myself to stop crying. I breathe in the scent of the rhododendrons and it reminds me of you and I know that I cannot live like this. And then I curse myself for my indulgences and I neck the last of the drink, wipe my eyes on my shoulder and turn back to Diana. She is right behind me. She holds me, and cries on my shoulder, and I don't know what to do, or what to say.

CHAPTER THREE - IZZY

I've had to move on to water but Diana is still going strong on the gin and tonic. I've had a few sandwiches – couldn't tell what was in them. I've also had a look at "The Box". That's what Diana calls it – it's her collection of stuff about Johno, about where he's been and a few tourist maps Diana's picked up. I have a quick skim through it all. I don't know what I'm looking for.

There's a squelch of decelerating tyres on Diana's gravel. A heavy sounding car. Diana is already out the front waiting for Izzy – she's just called. She's looking forwards to meeting me apparently.

Back in the box there's a few scrappy credit card reports, he's taken out a lot of money in Delhi and been charged the extra for it, he's bought a ticket at New Delhi rail station but for where I can't understand – seems its in Indian. There are a few other things, money spent at a pharmacy. A hotel booking in another city in India. On the tourist map these places are joined up with pen. Plotted out by Diana. The map is useless – I see this straight away and I write "map" on the back of my hand.

There's a crying kid in a buggy that looks like a four-wheel drive being pushed by Diana. There's a tired looking Isabella wearing what could be Johno's clothes. Isabella gives me a big long hug.

"I'm sorry you weren't invited to the wedding." posh West London accent - but with the grit of loss.

"It's ok. I'm sorry to hear about Johno." I say, as if I know he's dead already.

"He never really mentioned you. But I think we met?" Asks Isabel.

"Yes, at a pub near Ealing. There was a private room, lots of screaming children, I'm not sure we had a chance to properly meet." I say.

"I suppose we didn't. We had mostly family at the wedding anyway." Says Izzy

"It's okay, I'm not much of a wedding person anyway." I say.

"Matthew's a bit of a loner." Says Diana

Izzy is pretty, but maybe not beautiful. I can sense she's smart. Smart enough to know Johno is probably dead already. She's telling me that by the way she looks at me, and by the way she holds the kid, like she believes in reincarnation. I don't believe in anything, but I think of reincarnation when I see her, Madonna and child the child is Johno – I'm thinking of this because I'm thinking of India – Asia – all those religions I've seen on the TV.

They are both looking at me now. And I feel kind of strange.

"Di says you're quitting your job to help us. That's really above and beyond. Are you sure?"

I couldn't explain the girl. I nod. "Yeah. I can always get another one." Izzy smiles.

"What do you do?" Isabel asks
"I'm a writer." I say
"Oh glamorous."

"Oh not that sort, I fill in the gaps on the internet."

"Oh right?"

"If you are reading the news , well, then stuff pops up selling you stuff? Well I write that stuff." I say, not wishing to talk about it.

"Advertising?"

"Sure." I say.

"It sounds like a good job."

"It isn't." I tell her.

She changes pace, she says. "Well I'm very grateful. We have some recent photographs, from before he went away." And with that Isabel looks in her bag. She passes the photographs.

In them there are only two of them. No baby, no baby lump on her. They look happy enough. He's slightly ginger, slightly ginger beard. Her hair more clearly died in the photo darker roots showing. Her in a dress, him in a linen suit.

It's from a wedding. Before he went away for work.

"You look very happy." I say.

"We are. We are still happy, deep down."

She takes a deep breath and I can see she just wants out either way. He's left her or he's dead. Either way would be better than this.

"Do you have a notebook?" asks Isabel

"No" I say.

"You'll need one." She says.

"Yes."

Diana steps in again – some of this seems rehearsed, as if they've already discussed what they will say if they found someone willing to go "We also would like you to keep your receipts," says Diana "the insurers would anyway. We have a little money to give you to start with. And can wire more when you are there. But please keep the receipts. Its important."

"Don't pay cash." Adds Isabel.

"Okay."

"We won't be able to trace you if you pay cash" Says Diana.

"Sure, good point. I'll buy a ledger and a notebook and I'll make sure I keep my receipts." I say, hoping to sound reassuring, already thinking I sound like a man playing the part of a private eye.

"Thank you" says Diana.

Isabel steps forwards and kisses me on the forehead. "Thanks Matthew." She says.

"What's his name?" I ask looking at a picture of Johno with the baby in his arms.

"Jonathan." Says Isabel

"Oh, that's very..."

"It's okay," and with that Diana starts crying. She suddenly can't stop. It's uncontrollable. She's a mess in seconds. She takes a napkin from the sandwich tray and wipes her face. Izzy is more resilient.

"We just need to know how he died." Says Isabel

But then Diana takes me aside and says in hushed tones "Please bring him home."

And I don't know if they mean alive or for a funeral and all I have to say is "Okay."

I hug her sincerely.

CHAPTER FOUR- THE ROOM

I'm in Johno's room. It's plain. Almost nothing in it from when he was a teenager. But there are a few school photos on the wall. Karate class. We are all there in our whites. Couldn't be less tough but we are grinning. Thought we could be ninjas, invisible fighters. Good times. Nostalgia. Easy happy days.

There's a bookshelf in the corner. A few books on it. A Martin Amis – it looks unread. A Roget's thesaurus. A book on sailing by J. Slocum. And a small atlas. I take out the atlas and turn through the pages until I get to India. Something falls to the floor.

Another photo. I think about my job – how this would all be online these days, the atlas, the novels on a tablet, the photos in a 'gallery'. I'm relieved to have a reason to quit.

I look at the photo – it's a little faded but not much – it's of a girl from our school. Anna – she must have been about 15 in this picture. He fancied her, maybe even loved her. I think they kissed a few times. She was found dead I think at University – none of us kept in touch with her so we never really knew. But Johno was keen on her. A lot. I turn the picture over - it just reads "Ha ha XX" - in a girl's cheery handwriting – a gift from her to him. She's there in it – smiling, happy, her face illuminated by a camera's flash – accentuating the smiles – really beaming, eyes really wide with luminous energy.

And that's it. The Atlas is unmarked. The Amis definitely unread. The Slocum very second hand, pages burnt by age.

I can't remember why she killed herself. She was probably the kindest girl at our school and maybe the prettiest. I think she went up north somewhere for studies, ran into some problems. I don't know.

I take one more look around at this room – its like a dead child's room on TV when they finally catch the serial killer and then they go to the parents and thirty years on they show how they've persevered the room.

No more nostalgia – I go back to the bookcase I put the atlas and the Slocum inside my jacket and wrap it up. I leave the picture of Anna inside the Amis book for someone else to uncover one day. If they ever ask I'll say I need it – a 'lead'. I'm a detective now. A missing person's detective. I need all the leads I can get.

Downstairs Diana is crying behind a door. The kid is crying too.

Izzy appears in the hallway as I'm letting myself out of another door.

She kisses me on the cheek and says, "Thank you. Remember to write everyday and tell us the news. Keep your receipts and please write everything down too just in case."

I nod. "I'm really sorry about what's happened." I say.

"We are counting on you, you know that don't you?" she says.
"Yes."

"If you need money there's more money, you know that also don't you?"

"Yes. Thank you." I say, then I hug her and walk away."

I walk past her tank of a car. I walk down the gravel driveway. I walk passed the mushroom things. I'm walking down the lane again. I'm getting to a road. I'm nearing the station. I'm moving at speed. I need to leave my job – I haven't done that yet. I wasn't sure until today. But I feel good for the first time in years and I'm going to follow you Johno. I'm going to find you. Dead or alive.

CHAPTER FIVE - CLICK THROUGHS

I'd written and sent the email on the way back in to London on the Saturday. They must have read it by now, today was Monday. They'd had a full day to digest it. I'd handed in my two weeks notice period. But I knew and they knew that I wouldn't be working it. This is media planning and creative where idiots panic that you'll steal their one good idea, their one good client.

Diana had lost her husband to a girl at his office, that's losing.

But these cunts don't care about that, what matters to them is clients and budget and planning and data and click-throughs. The moment I'd made the decision to go I was already out of the door. I'd planned my exit well. I left my laptop at home. They could ask for it back but I'd be gone. I'd brought just enough cash for the first round of leaving drinks. Anyone who thought they might be a friend of mine couldn't rely on me for a second spritzer. They would have to open their wallets.

Everyone sits down to work in the open plan. I don't. I make a cup of coffee and then go and read a magazine by reception. Lottie is a temp and she's nice, she keeps her flat pumps under the desk and wears Nikes in and out of the office, she's normal and wants to be a teacher one day or something. She's kind to

me. I'm reading Bella from under the coffee table and Lottie
asks if I'm enjoying it.

"I'm leaving you Lottie." I say.

"Oh" says Lottie. "Can I come with you?" and she giggles.

At that moment Rossie and Russell appear. Their ridiculous
beards and spectacles ruin any serious aggression they are
feeling towards me right now.

"Shall we?" I offer.

"Yes please" says Rossie

"Yes." whimpers Russell

I follow them into their boardroom. Its a work in progress
and probably always will be. I don't sit down. I sip my coffee.

"Guys, I've loved working here but my friend is in need of
help and I have to go and rescue him from India." It sounds like
a lie.

"Right?" Rossie

"Oh, god really?" Russell

"Yes. It sounds like a lie but he needs me." I say.

"You understand that if you leave here, that's quitting?"
Russell asks.

"Yes. Look I love working here but you know when
something is your calling.?..." I say.

I look at Russell and then at Rossie, I know that both of them
fancy themselves as the adventurous types, always signing up
to Tough Enough weekends or Muddy Spartan races. "...An
adventure?" I add. Neither of them have the gumption to turn
down a fellow adventurer.

"Well, we'd like to offer you a rise, make you a partner, how
about that? Offers Rossie. Russell flexes his fingers. I get a text.

"Just a minute." I say and look at my phone. The message is
from the girl. It reads: Look can we meet and talk?

"Do you want to take lunch to think about this?" asks Russell.

I'm texting the girl back: Are you around now? We need to
talk.

"Yes, maybe I'm being a touch rash." I say.

-

I waited in anticipation for her outside her office. She was late. Across the road a motorbike roars to a halt. A bearded Percol wearing biker pulls up with a beautiful woman riding pillion, it was her, she hands him her helmet and gloves before she sees me. Something glints in the daylight, a rock as big as the Ritz on her finger. She smiles at me from across the street. The biker kisses her and pulls away. Traffic fills the street between us. I turn away again.

-

"The truth is I'm heartbroken, I need a break." I say
"Give me a hug," says Russell.
I hug him.
"I'll send a postcard." I say.
There's some nodding from Rossie.
"Look Matthew, if you don't want to work these two weeks that's better for us. The client is a little touchy about finding his copy across other platforms. If you can leave your phone and Mac with Lottie, we could I don't know, split the weeks, pay you for one and give you the other off." Says Russell getting down to business.
"Thank you for being so understanding guys." I shake their hands. I walk out of the boardroom.

-

In the reception I say to Lottie "Look I'll drop my phone and computer next week?"
"Oh alright then, sorry to hear about the girl." She says.
I walk out of the open plan and into a corridor of other open plans.

Down in the street I cross the road to Coffee Spot. I tell the waitress that I'm leaving the country and I hand back my loyalty card. It has two free coffees on it. She insists on making them.

I'm down the street with my two coffees. Rossie comes running from behind.

"Lottie says you didn't leave your Mac." He asks.

I shake my head and hand him the two coffees. I walk away from him at speed. He tries catching up but spills the coffee on his jeans. He drops both coffees and tears at his burning crotch. I just walk away and wish there was a door I could shut on him, her all of it.

CHAPTER SIX - GATWICK SKY CITIES

I hadn't thought it through; I don't think Diana or Izzy had either.

But I'd quit now. And then I went to buy a plane ticket to Delhi and a return for three weeks later. Should be enough time.

Back in Stroud Green I'd advertised my room and after a couple of days of emails back and forth a Jewish Serb 'Nico' came round to look at the place. He was in town for a conference on warzones and I did him a deal. He seemed alright and promised to water the one plant I have.

The plant was a chilli plant I'd grown from seed after a date It had been an awkward meal with someone I'd met online – she chose the 'restaurant' and turned up with her kid. I'd taken the seeds we'd been given with the bill and grown them and a couple of small nubs of chillies had appeared. After Nico left I threw the plant away. No more nostalgia.

I had a couple of tote bags from days at advertising seminars and then an old sports bag with some gym kit I'd never used it smelt like cum and death. Neither seemed practical for the trip so I went down to the discount sport shop in Finsbury Park and bought a backpack with "Traveller 4 Life" written on it. I felt like a tit but the moment I was abroad hopefully no one could read it right.

I packed some swimming shorts, a new notebook I'd gotten from Amazon along with a torch and a first aid kit. I called my doctors about malaria and everything but there was a waiting list and I wouldn't be away for long.

"Not much Malaria in Delhi according to Google" says the receptionist.

"Oh."

"Yeah. You should still come in for a prescription."

"Okay."

I never did. I did the on-line forms. Did the in-person meeting and I got my visa. Two weeks later I had my flight.

This all seemed like a holiday. The truth is I felt for Diana, I felt for Izzy and for her kid, a bit anyway, but Johno and I hadn't been friends with for a long time – and I felt nothing towards him, he could be dead, and that would be sad, but I don't think I'll cry if the time comes and I'm staring at his body in a morgue.

I had said yes to all this out of a selfish desire to get out of London.

I wanted to 'find myself' more than I wanted to find Johno. I hate those kinds of people though. I don't leave the m25 it isn't what I do.

But that's what's happened by mistake and I find myself at Gatwick waiting for my flight. No one to see me off. I've got the laptop and the atlas in a tote bag. My backpack with clothes, torch and a couple more books, is all checked in.

I check my emails. Pop-up's on the side of the screen are some that I'd written. A car ad. A menswear ad. A paternity check ad.

Rossie wants the laptop back as soon as possible or they are taking it from my final wage. They'll let me the phone.

I drink coffee and eat cake. They have tea in India don't they. Tea, religions and a lot of people. And Johno, dead or alive. And that's kind of all I know. That's as much as I know. Whilst I'm waiting I look at the shops around me. There's some menswear. Some perfume. Alcohol deals. M&M chocolates. I move from the cafe to the oyster and champagne bar. I buy a glass of red wine and double check I've got enough Valium for the flight.

Then I see the bookshop. I should get a travel book, or something. A dictionary. The phone rings. I've saved the number now so I know its Diana.

"Hi, I'm at the airport. Packed and ready to go."

"You will tell us when you've landed." Diana reminds me.

"Yes"

"And you're going straight to his hotel?"

"Straight off the flight and yes. I have to change in Qatar, same as he did. Same as Johno." I say.

"But then straight to the hotel. And you'll call us?" she sounds concerned that I might not stick to the plan. I reassure her.

"Yes, of course I will."

"Thank you so much Matthew."

"No worries."

"Isabella really is grateful, she's looking forward to your call."

I can hear the way she looks, resignation, hope and trust, she trusts me. I don't want to let her down. "I'm just glad I can be of help. I have to go to the gate. I'll call you. I promise."

"Thank you. Much love and, well, good luck." Says Diana.

"Thanks Diana. Bye, bye."

I hang up and finish the wine.

I walk over to the bookshop. In the travel section there's guides to most places but no India.

"Do you have any books on India? The er, rough guide or lonely planet." I ask.

"No sorry, all out of India. Try fiction maybe. That Slumdog Millionaire book is popular. Or Life of Pi – they made both into films. Lots of Indians in them." Says the clerk.

"Thank you. I'll have a look."

I walk straight back to the bar and order a big glass. I have two thousand pounds in my account from Diana & Izzy. I feel good. I text my dad as I know my mum doesn't use the phone anymore.

Away for a few weeks on holiday. Back soon. Don't die yet, Matthew.

CHAPTER SEVEN - QATARI BARISTAS

Qatar airport is like Westfield Stratford after hours. Same shops, same cafes but almost entirely empty. I go to a Camden Coffee shop. I'm starving. I have twenty minutes 'til my next flight and I get an egg roll and coffee and a beer. It all goes down together and I walk past all the menswear boutiques, the handbag shops. The cleaners are Arab; white eastern Europeans run the food court and coffee baristas are Indian, Pakistani or Bangladeshi. It's just like home. I feel at home. The tote bag is boring me already. I've definitely over packed.

There's a couple I recognise from my flight arguing, they are rushing ahead to a travelator. I hope they aren't going on the same flight as me. Already crying, great holiday. She's carrying both their bags. He's searching his pockets for something. He turns around and runs back past me. She drops the bags on the floor and screams at him.

"You always do this!" says the woman

I travelate past her now. She grits her teeth and shows a chipped tooth. I fall for a moment – I'm a man with a tote bag and a shirt and jeans. I'm in a shopping centre airport. I'm falling for another girl with another fucked up mouth. I keep travelating.

I get to the next gate. A smaller aircraft. Comfortable. Two spare seats next to me.

I'm about to take the last of the Valium when she and him sit down next to me. His passport is in his teeth. They are both exasperated and angry. I can hardly believe it.

"Are you going to India?"

"Yes – she says. Its one of our favourite places to meditate." Says the screaming woman.

I offer her a Valium, then him. Both refuse. She opens up a magazine on baking, he stuffs his jumper under the seat in front.

A few hours more sleep.

CHAPTER EIGHT - HAUS KHAZ

I carry a picture of Johno with me. Folded in half – on the other side is Izzy. It's taped back. I figure I can flip it over in case I forget why I'm here – who I'm doing this for because I've definitely decided it isn't him. That's how I think. I'm thinking ahead. I'm thinking when I forget why I'm here I'll look at the card and remember I'm here for Johno's kid. That's probably the truth.

There were times he could've been a friend, could have gotten back in touch. Helped me out when I was in trouble, or reached out to me when he was in trouble, but he didn't. And like a school kid his mum's now had to get in touch, she's had to bring us back together again. We weren't friends until she told me last month that he still thought of me as such, or had done before he'd disappeared. And I don't think we were friends. Who are your friends? The few that haven't left London for children are the guys in the George, they won't miss me, I'll be back before they notice anyway. The pub quiz on Tuesday's will be one place emptier, a corner at the back of the Moth club will have one less creep in it on Saturdays. Friends are in truth few and far between in this life but Johno isn't one of them. I'm here for his kid, and because of her, because I had to get away.

The picture is also saved on my laptop. I've also scanned most of the items from the box onto my laptop too. And I have his picture in my phone's gallery in case I need to send it to someone here.

The picture is in my wallet. I glimpse it when I'm shuffling for my passport and visa. The couple have stopped arguing and they are now picking a line at entrance. They seem to know what they are doing. I'm in a long line. Ahead of me some teenagers from maybe Birmingham are moved out of line. They've come this far without a Visa – they are moved to another line.

They look briefly at my passport and send me into India. This is almost as far as I'd planned. I walk through the airport. Hot, I'm already sweating. Shit.

I get out onto a concourse. There's a half-run towards me of men. They all want to help. I walk away from them to the taxi rank. Funny little scooters with hats on are one option. The other is normal cars. I don't know what to do. A kind looking man walks up to me and tells me that the scooter taxis are bad.

"Crooked sir, all crooks. Don't listen to them, come with me, where you going?" he takes my arm.

"Erm. You have a taxi." I ask.

"I'm taxi driver sir." And his head wobbles and he and I both know he is lying. But its day one so I give him the benefit of the doubt.

"Okay. How much to here."

I show him the address for the hotel Johno stayed in whilst in Delhi.

"One thousand."

I do a rough calculation. That's about ten pounds. You can't get anything for ten pounds back home let alone a taxi ride.

"Great. Just this bag." I point to my pack.

He walks me up to a taxi and then writes a note.

"You wait here." He says.

I stand in the heat. The whitest person here. I'm sweating buckets. I'm paranoid my laptop will get stolen. Shouldn't have brought it. I'm looking around. Other passengers disappear on the scooter taxis. The arguing couple load theirs up with luggage and take off. Suddenly the airport seems very empty. Its one of the busiest in India I read on the way here, but now I feel quite alone. Unsure what to do I unbutton my shirt a little to let some air in.

Another man arrives. The first guy shouts at him. He pulls a polo shirt on top of his t-shirt and opens the car. I get into the back seat with my luggage. It's a white taxi, no seatbelts, and no air conditioning. I wind down the window. The driver smiles at me in the rear view mirror and reaches back for the note – I pass it to him.

"Ah yes I know this place. Which block?" Although he has a car this new man seems less certain than the previous that he can help me.

"I'm not sure. It's called the New Palace."

"I know this place." He says, suddenly changing his tone.

"Okay?"

"Which block though. This is south of defence colony."

"I don't know. "

"Yes it is. Near the tank."

"Tank?"

"Water tank." Says the driver as if I should know.

"Okay. Let's go."

He smiles and copies my "Let's go!" in his best Dick Van Dyke London accent.

The car starts and we are off.

The start is normal. Then it's weird. I'm only telling you this because it was interesting to me. If it is to you too, then that's good. You see I'm trying to paint a picture, so you understand what happened.

I had no idea where I was. But we moved fast for the first bit. I slumped deep into the seat. I suddenly felt terrified. I was the only white guy in this swarm of cars, bikes and scooter taxis. I hid behind the seat column. I was scared. For the first time in a long time I was really scared. What if I got kidnapped?

Suddenly we are stuck in traffic. I tense up, look around me. Faces looking in but none of them seem like they really care. Maybe I'm okay.

-

It takes an hour to get to wherever we are going. Then he pulls over. I'm stuck to the seat.

"Are we here?" I ask.

"Not here – what is the address?" he asks

I open up the laptop and look through some of the scans. The battery is dying.

"It's near the police station."

"Yes I know, police station."

We take off again. Turning off the main road. I guess we are in the suburbs. There's sign for a metro. There are people selling fruit at the side of the road. Livestock, dogs. Life on the streets. Shops and stalls and people cleaning rubbish with rubbish and putting it into rubbish heaps and setting it on fire. More of these fires the closer we get to wherever we are going. The light is low and filled with the smoke of rubbish. Everyone is Indian. I hadn't thought it would be this big a deal. But I feel isolated. Really, really alone.

"Here boss. Police station."

"Okay."

"You get out here. Easier to walk."

I doubt this very much but I sense this is the end of the ride. I want to ask him to take me to the hotel but he seems kind. I can't bring myself to.

"Fifteen hundred."

"They said one thousand."

"Now one thousand five hundred. Journey longer."

"Are we there yet?"

"Police station. You give me fifteen hundred."

I don't know how to argue yet so politely I say "Okay. Seems reasonable."

I give him the notes and get out. He drives off. We're on a crossroads. There are people pushing sticks through grinders. Fruit that looks rotten. Pastries covered in oil that can't be good for you.

No one here is interested in me. I turn in a circle. Nothing looks like a hotel. There's the police station, I trust the police here I tell myself. So I go to the police station gates.

A moustachioed man sits with a short cane in his lap by the entrance. He wears a beret and full uniform. He could be a French soldier.

"Hi?"

"Hello sir." And he taps the cane on the ground.

"I'm looking for the New Palace Hotel."

"Ah the Palace."

"Yes. Its near here I think?"

The man twiddles his neck buttons, and then looks at the ground and say "Very far."

"Oh?"

"One hundred kilometres." And he draws 100 in the dirt with the cane

"Oh. Okay." And I walk away.

There are some dogs killing each other. One has a lump out of his neck and I can see his vertebrae. Flies are already clinging on to him.

I walk back towards the main road. My blue shirt now several shades darker with sweat.

35

There it is – a sign for the new Palace. I look back at the
police station and at the main road. In truth by now I'm
completely disorientated. I could be anywhere.

It's not a hotel. It's the end house in a street of these houses.
They are large white sugar cube sort of things. Big. Like a few
houses all-together. There are sleeping dogs outside it. Ones
without bits missing. There are no fires down this road. I walk
up to the house. Underneath the Palace signage it's repeated
in the script – Indian? Sanskrit? Whatever it's called. Its
everywhere here – will I need to be able to read it? I'm not sure.

-

I try checking in. It seems family run. The boy who checks
me in is about my age but something has stopped him from
ageing. He wears jeans and is clean-shaven. Youthful. I look
down at myself and compared to him I look like a piece of shit.
I'm a dusty sweaty mess. The sweat now cooling on me like
meat in fridge. I'm a countertop turkey carcass two days after
Christmas.

We go up to my room and it's big. I wonder if this is the
room Johno stayed in. He shows me how to turn on the hot
water. He shows me how to use the air con. How the fan works.
"Noisy" he warns me. I nod.
Then I take out the photograph of Johno and Izzy. He takes it
from me straight away and turns it over.
"Your brother?" he asks
"No, a friend. "
"She's married?"
"Yes – they are married." I look at the man's eyes, to see if he
recognises the picture "Do you recognise him?"
He shakes his head.
"He stayed here." I say

"Maybe."

"No, not maybe, he, he definitely stayed here. "

"Maybe yes, I don't know."

"I'm looking for him."

"Englishman?"

"Yes."

"India is a very big place." He tucks the picture into his own shirt pocket.

"I think he's here in Delhi." I say.

He turns and says, "I ask my father. "

"Okay."

"He's not here." And he swings his arm around the room as if Johno could possibly be hiding in a cupboard here, playing hide and seek in an Indian bed and breakfast.

"Okay." I say.

"You ask again tomorrow."

"Okay. Okay. Thank you."

He told me his name when we've first met. But it didn't seem important so I let myself forget straight away. Now I want to thank him by his name but I can't. I feel bad. I'd have remembered it if he wasn't Indian...probably anyway.

"Thanks. Okay."

"You can take a shower. You can eat something."

"Yes, that's also what I wanted to know."

"Good food near here."

"I'm looking for this place. You know this place."

I take out my notebook. I have a couple of bits stuck in from the box. A receipt for a meal with a name in script on it.

"Very expensive. This means Fire Balcony."

37

"Oh."

"You cross main road. Fifteen minutes. You ask there."

"Okay."

"Is it safe?... To eat?"

"All safe." He says smiling.

"Okay."

He closes the door. I've forgotten the internet. Do they have it? I need to email Johno's family. Tell them I've arrived. Tell them I'm in the hotel and that I'm making enquiries. That I'm going to the place we know he ate.

Suddenly I'm hungry thinking about it. Thirsty also.

I shower, careful not to drink any of it. I have no idea if I can drink it here. I really should've got one of those books.

-

On the way out Sam (that cant be his name) gives me a bottle of water.

"Do you have Wifi? Erm, the internet?"

"Very fast fibre optic sir, but not working today, tomorrow morning you try as well."

"Okay. Thank you Sam."

"Okay no problem."

"Okay."

-

I leave their hotel. Dogs are still lying out front. I let myself out the gate at the end and I'm suddenly buoyed by the warmth. The sun is going down and its cooler but still warm. I feel it lift my body up. Like a perfect bath.

Trees droop over roads. Cyclists, cars and scooters pass me by. I have my wallet and phone with me. As the light quickly dims my thoughts turn to personal security – that's a thing right? I tap my wallet in my back pocket and my phone in my pocket.

Back past the police station. Their gates are closed now. Some stalls I'd passed by earlier are now closed, others are opening up in the same spot. There's food, I couldn't tell what it is but I'm sure it'd make you sick, there's fruit juice stalls, what must be a tea stall with steaming copper pot – it smells good but its on the street, where are they cleaning this stuff?

A few minutes of gawping, I see an English Wine shop – an off licence – government licensed – what does that mean? I get to the main road. Sort of a relief after the busy side streets to just have cars. Can I trust anyone here? I give the receipt to a man selling some kind of leaves at the corner of the road.

"Do you know where this is? Its a restaurant?" He waves his hand over the road – there's a black void across it. "This way?" I ask. He doesn't reply, only gestures with his hand as if to say "beyond" the darkness.

The sun has set. Cars pummel down this main road. There are no crossings. I see a man pushing a barrow cart and a couple walking out towards the main street. I follow them. We make it to the central reservation. Then they quickly frogger across the next two lanes safely to the other side.

I can't see a gap. I'm there for about five minutes. Half have headlights half don't. Between the traffic and the pavement is what must be an unofficial contra flow of bikes in the street. There's suddenly a gap and I get across it. I look back. Grateful. A small river I've crossed. I've been here a few hours and already feel things are changing around me, things shift here in new ways.

-

A long dusty road. I can't see anything, there's only the occasional street light. Most of it is darkness. This is the void I saw. People drive up and down this lane in cars. They all must be going somewhere. At the side of the road more sellers selling stuff. I have never seen things like this before. I have no idea what it is but people are buying and eating it, it looks popular, something that looks like a Yorkshire pudding with mint sauce. Who knows? What would Johno have made of all this. How far did Diana and Izzy get with this? It's no longer a question why they didn't get anywhere out here, its dark and confusing and scary, kind of. They said they found nothing, I'm not sure they'd even left the hotel, from what Diana said they'd spent most of the time taking tea with the police.

The long dusty road turns into streets. There are buildings, fewer cars, and some motorbikes. And then neon, lots and lots of neon. Each building has dozens of signs, roped electric cable languidly draped from balcony to balcony. I'm looking for the Fire Balcony. I'll ask around.

The main street here is full of Indians, I don't know why that's surprising but it is. They are looking around like me; maybe they are tourists like me. Some are queuing up outside a bar entrance. They are smart, smarter than me.

I still have the bottle of water in my hand and I drink some of it, then pour some into my hands and drag my hair back and pat some onto my face. Although it is cooler I am still sweating.

I sit down at the side of the road for a moment. A boy approaches me; maybe he's in his teens.

"I help, I guide."

"I'm looking for this place. Do you know it?"

I give him the receipt. He takes it and runs off.

I step up as though to run after him and then I stop. Would he lead me into an alleyway and stab me for my phone, kidnap me and sell me to Isis. Kill me. Hurt me. Rob me.

The step I've been sitting on is outside a sort of shop. I take out my wallet – If I'm going to be robbed I may as well spend something first. I buy a coca-cola – the only thing I recognise. I neck some of it. Then I walk back down the main road towards the other bars.

I see a few other Europeans – they are out in the street drinking tea with some aristocratic looking Indians – where am I. I figure the Europeans might be able to help. I walk up and ignoring the Indians interrupt.

"Hi I'm looking for the Fire Balcony."

The European looks over the Indian man he's talking to. He sips his tea again. The Indian man touches my shoulder, I startle backwards. They both laugh at me. The other European steps in. The Indian woman is taking out her phone.

"You need to relax," says the Indian man. "I'm Kish, this is Lukas and Ingir."

"Hey"

"Hallo

"Hi

"And this is Misha

"Hi, sorry excuse me." I've already lost track of who's who, and who's named who.

"No problem, you seem tense.

"I'm lost." I admit.

"Lost is okay." Says Kish.

I turn back to the European's and offer my hand "Matthew, from London.

"We're from Sweden, originally," says the woman and she shakes my hand "We live here now."

"Oh."

"This is our place." Lukas says and points at the warehouse space. Its full of brand new Apple computers, drafting boards, models of buildings. Ingir is dressed in tones of beige from head to toe. I look at Lukas – he's in greys – grey desert boots, grey chinos, grey long-sleeve shirt, greying hair. Only his designer Perspex glasses stick out – black tortoiseshell. Ingir lifts out a beige purse and lights a cigarette. It smells funny, cloves & liquorice.

"Kish is an architect." Says Ingir

"We've got work in London."

"Oh."

"So you're lost," asks Misha.

"Yes." I say

Lukas asks, "What's the name of it?"

"The Fire Balcony?"

"No, the place you are after is Concrete – its down there on the left, on the top floor is a fire pit, that's what's on the advert."

"Thank you."

He adds "No problem. Kish is right though, you need to relax"

The Ingir says, "You look scared." And I panic that I'm panicking.

"I just got off the plane, it's all a bit overwhelming."

Ingir laughs and says, "This isn't overwhelming." As if she knew what was coming… "You wait." She adds.

"Really?" I don't think they are just boasting.

"Good luck."

"Thank you."

I start walking down the street. The kid from earlier is running towards me. He is dragging someone behind him. I stop in the street – maybe they are both here to kill me. The man lets go of the kid, he reaches out his hand.

"I think you're looking for my bar." He's wearing Ralph Lauren, a gold earring, big watch, smiles, super confident.

I shake his hand. I look at the kid. I want to tell him I'm grateful he hasn't killed me. I smile at him instead, he grins.

"You give me money?" the kid asks nicely.

"Sure." I give him a hundred rupees. "Thank you kid."

"Thank you sir."

-

Concrete is Bhupen's place. From the outside it looked like a Neon mess and was just one of many doors to one of many bars. But inside it is slick, really slick. Bhupen leads me through it. He smells good, some expensive cologne; he wears boat shoes without socks, a Ralph Lauren shirt, big watch, and lots of rings.

Every light in here looks like it's from the past or the future. Tables are concrete, the floor is concrete, and the walls are concrete. It's a proper club. We go into a lift.
"I'll give you the tour".
"Okay thank you. My friend came here, I'm looking for him."
"White guy?" asks Bhupen, and I nod.

The lift stops.
"This is the second floor lounge." He walks into the space - It's a massive bar – also concrete with low lighting from copper and glass lamps inset into the walls. It is empty.
"It's early – people move here after they eat."
Back in the lift.
"Yeah English, my age, beard."
"No one I've seen."
"This would've been last year."
Third floor stop.
It's a full on dance floor – already a massive light show is on. Staff at the ready.
"Hmmm. We get lots of tourists." But he's thinking.
I start shuffling in my wallet "I have a photo somewhere".
Fourth floor. Bhupen gets out and I follow him. I'm on my phone bringing up the picture of Johno. Bhupen has stopped in front of a fire pit. It's a mix of copper, wood, aluminium, its massive. Couples are arranged around it on tables. It's metres wide. There are waiters carrying trays with cocktails. Away from the pit groups of men are eating burgers and ribs. People

are talking in English and in Indian.

"Wow." And I'm amazed not at the place so much but at seeing the place here. What is this doing here, this isn't the India I was led to believe existed, where's the grime. I'm saying "wow" because I had no idea what to expect, and this isn't what I expected, because...

"This is the fire pit balcony."

"You wouldn't think this would be here."

"In India?" he looks disappointed in me"

"Well up here...yes in India."

"You think we all live in mud huts? Come on my friend, sit down. Sit down." And he walks away. Maybe I'm just one more tourist he has to put up with today to keep this place going, but looking around me I think the Indian's are all better dressed than me and all more handsome or beautiful than you'd find in any London bar.

I sit one row back from the fire – I'm warm enough already but up here people are in their winter jackets and the women in wool shawls. I'm sweating, constantly.

A waiter approaches with Bhupen.

"You're in good hands here – the coconut curry is good. My friend." Says Bhupen and goes to leave so I show him the phone.

"Johno is his name."

He takes the phone and zooms in and out of the picture. He shakes his head.

"You're looking for him?"

"Yeah. Has he been here soon? I know he ate here about a year ago."

"He's lost?"

I tell him the truth "I don't know."

"India is a big place."

"That's what I've been told."

The waiter is looking over at me. I have the receipt back. Johno ate a burger and drank a beer.

"Do you have beer? And I'll have the burger?"

The waiter nods. Bhupen leaves saying, "Enjoy your food. See you in the club later my friend."

I look around. The groups here are celebrating. The couples on dates or anniversaries. Families out for birthdays. Young men out to find dates. Girls out to go dancing. It's just like home. Except for me. I'm the strange white man in the corner drinking a beer. Talking to the staff because I know no one here. What was Johno doing here? Who had he come to meet?

-

The burger is filling. The beer is cold and thirst quenching. The bill comes to about £30 without tip. I take out my wallet and pay with a card – Diana asked me to pay with a card when I could – its all got to be invoiced, all got to go to the insurers, they'll understand the beer – would a professional drink on the job? I don't know. I think of missing persons detective and I go back to Marlow – the Long Goodbye, Big Sleep, I've never been to Hollywood, I've never been to California, missing persons cases in the UK end up with a body in the woods at the side of the road, you never hear who find them except when its a dog walker, I guess they are out in the morning, the dog sniffs the body, they find the corpse. Maybe I need a dog out here, a dog to help sniff out Johno. Or Johno's corpse

-

As I walk out of the entrance Bhupen runs after me.

"Leaving already?" he asks.

I nod.

"The dancing starts soon. We can have some drinks?" He

looks disappointed in me; I feel I'm letting him down.

"Thank you but I'm tired. Great place, thank you for your help."

"No problem, tell your friends." And he's all smiles again.

I wasn't sure what Johno was after out here but I wondered if it was Concrete: the overpriced burger and western beer. Part of me isn't ready yet for what's to come but in that moment as I stepped back out onto the loud dusty street, the neon, the shouting, the sellers the motorbikes, I knew that this bar wasn't what I was after out of this trip.

And then the guilt hit. I wasn't on holiday. I was here for a reason. I walk back the way I got here. The shop I bought the coca-cola from is still open and outside on small stools is the kid from earlier drinking tea. I stop at the shop and point at the tea.

"Can I have a tea please?"

The shop owner tweaks his moustache and then empties the copper urn. He puts the urn back on the heat and adds milk, water, tea and then black pepper, he fires it up. It starts boiling rapidly.

"Sit sit."

I sit down next to the kid.

"You want one more?"

The kid smiles.

"One for him too." I say

"You find the bar?" asks the kid.

"Yes"

He says "You like it?" and studies my reaction.

"Yes sure."

"I've never been inside." Adds the kid.

"Oh"

I take my phone out; I show him the picture of Johno.

"You ever see this man?" I ask

The kid shakes his head. The shop owner gives us the tea. It's hot and sweet. The owner looks at the picture. He nods.

"I seen this man. He was here. Maybe last year." Says the tea maker.

"You have?"

"I remember because he had this red hair. Like he's been on a Haj. He drinks tea here too. Like you."

I look at my cup. The kid finishes his and throws it on the floor with all the other cups.

I ask him "Did anyone ever ask you about him before?"

He shakes his head. "No, not this man."

"I'm the first person to ask you?"

"Yes about this man, yes."

"Did he say anything to you?" I ask.

"He drank my tea. He liked it but I remember this man and he said it was just a little too sweet." He smiles. I sip the sweet tea, think of anyone arriving here for the first time, that is what they'd say.

"Do you know where he went?" I ask

"No no no." he says and starts to wipe up the tea station making it good for a next round.

I think, and add. "Was his with anyone else? Was he in trouble."

"I don't know. Sorry."

"Thank you." And I reach out my hand.

He shakes it and says "Maybe you come back tomorrow for tea."

"Maybe, thank you. I'm Matthew."

"My name is Rakesh"

"Nice to meet you."

"Does everyone speak English here?"

"Yes, we all love to speak English."

"And Indian?"

"Hindi." He corrects me.

"Hindi – yes, Hindi"

"Yes, but here not with you."

"Thank you, for explaining."

I look for a bin for my cup. And then Rakesh reaches out and takes it from me and throws it into a gutter.

"Your first time India?"

"Yes, goodnight."

"Good night."

CHAPTER NINE - ON THE STEPS OF THE MOSQUE

Last night I'd retraced my steps. Cross the main road, passed an arcade of shops I hadn't seen before. They were familiar, an Indian restaurant, a trainer shop, diy supplies. Familiar and different. I couldn't know that this was the most middle class area in Delhi. Sure it could get fancier. But this area Haus Khaz is fancy enough. I'd stopped for a final cup of tea on my way back to the hotel. Tea from a stand I figured was okay as it was boiled. There was a cow in the road and I thought back to my burger. What could've been in it? Who knows?

Sam had given me access to the internet and I'd written back to Diana and Isabella. Reassuring that I'd arrived. That I'd traced his first steps and that everyone was being helpful. I suspected that they'd already gone over this ground already but they'd not been entirely clear on this and so I felt it necessary to tell them about Concrete, about the Tea shop, Johno's red hair.

Sam's father comes out of a room and sits with me as I send the email as if he's scared I'm doing something illegal. That maybe I'm writing a bad review of his hotel. He looks over what I'm writing, I don't mind, there's nothing to hide. He nods as he reads.

When I finish typing I turn to him. He shakes my hand.

I start again with questions. "I'm looking for my friend?"

"I know you are." He says and catches me off guard.

"How." I ask.

"My son." He says.

"Of course. He stayed here last year?" I ask

"Yes. He said he was on holiday."

"He never went home. I'm looking for him, for his family." I tell him.

He nods and says, "Family is very important."

"Do you know where he went when he was here?"

"No. We have many people stay here. Every night six, seven people, sometimes more, ten people. Where you all go – I don't know."

"Sure." I say.

He hesitates and says. "A man came here to look for him before.

"Oh."

"Indian man, from the police."

"What did he ask?"

"The same as you."

"Did he say anything else?" I ask.

Sam's dad shakes his head. This can't be as far as I get. "Now today. You take the metro. You can see the sites. How long are you staying? Maybe today you see the Red Fort. Tomorrow Qatab Minar." He says excited about all that Delhi has to offer.

It seems the question time about Johno is over, so I just say, "Okay."

He tells me. "You see Delhi today."

"Sure." I say.

I turn to go and then think to ask "How many nights did he stay here."

"I can't remember." He says.

And that's that. Sam has overheard us and he runs off. His dad

is looking through old brochures for the sites in central Delhi. He hands one to me. As I unfold it a picture of Ghandi appears
"The Red Fort." He says.
"Thank you." Ghandi looks up at me from the sheet. I'm embarrassed that he's one of the few famous Indian's I could name. Maybe the only one. He's reassuring though in his spectacles.
Sam says "You take the metro now."
I'm tired, hungry, so I ask "Okay. Where can I get some food."
He smiles. – "Anywhere!"
"Is it safe everywhere?" I ask.
He beams at me. "Maybe, maybe not for you. For me its okay."
"Okay."
Sam comes back, he has a giant ledger with him. A big visitors book. He turns through it, back in time through all these people. Then he stops and turns the page to me.
"Here."
He's pointing to an entry in this book, this guestbook. And there it is, my first clue.
Helpful, hot water in 8 needs fixing. Lotus Temple illuminating. Found Orcha on the Mosque steps saw the chowk – crazy. Thanks Sam and team.
He said he didn't have an advisor account, so he wrote in here.
I look across. I would soon learn that everyone that stays in a hotel, hostel, guesthouse leaves a trail – at each point their name, passport number, nationality and to-from fields are filled out. Where have you been? Where are you going? You don't have to say why, you don't even have to go there. But alongside Johno's name and nationality was Dubai, then Rajasthan.
I look over at Sam.
"Did the people who were here before look at this?" The guestbook has thick faux leather on the outside and is hundreds and hundreds of pages thick, I'm having trouble holding it, the

weight of visitors.

He shakes his head.

"What happens to all this information? Do you send it in to the government?" I ask.

I see on his face that it's a no but he humours me with an answer. "Sometime we will, but computer not working."

He gently takes my hand, I hand him back the heavy book and we walk to the stairwell of the house.

We duck under some cloth hangings and there are some large boxes. He opens one of them. It is stacked with books.

"We have many ledgers." There's also a box of 3.5" floppy disks in a corner, a broken looking printer too – detritus of digital. So I ask him "And all of this is online?"

He lets out a little laugh – as if I should get it, the absurdity of it all "No sir, computer is too slow. So we just keep for the law." he says.

"Thanks Sam." I say.

"Today you go to Lotus temple?" And he makes the shape of a lotus flower with his hands.

"Er. Sure, and the mosque – what's this Orcha, in his book?" And I point over towards the guestbook.

"I don't know, but orcha means hidden place." replies Sam.

"Oh?"

He turns and looks for something, it's a bad map with almost no roads on it but with colourful tourist style photos of key landmarks – he presses it hard into my hand.

"I think today you go to mosque, this chowk is very busy for you, you wont like it."

"What is it."

Sam says "Chowk - it means a market."

"I'd like to see it."

"This one very busy, lot of hassle for tourist."

I catch myself nodding a lot." Okay."

He continues "You take metro, you see the mosque, you come back, you see Lotus temple this evening, it is best."

"Okay."

So Johno had gone to Rajasthan. I knew this already. In 'the box' Diana had worked out he'd gotten as far as a city there called Bundi, then there was a bit of confusion. Looked like he'd gotten a ticket straight back to Delhi via the Taj but that was as far as the path had run. Nothing after that. So far I'd found out exactly what she'd found out. I was going over old ground. But that's okay. Because I was still finding it out for myself, I was following him to his grave, or to his cave or wherever, but I was doing it myself, piece by piece, clue by clue, and that was okay, there was no hurry to get back, no rush at all.

-

At the metro I'd bought my connect-four counters to get through the turnstiles. Had my notebook and bag scanned by the army and only gone one stop south before getting back on track to get to the mosque. It is air-conditioned but I'm soaked. It's cramped. Thick-rimmed glasses and backpacks are popular amongst the young men here – going to work, college, university. Fewer women on the metro, signs everywhere against harassment, special designated seating for women.

I make a point of asking at each stop for "Mosque" – no one is suspicious – its one of the biggest sites in Delhi, there is none of the stigma here that mosques and Muslims seem to befall in the west.

I change once. And then queue to get out, back through more scanners. There's a resigned sense that some atrocity will happen here on this metro one day. We queue, the warm air from outside making it more and more uncomfortable.

Then outside. I still must have gotten off a stop early or at least in the wrong place. Whoosh, neigh, caw, crow, hiss, bark, moo. I'm standing at a roadside. A smell of sickly sweet rotted fruit, cow shit and incense covers me. This smell will not disappear for the remainder of my days in India.

I was naïve to think I was in India the day before. This is it.

Beep beep. I'm standing on the pavement but its being used by mopeds as well. Nothing is familiar. The signs that giddy mix of script, numerals and English. Coconut husks, plastic, metal, cardboard, rubble, sheet metal, all of it piled up alongside shops, cafes, sexologists, tourists shops, clothes shops, incense shops, fruit sellers, drinks sellers, luck number hawkers.

It is all here. All of life is here in this one Delhi street. I have a tourist map inside my notebook, which is inside my bag. I take it out. Twist it, turn it, I'm getting some looks. A young man in a shirt approaches me. I reek of tourist, I'm super pale, with a map, clearly lost, a little scared, drenched in sweat, cold with fear.

He's talking.

"You look scared." And starts moving around me working out who I am, where I'm from.

I'm terrified so I squeak out "I'm not I'm just..."

"How long India" he asks confidently.

"This is my second day," I say, and then think I should've added several weeks on to that.

He stops his spinning around me and asks" Second day? Englishman?"

I nod, "Yes"

"Yesterday you come England, today Chowk" he says and gestures at the chaos.

"Yes"

"You look scared, if you look scared people take advantage of you." Says the stranger that I'm certain is about to take advantage of my ignorance.

"I'm not scared" I say completely unconvincingly.

He turns kinder, more softly spoken he says "But you look

frightened, no need to be frightened"

"Oh?"

He starts pointing down the street, "Here is shop, here is restaurant, down there is Karim's - you know Karim's."

I shake my head.

"Hildrams is on the corner – that is simple for if you don't want Delhi Belly – you know Delhi Belly?" he asks.

I smile and try and laugh – the truth is I'm scared. No one talks to strangers in London , and not strange young kids hanging around outside tube stations.

He keeps going, and says "Would you like to take a tea with me?"

"I'm looking for the great mosque." I reply and start moving away from him.

He steps with me, and says "I show you, but first we take tea."

I take another couple of steps away from him "Er..." I don't know what to say.

"Tea, it's good, here you follow me." And he walks away.

I call after him "And then the mosque?"

"Yes." He says without turning back.

"Is it far?"

"I show you after." Again without looking at me.

I shrug, there are half a dozen men who all seem to be stepping towards me ready to take over the vacuum this first stranger will leave, so I skip after him and call out "Okay. Wait up!"

-

He leads me down an alleyway. To one side a man dices a trees worth of herbs in a dicer mounted on the back of a motorbike. A cow shits in the distance. Bamboo scaffolding and piles of rubble. A few low plastic seats. I put my bag down.

He speaks to the four guys loitering there. Dusted with rubble and dirt the guy on the floor takes the copper pot and heats it up. He adds the milk, tea and brings it to the boil, the creamy bubbles threaten to fall over the top of the pot but never do.

He serves me a cup and the man who brought me here a cup.

"Thank you." I say to the tea man.

"100 rupees "– says the guy I followed here and he puts his hand out. "Oh okay." I say to him and look at him "Last night I paid 5 rupees, today I'm paying 100." I say.

He shakes his head. "Less than one English pound. You know what the exchange rate is today?

I shake my head. I sip the tea and hand over a 100 rupee note.

"Good tea" I say, then finish the cup. "Can you show me how to get to the mosque?" and I stand to leave.

He doesn't move, he's staring at his own cup when he asks "Where will you go next?

"The mosque." I say.

"And after?"

"I'm not sure."

"Maybe you like to go to Kashmir?" he says, like I should understand that, as if I've missed something. I sit back down.

"I don't know where I'm going next. I think Rajasthan."

He shakes his head "Rajasthan is very far."

"Okay." I don't know what he's fishing for or suggesting but I'm too lost and too scared to stop him.

"You shouldn't go to Rajasthan. It is a bad place. Too far. No Kashmir is better. In Kashmir my family has a boat, very beautiful, come, on the way to the mosque I will show you, you can make a booking."

"I just want to get to the mosque."

"It is on the way."

"Okay."

I stand up and wave goodbye to the guys manning the tea stand. They are smiling and laughing, they seem nice.

"You have a girlfriend?"

I pause. A small knot starts to form. "No."

"You are single man?"

"Yes."

He leans a little closer. "Bachelor then?"

What does he mean?

He stands and starts walking further into the alleyway. "We go this way."

"Okay."

"You still scared?" he asks me.

"Thank you for the tea. I think I won't make a booking for Kashmir today. How do I get to the fort?" I take out the map Sam gave me, and then the leaflet. I tap on it and say "Ghandi!"

He looks like I've just spat at him, his face turns strange. "Why? Maybe you can come back later and book?"

"I'm not going to Kashmir."

"You are alone in Delhi.

"Yes." I say, and I start walking away back to the main market, he follows me and stands in front of me, I try to duck around him but he won't let me pass.

He touches me on the shoulder, I don't know what's going on , I just want out – he says "You need a guide?"

"Can you show me to the mosque? I say firmly.

"Five hundred rupees – I'll guide you to the mosque." And he won't move out of my way. I start to reach for my wallet – if that's what it will take.

Suddenly "HEY!" shouts another voice, strong, tough. "WHERE ARE YOU LOOKING FOR?" shouts the man back on the market street.

This guy is dressed head to toe like Kanye West, trainers, ripped jeans, oversized t-shirt, jacket, sunglasses. He shouts at my "guide" and the guide disappears.

"You want to lose all your money, you follow that guy." He shakes his head as he talks to me.

"I want to go to the mosque." I say

"You are Muslim?" he asks kindly.

"No."

"It is very beautiful place, very peaceful." He says.

"Yes. I've heard."

"I will show you."

"Thank you."

He lowers his glasses at me and winks. "You look scared."

I take a deep breath. "I think I am."

"It is okay. If I come to London maybe I'm scared too?"

"I don't think so."

"I'm Harry" he says.

-

Harry, which can't be his name, leads me to the mosque. India is a Hindu nation, at the moment I don't know what that means but I imagine flowers and orange cotton. But old Delhi is a mixture of Hindus and Muslims, not quite cheek-by-jowl. Instead in the rickety medieval alleyways there turns a real divide. From vegetables, herbs and breads to live chickens and fire pits with cows' heads, their eyes glazed over with heat. The smell changes, somehow thicker. Women fully hidden behind their robes ride on wooden carts past drainage ditches full of dogs. Young boys in their low brimless caps scatter in all directions with backpacks weighted with books.

Then I step out and see the mosque. It directly abuts these webbed streets. Large steps lead away from the smoking meats and up to the mosque and then the sky. Heavy late afternoon air thickened with fumes from motorbike taxis. There are shouters selling wares or angry at the gridlock in front of the mosque; disabled beggars, bicycle taxis, taxi taxis, coaches. More and more and more of everything.

I pick my way through the traffic. I'm used to London. I know when to cross but even here in the slow day lit jam it feels unsafe.

Again I think of Diana, in Surrey, her G&T cold, lawn mowed, streets empty. She could never have found him here could she. Maybe I underestimate her. Perhaps she's the adventurer and I just don't know.

I get to the top of the steps and something strange happens. The noise disappears. They are only a few feet away shouting, screaming, revving and beeping and their volume is somehow cut short. The air clears as I reach the gate.

Three men start to approach me. The first looks to be a man from the mosque, he wears simple white robes and points at my shoes. I take my trainers off and put them in my bag. As I'm doing this the second man offers to show me around the temple and says he is cheaper than an official guide, at this point the third man interrupts and says he is official guide and I will pay a fine if I take the cheaper guide.

I ask "Do you know a guide called Orcha?" The two guides shake their heads.

"No guide here by that name. I am a very good guide."

"This man is not an official guide."

"I am an official guide." They say in unison.

To all of them I say "I don't need a guide, but thank you." I leave and they curse each other in Hindi.

I walk in bare feet over the dry pigeon droppings and up to the gate. My bag is scanned. I pay my entrance fee. It is 10X the "local fee."

And then I am lifted away: a cooling breeze rushes through the gateway moving me inside. Immediately calming, the street noise even quieter; I stare up at the towers, columns and turrets. I have never visited a mosque in the UK, they have a bad reputation.

This place is exquisite, the warm flagstones carry me across the giant courtyard, birds fly in swarms, children run.

Cooler still are the covered alcoves at the back of the courtyard, here families sit and eat or sleep. They have a lot of clothing with them. Perhaps they live here.

At the front of the mosque men crouch, prone and in worship. I imagine arriving here, hundreds of years ago and this would have been the same, up away from the streets and chaos, a place of refuge, calm and thought, clean, and seemingly a space for all. You can't help but feel like you've arrived somewhere important, that makes sense.

I still don't know what Johno was doing in India but perhaps that calm was what he was looking for. Maybe this Orcha worked at this mosque.

At school we'd sung the Lord's Prayer in assembly hundreds of times, no one in class ever knew what it meant and I still don't now. We'd go several times a year to the local church and have to sing, damp and cold and unwelcoming. Not like this place at all. Forbidden really amongst the West but I got it. This was my first religious experience in India, and it would've been Johno's too. My thoughts take me away from the courtyard, and I wonder if he got really stuck in, joined an islamist group and is now somewhere across the world.

Back in the courtyard a dozen tourists, the women still tying their borrowed scarves into their hair gasp and photograph the place. My experience was not my own. Johno would've seen this too. And I know he'd have been happy here, awed, inspired, but this wasn't where he stopped – we know that already. But it also wasn't where he went, off to become a scholar in a distant city someplace. I can't say for sure, but I have a feeling that wasn't his thing.

The sun is low already, security guards calmly begin to sweep us all out of the mosque and it is sunset when I get to the gate. I'm putting my shoes back on , struggling with the gritty socks. The world turns a little ochre in this light. The gate is locked.

Street noise grows. I'm following you Johno, I just don't know what you saw here. What is Orcha. I can't face the street to the station again. I have this money so I might as well use it. I hail a motorbike taxi.

"You like Tuk-Tuk?"

"Took took?" I ask.

"Tuk Tuk" he says, slams his hand hard on the back seat and adds "Taxi!" He bangs on the taxi. Dressed in what seems to be the motorbike or took-took drivers grey uniform.

"Yes please, take me to the metro station."

"Very good sir." Says the taxi driver.

CHAPTER **TEN** - PLANES TRAINS & GUAVA

Somehow I got this far.

I'm really hungry – a couple minutes ago I pointed at a pancake thingy and now it's in front of me I have to work out how to eat it. There are rats on the floor here, and across from me the open door frame a cow on the platform and a kid being suspended over the tracks whilst it shits.

After the mosque I got a ticket for a train down to Rajasthan. I checked in with Diana and Isabella on email and paid Sam and his family for the room. An early taxi all the way round to this station – it's not the main Delhi one it's something else. And now I'm here.

I bite into the pancake and its good. Its curry and its morning but already that doesn't seem so weird, there's a microwave blasting in the background that is strangely reassuring. The rats are now eating out of a bin. No one cares about the rats, they are just there. Only I care, same as no one bats an eyelid at the family shitting, pissing and cleaning themselves on the far platform, they tuck under the hose meant for the trains and wash head to toe in all their clothes.

I'm panicked I'll miss the train but I've now asked every member of staff in this café and they've told me that it will appear at this platform. I've got the packing down to one bag. I left a sweater and towel at the hotel. I bought a scarf from the side of the road that looks like I could dry myself with it if I need to.

I toy with the Slocum book, flicking to the pages in the middle, reproductions of old photographs of a man and his boat.

Outside of the book there are whistles, announcements, suddenly the platform comes alive. People cross from far platforms right over the tracks. Luggage, motorbikes, parcels and heaps of textiles are stacked up at the platform edge.

"This is your train." Says the waiter from the café in blue and red Polo shirt.

"Thank you."

The train pulls in.

I leave a tip.

I'm grateful for my one bag as I move along the platform.

I'm looking for the sleeper carriage. The waiter runs up besides me with my tip and puts it back in my hand. Then he takes my ticket and waves me along the platform. I reach my carriage. He hands me the ticket and wishes me luck. I've made it.

-

For the rest of the day this would be my ride. A streaky blue carriage in what I learnt to be the travellers' favourite 'Sleeper Class'. Six bunks in the main bit and two on the side, no privacy. The bunks are up as we all sit down on the lowest and arrange our stuff. There are four of us here. One guy has a brief case. Another a backpack and a boy, pre-teens. Briefcase guy has a shirt and trousers western style but the father and son wear traditional Indian stuff, I don't have the words at this time so

63

to me its just stuff. They all take their shoes off and relax into their beds, like daybeds, divans.

We nod briefly to one another. The briefcase man padlocks his case to his upper bunk.

I stare out of the window as Delhi turns to suburb and then to plains.

Endless endless countryside, seemingly all turned to vegetable patches and irrigation ditches.

My wonder is only interrupted when we stop at a station and a new member of our carriage wants to fold his bed down. Its fine by me and I'm half asleep for large parts of this journey. The father and son come over at one point with some newspaper, they unwrap it to reveal some squash balls.

Cutting into them they offer this fruit to me.

"Amroom?"

"I've never had it, are you sure? Is it good?"

They sprinkle it with spice and pink looking salt and hand it to me.

"Thank you."

It's like custard in taste and texture and the salt cuts through the sweetness an extra hit, its incredible.

I nod, and make mmmm sounds "Very nice." I say.

-

We stop again and this time a man swinging a large flask of tea comes down the aisle. I buy a cup from him and soon after a samosa from the next "wallah". I'm learning slowly. Hesitant at first about all of this food. The samosa tastes good, the tea is sweet and milky and also spiced. I don't know what to do with my rubbish, there are no bins. The boy sees this and takes the rubbish and throws it out the window.

I suddenly say "No!"

He stares at me. The father stares at me too.
Realising that's just what's done I add "Sorry, nothing."
I bed down on the vinyl mattress seat and get some rest.

-

There's no way I'd have known when to get off the train if it
wasn't for the man with the briefcase nodding seriously at me. I
don't have time to put my shoes on and I just make it out of the
door before the train moves again. From my carriage the father
and son are waving at me.

"Amroom, Amrooom!" I shout at them "Thank you!"
"Amroom" they reply, smiling.
I wave goodbye to them.
I turn straight into a throng of tuk-tuk drivers. Thirty deep
and I'm the only customer. They are standing by the sign I'd
missed at the station. "KOTA JN"
They all walk towards me at once. Shit.

-

I'm walking at a slow place through Kota. Its hotter than
Delhi, I'm carrying everything I have and I'm sweating more
than ever. I'm not sure I care. Kota is two streets of markets,
shops and hotels and I'm here for the bus to Bundhi.
Each of the thirty tuk-tuk drivers now slowly drives past me.
Each kindly offering to take me to the bus terminal. I admit
to myself I should've taken one of them, but what are you to
do when thirty guys touting for business all come at once. I'd
panicked and now in this hot hot heat I was paying for it.
Also I was one stop away from Johno's last known
whereabouts and I think part of me wanted to delay getting
there. Delhi had been an easy place to pick up the 'scent'. I'd

65

walked in his footsteps from the hotel, to the bar, to the mosque, even paused in a taxi at the light display from the Lotus Temple. And here I was, 500 miles further on and with a few miles left to go before I caught up with him and would take him home, before I lost track of him forever and would go home empty handed, or before I would find out what he did next and follow him one step further.

I wrote copy for shit ad sites. Nothing qualifies me to do this. Does Diana want me to fail, would Isabella rather I not find him. Then they've done all they can. I've come out here and gotten nowhere, not found him, come back empty. They can move on. Maybe that's what they want. They chose a guy who hardly knew their son / husband anymore, who by his own account was lost himself and set him off in the vague direction of a dad abandoning his own life.
A couple more tuk-tuks smile and tease me.
Fuck this. I stop the next one and get in.
I ask for the "Bus station?"
The taxi driver accelerates away "Yes! Let's go."

-

A few hundred metres down the road I pay a few hundred rupees and am left by a roundabout. He waves the wave that says all will make sense if you stay here long enough and see what happens.
Sure enough a bus picks me up. I get on and buy a ticket from the conductor and then force myself into a seat, my pack on the shelf above me and I'm now counting down the miles until I see where Johno ended up.
There's a young kid next to me. He starts talking. Perfect English. It's been a long day and I don't want to talk.
"Englishman?" he asks

"Yes, from London."

"Manchester United?"

"Yes." I look out the window, maybe he'll get the hint, but he doesn't.

"Camden Town?" he continues.

Still looking out the window I say. "Yes."

"You like wrestling?"

"I don't know anything about wrestling. Indian wrestling?"

The boy looks horrified, he shakes his head and says. "No WWF!"

He takes out his smart phone and searches through it. Folders of videos appear. He turns the music up. He smiles. The people in front turn around and then shrug it off. And we sit there, for the next forty-five minutes watching American wrestlers in fancy dress fake hurting one another. Every time a video finishes he loads the next one.

-

I settle in to the rhythm of the bus. Everything shakes and hums and slowly the drone overtakes everything else. Besides me the boy is still drooling over the WWF heroes and their gaudy costumes, throwing each other across his screen. But my thoughts turn to a girl back in London, and what happened there.

I'd been asked to go to a conference on ad-copy called "Keep it Short". Dogshit the lot of it but at least it got me out of the office. People who wanted the job off my back had all paid fifty quid to come hear six of us talk about our experiences of writing inanities. They'd lumbered in and sat down in the auditorium as the five of us prepared in our own ways for the gig. I drank from the free bar and took a piss, others arranged keynote slides or witty photocopied 'zines that betrayed how at some point they'd decided to kill off any real vestiges of creative life they had left inside of them. I wasn't better than them, I knew that, they probably hated me too. I'd sold out too. A piece of crap too. But this afternoon we would present ourselves as the eminent successes of web.

It was as I was leaving the bathroom I saw her. She was chewing on an unlit cigarette nervously outside another conference hall. In her hand some photocopied 'zines in a style I recognised. I looked at her face and recognised her. It was Carol from college, or Cat as we all called her, she hated Carol, said it aged her from birth. Cat and I stood in the hallway for about 10 seconds. We both knew that I'd tried to have sex with her on someone's rooftop a lifetime ago. I hadn't been the kindest of men. She gave me her business card and one of her 'zines. Then there was a buzzing sound and both of our afternoons were about to get less interesting.

I'd lost the 'zine before even getting sat in the auditorium but somehow had retained the card. That afternoon I put a spin on my failure to convert my masters' thesis into a novel and talked about all the fun times that we had at the agency writing copy. Afterwards my wallet filled with business cards from these kids that would stab me and leave me for dead if they could.

It had taken me six months to find her card again but then about two minutes to contact her. She was happy I'd got in touch.

We met the first night at a pub she chose. She brought her new comic for me, freshly printed, before it came out on Amazon. It was impressive, gloss hardcover, beautifully printed. I flicked through the first pages. It was about an artist joining the IRA in the 70s. Her father if I remembered. We got drunk that first night and reminisced a little. Later...

"You were a pain." She said.

"Was I?"

"Yes. More than a pain."

"Formative times."

"You hurt me that night, on the roof."

"I didn't mean to, I thought you fancied me too."

"I did. But that doesn't mean I wanted to screw on a rooftop. It took me the rest of that term to get over it. You shocked me, what men can do. You never did that again did you? Try and force someone I mean."

"No, I didn't mean to, I wasn't well that night."

"I know. But it's no excuse."

"I know that now. I'm sorry."

I'd turned away. That night we had both taken a couple of ecstasy, I'd also taken a little extra speed and some cocaine. But I knew that was no excuse. There's never an excuse.

We turned back towards each other and kissed briefly on the lips. And then she picked up her coat.

"Will I see you again?" I asked her.

"I'm not sure – you were a dick to me."

And then she walked away.

-

Dust and shouting. Something I would get used to with time. The engine over-revs as we pull into a concrete courtyard. This is the end of the bus journey. This is as far Johno got as far as anyone knows. I think about his kid being here, not a place for a newborn, all this dust and sand and piles of rubbish and everything looking broken and rusted.

I lift my bag down and pick my way out of the bus.

The courtyard gives nothing away. A small kiosk sells tea and puffed pastries with the parsley liquor. I walk out of the gates and onto the road. It can't be hotter here than Kota Junction but it is.

Caw, Caw – monkeys chatter behind me. I smile. I've seen them once before in Gibraltar, but here they seem really at home. I like this place already.

I take a tuk-tuk up the road into town. It's a real rattler. Transported to wet Saturday afternoon watching Octopussy. The same frenetic drive through markets, garlanded doorways, passing antiquities or fake antique stalls, through ancient gateways and cobbled street ladled over with dung.

The driver is taking me to the backpacker hotels. He keeps taping on my backpack and saying "traveller" turns out everyone here reads English and my stupid backpack means I'm the traveller so its hostel time for me.

He dumps me at the top of a road, I turn back and can't see anything, it's just a dizzying myriad of streets that tumble away form me presumably back towards the bus depot.

Above me are gated sections of old winded roads and far above a magnificent castle set over the hills. It is all too much to take in.

Immediately around me there are stoops outside houses or shops, its hard to tell. Then a little further up signs for hostels and hotels.

The driver turns back on himself and waves me in the direction of a hotel.

"Good hotel, not expensive." Says the driver.

"Thank you." I say, and shake his hand.

"No problem."

-

At the first hotel they wanted the equivalent of twenty pounds for a small room not overlooking a lake that I hadn't seen before but now that I can I figure I can do better than this room.

Over the road there's a room in a Haveli for three pounds and it looks out onto the lake on one side and the castle on the other. It's courtyarded in the inside and monkeys play freely between the five floors. There's no air conditioning but a room for the night that's the same price as a cup of coffee in London seems good to me.

-

That evening I email Diana – I'm in Rajasthan, I haven't learnt anything yet about Johno. I hope she and Izzy are okay. Some platitudes. Moments later a reply asking if I need more money to help find him. Money won't find a guy who's dead or hiding. I've hardly spent anything anyway. I reply that I'm fine for money but I'll let her know if I need anything.

It's dark already. On the rooftop there's a traveller couple, they look really in love, in matching faded clothing, flip flops, hair like rope. They eat up there, a woman appears from nowhere and offers me supper. I thank her but sat alone with this couple up here doesn't seem right. It's their night, they can have the roof. I walk back down stairs and out into the street. Come on Johno, show yourself.

The dark streets have a fug, hundreds of kids on motorbikes run the gauntlet of these narrow ways. I step out of the way and up on to a stoop. A man dressed as a 70s John Lennon offers me a seat, it's a tea shop, step down it's a street , step up it's a shop, nothing complicated about it. Tea is started, black pepper, cardamom and sugar cane is ground together and added. It's thick and strong and the pepper burns the throat. I pay John Lennon. It could be him, maybe this is where people come to hide, he didn't die, he's here making tea, staying out of trouble, and maybe Yoko sometimes comes here and hangs out with him. Maybe its John's castle.

There's a darkness on the edge of town. As the shop front lighting end there are dimly lit barrows of food for sale. Script on all of them. I see someone doing the marsala pancakes again and I order one. I sit on a child's plastic chair and wait. People giggle around me, maybe this isn't where the tourists eat.

The food arrives, some kind of thick whey and a spiced ketchup is on the side. Costs about fifty pence. I take my time to eat it. Cover my hands in pancake and lentils and whatever else is in it. I see the kids eating their noodles and pastries – afterwards they wash their hands carefully using a steel cup and bucket.

I walk away, stop at a sweet shop and buy something that looks like fudge but its some kind of sweet bean mix. I get back to the hostel. Isabella has written an email to me.

Dear Matthew,

We are grateful for your help so far but know from bitter experience how quickly people get caught up in a place. Please ●o not lose hope or sight of your goal – to fin● my husban● an● father of my chil●. There is an allure of travel that I know is easily ●evoure● until it consumes you. Please ●o not be ●istracte● by the all that In●ia might have to offer a man like you – I expect there is much to occupy you without thinking of Johno an● the reason you are there. You are working for our family an● we trust you to make goo● on your promise to us. Please ●o not let us ●own. Trustingly, Isabella.

In the mirror some pancake on my face and powder from the sweets, I wipe my face with the back of my hand. Button-on the fan and lie down. I'm asleep before I think of how to reply to Isabella.

CHAPTER **ELEVEN** - LASSI

Half an hour later and the heat has woken me, the fan is no longer spinning and there's smoke in my room. My laptop seems to have burnt out somehow – smells like a biro in a toaster. I unplug it and look out the window. Seems the whole haveli is without power now. Up through the courtyard's well is candlelight. I pull some long swimming shorts on and a t-shirt and shoes and go for a wander.

Up on the rooftop the candles burn. Insect flick and flitter in and out of the light. The woman from earlier is there – her partner missing. There's a full ashtray in front of her and more butts at her feet and she's got one on the go. A bottle of water. A diary. She's reading a paperback. "Pensees" by Pascal.

"May I?" She nods and ashes.

"I couldn't sleep. I'm not used to this heat." I add. To try an explain why am here, not that I needed to I guess. The girl says "This isn't hot."

"No?" I ask.

"No. Last summer was hot. This is cold. Too cold."

I look again and she's wearing a thick hooded sweat made of that coloured woven stuff popular in the 90s. Vaguely ethnic not that I'd seen a single Indian wear anything other than a collared shirt, vest or dress in the last week.

"We've had an argument." Says the woman. As if I'm supposed to understand.

"Oh. I'm sorry. How long have you been here?"

"In India? We go back and forth from here to Thailand depending on the weather. How about you, let me guess. Two days?" she says, reading me straight away.

"Close. Three."

She looks me up and down, points at my face "I can see it."

"Where you here last year?"

She's looking back at her book. "On and off – as I said we've travelled."

"I'm looking for a friend." I say.

"A year's a long time." Her accent shows more now.

"Where are you from?"

"France. He is from Israel." And she tuts and nods her head towards the bathroom. She turns the page of her book back and forth and then starts in the same place again.

"My friend was called Johno, ginger beard, my age. He had come via a business trip so maybe he was smartly dressed?" it's a stab in the dark but maybe this girl knows. Sure India's big but maybe...

"To be honest I try not to get to know anyone here, too many fakes you know, too many people on holiday here, they give nothing back, we are travellers you know, not just holiday making, we live here." Says the girl.

And Thailand? I ask

Then she deadpans "Thailand too is also our home." I guess she's being serious. Since we both can't sleep

"Where in France are you from?"

"Near Lyon, but I haven't been home for three years. It isn't home." She starts reading the same page again.

"Do you think your boyfriend might know my friend?" I ask.

74

"Juli? No, he likes people less than I do. Particularly business people." I think she's now getting pissed at me.

"Maybe if I showed you a photo."

"I wouldn't recognise him. Maybe if you had a map of his aura I could sense it. Colours, you know I'm synaesthetic."

"Sorry?"

"I hear colour and see sound, auras a magical field." It is then that I realise they aren't cigarette butts. This girl is out of her mind. At that moment a young teenage boy arrives from the stairs carrying a milkshake. He leaves it for the girl and runs away.

"It's bang. You want to try it?" she asks and offers me her milkshake.

"Bang?" It's a milkshake – is it refrigerated, it looks thick, not just a milkshake but some kind thick diseased milkshake, my stomach groans in fear.

"Marijuana. Go on, try it. You'll be home in a few days anyway, you can tell you friends "hey I did marijuana milkshake with a pretty French girl on a roof top overlooking an ancient city surrounded by monkeys.". You know that's what you'll say. So go on" She licks a bit of milkshake from her fingers that's dribbled out.

She's pissing me off, and now she's daring me, I take the bait. I reach for the glass and try and sip it but its thick and a quarter of a pint goes straight down.

"Whoa."

"Sorry – it's yoghurt?"

"Oui. You know Juli is out at one of the temples up there."

She points to a distant light far up on the opposite hill.

"Every night there is a ceremony. You meet the holy men, you drink a bang. Maybe spoke a chillum and then you wait for the sunrise. You can ask him when he's back about, about your friend." She says. But I'm already miles away.

-

The following morning. Back down in the alleys and streets.
I pause at a man frying samosas and boiling up tea and I sit
and wait as he drains the samosa, strains the tea and then goes
down the line of Indian men and children who eat here.

Newspaper, samosa and a little curried liquor goes on top of
the fresh pastry.

I'd overslept a little and when I'd woken had no memory of
the night before. But I had bumped into Juli in the stairwell and
from what he said I'd bored Mathilde , the girl, with my story
of heartbreak and then fallen asleep. Juli had returned early in
the morning and helped me to my room.

With my laptop looking like it was out of action I'd emailed
from my phone to Isabella and Diana. I'd wanted to reassure
them that I was on the right track, that I was honouring our
agreement. That I was fundamentally not ripping them off. I
was struck again at what curious set of circumstances had
brought me here. A missing person, a time of my life when
I needed an 'out', a family incapable of letting go, a country
without end. Here leaving no stone unturned would be
impossible. I could turn a few over and perhaps draw some
conclusions.

In my half awake state this morning I had forgotten to ask
Juli about Johno. I had a printout with me of his face and I
intended to spend the day asking after his whereabouts.

After the tea and samosa I went back to the tea shop that
I'd been to a day earlier. Again John Lennon was there, he
beckoned at me to crouch on the floor. Across from him on the
opposite stoop an obese man sat shirtless on a rug, leant back
against a stack of pillows, he squinted at me and spoke briefly
to someone unseen further inside his home. John Lennon
begins his ritual of milk, tea, cardamom, pepper, and cane sugar.

76

I put the picture of Johno down on the table. John serves me the tea. He shakes my hand

He says "Hello. Davindra"

"Matthew" I say. I like this guy.

"You like my tea so you come back?"

"It's the best I've ever had. "– This was the truth.

"Thank you."

I tap the picture of Johno, and ask him kindly, with the least amount of private eye. "Do you know this man?"

He looks at the picture "He is your friend?"

"Yes, I think he came through here."

"Let me have a look." He holds the picture close to his face. He stands and pushes back a curtain. There on the wall are elaborate paisleys. He thinks hard, closes his eyes as if meditating and then says "Jonathan, yes, here, here!"

He stands and is pointing to a paisley on the wall. I stand up and look a little closer. Each paisley's petal is made up of a quotation and then a name. And there it is: paper in a forest, marks on a tree, snake scale in a shower, a quote in Johno's hand signed off with his name.

I read it out "Eheu fugaces labuntur anni Johno 20XX"

"Englishman, orange beard like he'd been to...Like he'd been to Haj. Yes but he was Christian, not Muslim ?

I can't believe it. "That's the guy! I say.

"It's Greek I think." Says Davindra

I nod, "It's Latin."

"Yes Latin, old language, almost as old as ours." And he smiles. I got the feeling Davindra was here when the earth came to light, he will be here when earth dies. He knows that he cannot die and that he will live forever, that is what his face tells me anyway.

"Do you know what it means?" he asks

"No, do you have a pen I can borrow."

He steps down to a small toolbox full of spoons, scrapers and so on. "Yes, yes.

He busies himself looking for a pen as I look at what other treasures are on the wall, what other clues I might find.

Amongst the other quotes are buddhist-lite, instagram-heavy "seek and you shall find" "better angels" "temple body" stuff – eastern pop philosophies filtered through western travel writing and guardian columnists with a bit of French, Japanese and Israeli thrown in for good measure.

-

I'm writing the quote down when a voice interrupts me.

"Slaughterhouse five." I turn and there's a Chinese looking man looking at me.

"Hi."

"It's from Slaughterhouse Five – Kurt Vonnegut." He says. As if I should already know that.

"Right."

"At least sort of, Vonnegut is quoting the Latin, something to do with lost years I think."

Who is this guy? "Thank you." It doesn't make sense, did Johno like books? I think in school he wasn't that into books, not like I had been.

"No problem, I'm 'Snake." He reaches out his hand.

I reply "Matthew. From London. You are from, China?"

"Korea. But it's okay."

"Sorry."

"You're the guy from London – you know Mathilde? She said you got laced on Bang last night and passed out. Says she had to help a boy from London finish his milkshake, said you were mashed."

What had happened – I couldn't remember. "Yeah that's me."

He continues "She says you're looking for a friend who's gone

78

missing."

I point at the wall "He wrote this – see Johno 20XX."

He squats on the floor, cross-legged. He looks at me and says "I'm sorry for your loss."

"He, he, he isn't dead." I stutter out.

He looks at the floor and says "How long has he been gone?

"A year." And he looks at me and then at Davindra who looks away.

Snake says "Well. Look I was going to go riding out to see the Baba in the desert but I've messed my leg up coming off the bike, if you can drive a bike you can come with me. Anyone that passes through here Baba is sure to know about."

Is Johno dead? "Well, I'm not sure. I was going to look at the castle and then get some lunch."

Snake moves a little and from under his t-shirt finds a five hundred rupee note and hands it to Davindra. "Does the castle know how your friend... how your friend went missing." Snake asks me.

"No but, whilst I'm here."

"Look , Baba knows who has been through here and who hasn't. He'll be able to tell you." And Davindra passes him a cup of tea.

I'm thinking, then "Do you know a guy called Orcha? I ask.

He shakes his head. "Can you ride a motorbike?' he asks.

"No. Could you teach me?"

"Sure. It's easy." He says and nods.

-

And so Snake and I found a quiet patch of dusty road. The sun didn't seem to rise that day and a soft cooling breeze eddied across us and in the sometimes shade of brittle trees and unfinished desert homes I learnt to ride a motorbike.

Snake was fearless, holding on to me as he gave instructions, edging me on with the accelerator. Once he thought I had graduated from his makeshift classroom of dusted road he gave me some directions and we headed of to see Baba.

I knew nothing about motorbikes, I don't think Snake did either. But we knew it needed gas and so before we hit the desert proper we filled up – bought a £3 old whiskey bottle from a corner store and had it siphoned into the tank.

The sun had finally found its place in the sky. I didn't know it now but I would later learn about Surya – the sun god. And perhaps it was him and his chariot that delivered me safely on this first ride.

Dogs, cattle, trucks, carts, unpaved road, gravel, sand and river crossings. All new all of the time. Nothing prepares you for constant newness, it is a profound feeling. More so than any drug. It is often described as a leap but this is false, it is the slow relaxed succumbing over hours and days, fear and excitement given way to acceptance and calm.

And Snake's calm gave me a boost as I piloted our motorbike through palms, past fields of puja flowers picked by women in gaudy florals. Past a closed up post office outpost where men played some kind of chess on the ground.

All the while Snake and I talk as only total strangers trusting on another with their lives can. We talked with total honesty, an outpouring of stress and rejection of the fake walls of machismo we've started to leave behind.

He's a water engineer working across the middle east bringing irrigation to deserts. He's disillusioned with it all and is out here, in another desert looking for some answers. I tell him about Johno, about looking for him, my honesty stops when I decide to leave out the bit about my being paid, I tell him also about the girl and he understands, he almost got married back in Korea but she had been having an affair with a much older married man, the failure of that relationship was what first prompted him to look for water in the middle east – a similar search to mine in many ways.

We twist and turn and suddenly the plain turns into a cliff. Some kind of weather formed this. There's a river and a waterfall. And the sun is coming down. I slowly wobble the bike towards the waterfall and park it up. We both almost fall off when we come to a full-stop. Snake screams with delight "This is where Baba is. Hey Baba!"

We start to walk towards the waterfall. The base of it falls into a cool looking trough of clear water. It starts some 50feet up. It isn't running fast, I guess its not the season for rain.

Then I see him, a slight man with dreadlocks and loincloth quickly picks his way down the side of the falls. He is Indian, handsome, light skinned, he wears necklaces, bracelets, no watch. From a leather lanyard he carries a fabric phone sling. He is also ageless. His skin stretches over bones and muscle. Like a skinny British retiree on the Costa – leathery tan.

Snake starts with "Baba – we've come to see the beautiful waterfall!"

"It's amazing." I say

"It's dry" says Baba, slowly disseminating wisdom. "Well mostly dry but, if you look at little closer you will see that the water still it flows." He turns away "Here look."

He walks back away from us just as quickly as he arrived. He gestures and we follow.

"See – still it flows." Says Baba.

From some unseen meandering the waterfall spits out from a tit-shaped rock. "You see the shape – very special water from this rock." Says Baba. Baba touches the rock with his fingertips and makes a silent blessing. He turns back to us and we three walk back towards the motorbike.

"Nice bike" says Baba

"Thank you, it's a rental." Says Snake.

"Not a Honda?" asks Baba

"No, something JVC something, I'm teaching Matthew here to ride." Says Snake distancing himself from the bike.

"He's a good teacher, I make a bad student." I say.

"You should've rented a Honda, more reliable! This has poor tyres for the desert. An old "Honda – that's what you need." Says Baba.

"Sure, next time we can rent a Honda" I say.

"Wise words" adds Snake.

"Sit, sit." Says Baba.

We sit down on the ground.

From Baba's phone sling he takes out an old Ericsson phone and puts it to one side, then he takes out a small clay pipe, some tobacco and some marijuana. At least that's what I assume it is.

"This is chillum, you know chillum?" asks Baba.

He crushes the weed in between his palms and then stuff the rough grinds into the pipe, then lights it. Cupping his hand around the pipe he takes a few deep gulps of it and then passes it to Snake. Snake refuses.

"I have to ride the bike back to the shop. Matthew will though." Says Snake without asking me. Baba passes the pipe. A little ash spills as I'm not used to it. I take a couple of deep breaths. I look at Snake, he is smiling. Baba steps away and brings a bucket, a stainless pot and some coals. He lights a the coals in the bucket and starts boiling up some cold tea.

"Thank you." I say, and pass back the pipe.

"Namaste." Says Baba.

"Namaste." Says Snake.

Snake is grinning. Why is Snake grinning?

-

An hour later I wake up in the shade of the plateau's cliff. Baba is lying down opposite me. Snake is shouting.

"Matthew, you should get in, it's great!"

I lean up, he's in the pool. The coal fire is burnt out now. The ash of several pipes has been knocked out in front of Baba. Snake pulls his t-shirt on and comes back to the fire.

"You passed out, must've been tired." Says Snake and laughs. Baba opens one eye and grins.

I look at Snake, ask him "Can we ask him about Johno."

He nods "Sure, ... Hey Baba?" Baba lifts himself up into a seated crouch.

"Yes?"

"Matthew here is looking for a friend." I start on the story "I think he passed through here, he visited Bundi, I'm sure of that. He has ginger hair, beard maybe, maybe he was reading a book – he could have carried the book with him – maybe you've seen it - Slaughterhouse Five it is called."

"Name?" asks Baba

"Slaughterhouse.., oh, Johno, his name is Johno." I say. Baba starts grinding up again. He taps out the chillum.

"No. " he says. Then he stares at me. Something in my face must look devastated.

"No, sorry – I meet a lot of people, many people from London, Chelsea, Manchester, all come here, all want to smoke my chillum, say they've met Sadhu, take tea. Many, many people." Says Baba.

"I understand." I say.

"I wish you luck with your search." Baba replies

"Thank you Baba " says Snake.

"Thank you Baba." I say.

Baba looks out at the motorbike. "Remember Snake, next time you visit I want to see a Honda."

Snake nods, puts his hands together "Yes Baba." I copy Snake and the greeting is returned by Baba.

I'm feeling relaxed, not high. But the slight fog means that it isn't until we are 100metres back towards the desert track to Bundi that I remember that other name 'Orcha'.

"We have to go back, I have one more thing to ask him." I say. Snake turns the bike back. He doesn't ask questions. Baba hears us heading back towards him. We pull alongside.

"This is still not a Honda!" he smiles.

"Baba, you didn't know Johno, but do you know someone called Orcha?"

Baba smiles. "Orcha? It isn't a person – it means Hidden Place. There is an ancient city called Orcha. Very far from here though."

Maybe I'm saying it wrong I think to myself. I say "No, I think it's a person – someone who would have met Westerners?"

"Orcha is the Hidden Place! I have never been but very beautiful."

"Thank you." I say.

"Good luck with your search. ...Snake?" says Baba.

"Yes?" asks Snake.

"Don't bring this again, it has to be a Honda."

"Yes Baba."

-

Back in Bundi I get off the bike at the edge of town and decide to pick up some food. I realise I haven't eaten since we left town that morning and the smoke and the sleep have left me with a big appetite.

I walk up through the market, take a couple of different streets. I pass the entrance to a foot well and peer in. Something to look at tomorrow.

I pass another samosa stall and buy a couple for a few rupees. In a small stall a man sits cross-legged sewing paper notebooks together – I buy one for the same price as the samosas. At a sweet stand I buy a box of condensed milk sweets. Maybe I am a little high.

I get back to the hostel. Walk past the kids of the owners playing in cool of the ground floor. I head upstairs to my room. And there, out on the landing is a man reading a paper. I'm opening the door to my room when he starts up conversation.

"You're the Englishman who was out at Baba's today?" asks the man not taking his eyes off the paper. I turn back to look at him but can't see past his Times of India.

"Yes – I say. That's right." I say. Paranoia - I'm worried it's the weed – that I've been caught smoking, that I'll be tried for drugs and die in an India prison.

"Here, this is a guava." Says the man. He lowers his newspaper and hands over the fruit – it's like a soft pear to the touch.

"Those sweets will rot your teeth."

"Thank you." I say.

"You've been asking about me haven't you?"

"I'm looking for my friend Johno."

"My name is Archer, or Asha, or…" he pauses.

I finish his sentence for him "Or Orcha…?"

"Yes." He says.

I look at him hard. His hair is thick grey and shoulder length, he wears a linen shirt, sandals, chinos. He smiles, looks kind, his eyes are wrinkled, his nose is roman, his ears pierced, bangles, necklaces, a watch.

"Nice to meet you."

"You've been asking about me."

"Yes. I think you met my friend."

"Perhaps."

I look at the guava.

"What do I owe you for the guava."

"It is a gift, from my garden to you. "

"Thank you."

"So what did you want to ask me."

There's a seat next to him.

85

I turn back and finish unlocking my room's door and put the sweets and guava down and then take a seat next to Archer.

"Matthew, good to meet you." I say.

"Very nice to meet you Matthew. You know my name."

"Yes."

"So why did you want to speak with me?"

"Well, I don't know if it's you. I'm looking for my friend, Johno, I think he came through here, after Delhi, he's gone missing. In Delhi he wrote that he'd found or met Orcha there, and I don't know what that means, or if it's you. But he's gone now, maybe, maybe he's..."

"Missing? Asks Archer.

And not having the guts to say dead I don't correct him. "Yes"

"I doubt that."

"He has."

"Some people go missing, other people take a longer holiday than they bargained for. Perhaps he simply didn't want to go back to work?" He laughs to himself.

"Who would want to work in an ugly city when you can be out here?" asks Archer.

I say "That's true.

"You for example, you are here on holiday, maybe you want to stay on a few weeks longer, you don't tell work, you stay, people get a bit worried but that's normal."

"I'm not here on holiday, I'm looking for my friend." I remind him.

"I was just giving an example."

"Sorry. – I'm apologising."

"I meet many, many people, we all do, there is a circuit here, invisible but tourists like this part of India, they like to feel they are explorers, another continent, another culture."

"Yes." I say.

He starts again, his voice calm, super confident. "I saw you on the bike today, a little unsteady. Your friend is a better rider."

"He's teaching me, we only just met."

"You trusted him?" asks Archer.

"Yes, I mean, it was fun. You know, try something new."

"Trust is very important. The guava is ripe, you should eat it now."

"Thank you but I'm not hungry, maybe later." I say.

"But you were going to eat those sweets now?"

"Yes."

I look back at my room. Then to his paper. On the front page the prime minister of India is visiting a hydroelectric facility.

"My friend might be lost. I'd like to find him. Did you meet him?"

"Do you know how many people who are lost, that I meet and that I help get on the right track?"

I shake my head. This man is frustrating, but I've no other options. I'll go along for now.

"Thousands! Many, many westerners come to meet me, I have a class, and sometimes I have one pupil, sometimes two or three thousand pupils. "

"Is it yoga?" I ask.

He smiles, maybe he can't be pissed off.

"It is similar to yoga. Very similar."

"I think you met my friend Johno, or he met you at least in Delhi, at the mosque, and I'm not sure, but I think he came here afterwards, maybe he followed you?

"Maybe he did".

"Well did he or didn't he?" I mutter

"You are sweating." He says "Perhaps you'd better have a lie down. Eat the guava, have some tea on the rooftop."

Just then Mathilde walks in carrying some shopping. Bottles of water and some fruits.

"Hi." She says.

"Hi!" Archer stands. He gives me his hand to shake.

"We should talk this evening? And get some rest, you look ill."

He says.

Archer walks away, leaving his newspaper. Mathilde watches him go. As he walks by her he touches her elbow with his hands. She smiles at him.

"I see you've met Archer?" she asks

"Yes, he's..."

"Brilliant?" She interrupts.

"Well."

"Isn't he. He's changed me."

"Has he?" I ask.

"Today, I felt terrible, me and Juli, we fight, I see archer for one hour of meditation, I feel better, we eat some fruits and then we drive on the motorbike to collect some puja flowers from the farmers."

"I think you might have seen me? I was with Snake – in the desert, by the waterfall. Archer said he saw us?" She looks uncertain

"No. We were alone. Maybe that was before.?" She's flakey, maybe she'd forgotten she'd seen us, or maybe she hadn't seen us at all. Maybe Archer hadn't but he knew, somehow he knew that I was looking for him. Next to arrive is Juli. His arm is in a sling."

"The fucking bike, piece of shit."

"Oh babes!" Screams Mathilde. Mathilde drops her shopping on the floor. One of the water bottles bursts open as she goes to hug her boyfriend.

"It isn't broken, just a sprained wrist but fuck that bike, never ride a Honda." Says Juli.

The water is gushing out over the edge of the courtyard landing like rain. I'm completely invisible now to Mathilde so I go back to my room. I smell the guava, its over ripe, beyond sweet. I put it in the window to get the smell away from my bed. I open up the box of sweets and chew them. Fuck you Archer. If you could see me now eating my sweets. I'm going to make you talk straight. Somehow.

-

That evening I shower, and head back out to the market. I see Snake back in the tea shop and stop to take tea with him.

"I found the guy." I say.
"Your friend?"
"No, Orcha, or Archer - the man I think he met in Delhi."
John Lennon looks up.
"Archer?" asks John
"Yes." I say.
John says. "Very brilliant man."
"Is he?"
"Yes, very, very clever man, many houses." Says John. I look at Snake drinking his tea.
It's a good one" says Snake sipping the tea.
"The best in Bundi?"
"The best!"
I drink my tea. And Snake is right. This is amazing. This is all amazing.
"Why Snake?" I ask Snake. " I mean, why snake the name?"
"It's me, it's my name. It's who I am. Why Matthew?"
"It is my name."
"I know but you don't seem like a Matthew?"
I finish up my tea.

I'll see you later – I say and pay up.
Where are you eating tonight?
Probably just from the stalls. You?
Maybe a samosa.

We get on me and Snake. And maybe he has a point. Maybe

out here I'm not a Matthew, who is Matthew anyway?

-

On my way to get my Marsala pancake I stop at an internet café. I figure I can type faster than on my phone and also there's something I want to look up.

A few lefts and rights and I'm in "Cyber Space" four new PCs heavily wired into various wall sockets. It is being run by kids in their early teens but as they type and game on two of the computers you can tell they're the new generation – faster than I'll ever be.

I rent a computer for a half hour.

There are emails from my old work – a begging email again from Rossie with a copied in Russell about the laptop. A kinder email from Lottie making sure I was alive. There's three emails form Diana and Izzy, one worried I'd gone awol, the other relieved I'd emailed them yesterday and the third was to ask when I would have any news.

I write to Diana and Izzy, tell them all that I've told you. That I think Johno was here. That there may be records of where he stayed. I leave out Archer for the moment – he's too much to sum up in a single email – and besides I don't know what significance he has. I reassure them I have plenty of money left. I also decide not to tell them about the motorbike – it doesn't sound safe riding through the desert and I owe them piece of mind.

I also email Lottie, describe the waterfalls, smoking weed with a holy man – she'll love that. Wind up R&R too hopefully. I tell her that I'll send the laptop back as well. Its fucked, I might as well give it back to them.

Then I open up Google. I type in his three names "Archer, Asha, Orcha". I press search.

And there he is: Archer. There are over a hundred thousand results. There are thumbnail pictures of him at the top of the screen. And the sides of my search page are filled with advertisements, with better written copy than I could've ever written for courses run by Archer.

I click through to images. There he is again in portrait – professional portraits in the dozens. Then underneath wide-angle photographs of gymnasiums and public squares filled with people seemingly praying to Archer. He stands at the front, dressed in linen robes. The faces of the faithful a mixture of western, eastern, Asian, African. All are represented here.

I click through to look at the courses. There are courses worldwide. Archer in Washington, London, New York, Sydney, Paris and so on. Pictures of him with celebrity fans, after dinner speaking for oil barons and democrats alike. He's stood with Madonna in Times Square holding a yoga mat whilst a dozen Archer fans do yoga poses on the floor.

Who is this guy?

-

Trust me. Hold tight. Don't let go and you'll be alright.

Easy to ask for trust, harder to give. We'd started dating again. Courting. In the most old fashioned way. Sat at a distance. The air between us weighted with the years past.

"I'm not sure I could trust you again."

"I'm sorry" I said. "I never meant to hurt you." We were going back over old ground.

"I know that, but it doesn't mean I can trust you."

"I liked you."

"We are going to have to take things slowly." She says

"Slowly is okay."

"Is it? For you?" she asks

"Yes. I'm not in any rush."

"Don't be an idiot."

"I still like you."

"I like you too, but trust comes easier the first time round, but the second time, I don't know, it seems harder. You'll hurt me." Going back over this, remembering this, the irony that it would be her that finished things. She thought that I might hurt her.

We took a cab halfway to the theatre and decided to walk the rest. Strolling at arms length across Blackfriars bridge like colleagues. A wind ripped down the Thames and she shivers. I offer her my jacket but she doesn't take it. Can't take it. She doesn't want to be smothered in down, she wants to be able to trust me again and she wants to love.

Passing lovers and first-date couples on the Southbank we share a smile. It is easier seeing yourself in the mistakes of other people.

In the bar before the show I see Rossie across the bar. I wave at him and he steps towards me. I can't put her through his bores too so I go and talk to him. Rossie's opener is "I didn't have you down as someone who liked a play Matthew?

"Here with a friend, we're here to support her sister – she's in it."

"Oh?"

"One of the chorus I think, I don't know." I say.

"There isn't a chorus in this one, its very modern."

"Is it?" I ask.

"Yes, stripped back, deconstructed. You know."

"Right."

"So am I going to be introduced?" he adds a wink. Just then the final bell rings out through the theatre.

"Ah, see you later Rossie, perhaps in the interval?"

"There isn't one." He says.

"Oh well." I shrug and turn away and go back to her. She's hanging by the door.

"You left me." she's upset.

"My boss. I couldn't put you through meeting him."

"I'm nervous, for her." She says.

"She'll be fine."

"Do you think?"

"Yes."

The play is pure tedium. Equally distilled and ragged with only pauses for laughter left over from the original. It has a musical interlude where phony hip-hop dancers mime sex acts on faux stone Greek god statues. After two hours it is finished. We both stand to applause.

"What did you think?"

"I liked it, a lot, very interesting." I'm lying

"You can say you hated it, at least I'd know you were telling the truth."

"It was good. Your sister was good."

"Could you tell which of the sisters she was playing?"

"Yes" – a mumble

"Go on"

"The taller one."

"Trust Matthew, that's going to be a problem for me."

"I'm sorry."

"I know you are, you've said that a lot." We walk up to the bus stop.

"I'll get the bus I think."

"Me too. Mine's the 87."

"Good."

She tugs at my jacket and pulls it a little around her. Then she looks up at me and we kiss.

-

I wake up in the havelli. Drenched in sweat. The sun is through the window and fills my bed. I look around the room. My backpack needs packing, the tote bag needs cleaning. The laptop needs sending back to Lottie. Phone needs charging. My face needs washing.

Leaving the room to go and find some breakfast there's a note on the mat outside my door. I pick it up and head up to the rooftop.

On the roof is Juli – his eyes closed, hands in the prayer position, chanting. I ignore him and sit at a table. Juli must've had one eye open.

"She's gone."

"I know." I say. "I mean, is she?" For a moment I think he's talking about you. But that's impossible.

"I have to let her go"

"Who has gone?" I ask.

"Mathilde, she has to go, she has to live her own life, who am I to hold her down, who am I to hurt her, you know, she left this morning, she leaves just some mantra for me to try and be more independent, you know?"

"I'm sorry"

"Why are you sorry"

One of the owner's kids runs up to me, smiles and gives me a laminated 'toast' menu. Egg on toast, nutella on toast, jam on toast, marmalade on toast, vegemite (Australian) on toast, marmite on toast, butter on toast. I order peanut butter on toast and a cup of coffee. The boy runs away.

"the coffee here is terrible"

"that's okay, I'm all tea'd out"

"you should drink hot water and lemon in this weather – it's cleaning" – he says.

I look at the note, unfold it. It is from Mathilde.

Dear Matthew,
Juli an, I argue, again last night for the last time. He has anger
issues an, I cannot be aroun, his negativity any longer. I am
travelling with Archer to U,aipur where I will take part in one of his
famous sunset healing ceremonies. You shoul, come. Archer says you
have a lot of healing to ,o.
Mathil,e.

Juli's eyes are still closed. The boy arrives with the toast. Juli
stands and sits opposite me. He takes one of my two slices of
toast and eats it.
"I can order more toast"
"One is enough" he says. I turn to the boy.
"More toast please"
"And hot water with lemon" asks Juli.
The boy nods and runs away.
"These people are so beautiful" he says
"Sure"
"Really, they've got such pure souls"
"I need to post a parcel, do you know where the post office is?"
"Not tainted by our western ways"
"I'm leaving today"
"Just a nation of innocents"
"Mathilde wrote to me" I offer. But Juli isn't on this rooftop.
He is miles away, his face is eating my toast but his mind must
be drifting over the desert.

-

There was no way I was leaving Bundi that day. I had no idea
where Udaipur even was. But Archer was there, and he wanted
me to follow him. He was the one person who might now

know what had happened to Johno out here and so I had to go. And besides Mathilde had asked that I follow her and out here maybe that simple request was enough.

I spent the rest of the day at the post office. I'd packaged up the Laptop in a thin cardboard box that the boy from the havelli had found in the kitchen - it had once contained noodles.

After queuing for some twenty minutes with men, women and children I was ushered behind the counter and into the office. Sat with the Chief Post Master I explained that I wanted to send the laptop to the UK, looking at a map I showed him that this was not the UAE but Great Britain. The two of us laughed more than either of us could really have felt at this misunderstanding. I then handed over the burnt out laptop and a few rupees and got a receipt. It wouldn't matter if the laptop never made it back - I posted the receipt separately to Lottie and threw in the notebook I'd bought the day before for her as a present – something to make her life behind the reception desk one degree more delightful.

After the post office I was spent. I bought a litre of cola to drink on my walk back up through town and made a point of stopping at every stall on the way up. Dentists, axe makers, bike menders and so on. I slowly soaked it all up as I got my constitution back. Constitution – something so often mentioned in colonial era novels. Here I got it, I just wasn't built for standing in a hot post-office for an hour.

I made enquiries as I went about the best way to get to Udaipur and double checked with John Lennon as I stopped by his place for tea. It'd be a bus first thing in the morning.

I stayed drinking tea wondering if perhaps Snake might show but he didn't. It was a quiet night in the streets. Few tourists. A half hour later John Lennon started packing up the stall. I was comfortable here, but it was time to move on.

CHAPTER TWELVE - UDAIPUR

Octopussy. There is no escaping that movie here. Knock of tuxedos for a few sterling. Motorboat rides. Café screenings. DVDs. Romantic nights at the hotel on the lake.

I'd arrived at sunset and the place was truly magical: I'd found a £3 a night hostel in a steep road flooded with shit. Picked my way through the turds back down to the water's edge and looked out and the thousand dollar a night hotel. No more female ninjas.

I'd wanted to get closer, take photo on my phone to send to somebody. And I'd walked out over a footbridge that linked the two sides of a slurry filled feed stream. There was another man my age stood there, in sandals, battered t-shirt and old cargo shorts.

"It's just another typical Rajasthani city with a fort. "cept for this dirty lake" He's American, younger than me now I look properly.

"How long have you been here?" I ask

"India? Oh, a few months now"

"What's this city like?"

"Full of tourists" With no sense of irony.

"Good to meet you"
I walk away from him to the other side of the stream.

-

The following day I'm searching for Archer. I'd forgotten to
contact Diana and Isabel and for most of the day my mind had
squandered my real reason for being here. Instead I'd busied
myself with getting my clothes washed, finding a tea stand that
wasn't selling cappuccinos and dodging knick-knack shops
selling repro paintings of James Bond.

I'd asked at the hostel for Archer and they all knew him here.
'Guru Archer' they called him. They hurriedly ran out of the
hostel and came back with a flyer with a picture of the man's
face on it surrounded by paisleys. Archer's class for that day
was to take place in an old cinema, some two miles west of the
centre.

I'd decided to walk there. It was hot here, perhaps the
warmest place yet. The streets were similarly narrow and
medieval at first before opening up into one straight dusty road
west. A man ground sugar cane into juice at the side of the road
and I stopped for a glass – it was the finest tasting thing I'd had
in the week I'd been in India and gave me a boost as I trudged
out of the city gates and up the hill.

-

Not the big crowd I'd expected. Instead there was a ragtag
bunch of us queuing up outside this 'old' cinema. Old meant
a few years old. All marble and concrete and unfinished.
Mathilde was there talking to a small group all speaking in
French. I waved at her and she smiled back.

"You found the note then?"

"Yes." I say

"I hope you bring a supple body for today?"
"I'm not sure"
"You'll be okay, we start easy"

-

We all file into the auditorium. There are no chairs. A young Indian man dressed all in baggy white shirt, trousers and shoeless wheels in a crate of bottled water. I notice straight away how warm it is in here. No windows, no air conditioning. Just strip lights and the little cooling from the concrete.

We stand nervously like kids on the first day of school. The man returns with straw mats and towels and we each take one of each. I follow Mathilde as she arranges hers and we form two lines facing the stage.

Next the man in white lights the incense sticks. He leaves a whole pack smoking on the front of the stage and then lights a second pack at the rear of the auditorium. We are all already visibly sweating just sitting here. The women too.

The man then arranges a mat for himself, no towel. He sits cross legged, makes the praying sign with his hands and then begins to chant.

Several of the group chant along with him. Its in Hindi, I understand not a single word. I look across to Mathilde, she has her eyes closed and seems to be moving her lips. So I close my eyes to and let it soak in.

The chanting sound grows as more people join in. How are they taking this in, how do they understand now what they didn't five minutes ago. Then there is a hand on my shoulder, I look up. The man in white is moving behind me. I start to move my lips, I start to make the sounds that the others around me are making, I don't need to understand, I just need to get the words out, I'm humming but it is enough and he moves away from me.

A tiny high pitch note cuts our mumbling. I look up. He now has a small bell in front of him. He puts it to one side. Next he starts to perform a series of stretches. Yoga. I'd never tried it back in London. It had become a fad synonymous with self-help and the encroaching avocado and smoothie west London clean-living lifestyle. A pyramid scheme for those in emotional not physical pain. I knew a half dozen yoga instructors back in London, often freelancers at the agency would be retraining, giving up their skilled jobs in media law or design for a life of yoga pants and foam mats.

I'd underestimated the difficulty. I wasn't the only man in the class, but I was perhaps the oldest, and the least fit. Other guys in their travellers' vests and baggy pants seemed to be having less trouble. I was still in jeans and a shirt. Out of depth and out of place. I look at Mathilde, she's not struggling at all.

The man now starts to move through us. My neck is by my ankles but clearly not close enough. He pushes down on my lower back forcing me further forwards. My shirt sticking to his hand and my back. He moves away and puts a bottle of water by my mat. I'm the first that needed this and I feel cursed by my years of living badly.

We continue to stretch, curl and lift ourselves around the mats. It is already midday when the first session comes to a halt. There is no sign of Archer.

Slowly we all file out of the auditorium. I drink heavily from the water bottle. Mathilde is waiting for me outside. It is much cooler in the hot sun and at least it is dry. She laughs at my state.

I walk up the street and find a tea stall. We have a break for lunch. A little further along is a stall selling a rice pancake and brown sauce.

"uttapam? You want to try?" – a teenage boy with sharp haircut and smart shirt.

"uttapam?"

"yessir, it will cool you down, coconut"

"Sure, how much?"

"fifty cents sir"

I pay my fifty rupees, a eat the pancake and nutty sauce. The boy is right. It is soothing. It is very, very good.

-

Back in the auditorium; some of the class walk in eating Snickers, Mars, drinking Cokes. Maybe they know something I don't. Maybe they don't like the food here. Mathilde is stretching on her mat.

"how are you feeling" she asks

"stretched"

"you like India yet"

"yes, I think I do. Do you think we will see Archer today?"

Mathilde shakes her head.

"I don't think we can be ready for him on the first day, maybe tomorrow"

The man in white comes back in. He lights up several more packs of incense and then sits at the front of the class. Again he takes out a bell.

We follow him as he sits cross legged.

"Now please, close your eyes." He speaks for the first time in perfect English.

I close my eyes.

"I want you to think why you are here? Why any of us are here. We are all so very lucky to have found each other, to have found this place, to have found this lake of energy."

There is a mumbling of agreement from the group.

"No please, no movement, no talking, nothing, eyes closed."

There is the sound of lights being turned off, the fluorescents in the roof somewhere going off one by one.

"Now open your eyes" he says.

The room is in near darkness. The smoke from the incense

helps pick out the man in white at the front of the room, but the group are rendered invisible.

"I want to you concentrate on your reason for being here, I want you to think of three words that describe your being here, and I want you to find those words slowly, when you have found those words I want you to say them in your head, again , and again, and again. Please do not ask questions, please do not talk."

-

Karate class at school only happened twice. I remember we'd lined up – only boys. One of the teachers playing sensei at the front. We'd all called him Mr Poo Manchu. Childish and racist but we were white kids in the shires. The teacher's real name was Malcolm Biggins but he must've become enlightened or perhaps gotten on to the karate and kungfu bandwagon that I now know, from days of getting drunk in front of Shaolin movies, exploded just before I was born. A macho yoga equivalent of its time perhaps.

Anyway Mr Poo would line us all up in our whites. And I might have been alone and also very naïve that this class would be a break from cricket. Young children marooned in a giant field with little communication for hours at a time in the heat, rescued by another bell - the school's ancient chiming clock that run out each timetable division.

We'd done some stretching as kids, I'm sure of it. Remember a kid pissing himself next to me. Mr Poo went to get a mop and we all stood there as the gym filled with the smell of piss. Johno had been there that day and we'd made faces behind the kids back. I can't remember his name, I think he'd left the school at the next half term.

Mr Poo had done his best but managed to tramp piss everywhere with the mop and the pissed-himself kid was excused. Mr Poo finished that first class by telling us all to make sure we used the bathroom before the next karate class and that was that.

The second class was a few weeks later. The pissing kid was gone. We'd lined up and done our stretching. Mr Poo had then taken us through some punching and kicking drills. Finally we were to spar. We paired off, Johno chose me, always good to pick a friend, like when racing long distance at a school sports day and you make a pact to take it easy until the last few metres. No need for competition amongst friends.

We watched the other kids sparring. Mr Poo seemed a little out of his comfort zone, he kept stopping the fights to correct a stance or punch but thinking back now he must've been worried someone was going to get hurt.

Then it was our turn, we were still grinning having joked during the last pair's spar that one of them had pissed himself. 'The Karate Piss' – a non-pun on The Karate Kid.

So I step up, and look at Johno, swallowing laughter. Mr Poo starts the fight and Johno punches me, hard in the face. I fall to the ground and lie still for a moment. I don't know if I blacked out or I was just in shock.

I wake up. Johno is stood in the corner of the room. Mr Poo has my head in his arms. My blood is on Mr Poo's tie. I reach up to feel my nose and it wiggles, and I'm in pain. Blood is gushing.

"it's a gusher" says of the boys.

I try and see Johno's face. I want him to be crying, I wanted him to be upset with what he'd done. But he wasn't. He turned back to look at me and was smiling.

-

It was still dark in the room. I still hadn't thought of my three words yet. Johno, Isabel, Diana – perhaps that would do, unless

103

like Scrabble there were rules against proper nouns. Or, unless those three words wouldn't do, because they weren't the truth, or at least not the whole truth. The bell chimed again. My eyes adjusted again and the man in white reappeared in the gloom. How long had he left us, I couldn't tell.

"Okay, we break for one hour, and then we will come back here for a bell ceremony. One hour exactly. Also remember your three words, we will be sharing them this evening" And then he left in the darkness.

Mathilde crawls over to me. I can just make out her face. She pulls her hand through my hair.

"You're all sweaty"

"Yes"

Still in the dark, she brings her hand down over my face. She puts her lips to my ear,

"Why are you here mister?"

The salty damp must between us is heightened in the darkness. She isn't interested in me. This is just post-yoga euphoria, this is confusion, this is darkness, this is me remembering this moment wrong, this is....

She kisses me on the side of my face. I don't know why she did it, and I don't think she did either.

Plink, Plink, Kerplink.

The strip lights come to life. By the time the room is bright Mathilde is halfway across the room again packing up her small bag.

We have a couple of hours before the evening. I decide to go down to the lake. I wiggle through the back streets, past shops selling repro antiquities. Corner shops stacked with toilet paper, cigarettes, Fanta, chocolate. Further back samosa stalls. Marble fronted hotels with recessed courtyard gardens and men in concierge outfits straight from a Hollywood film.

I get down to the lake. There are steps leading into it. A sign says "BEWARE - GHATS - SLIP".

On the steps three men with well-barbered white hair and two with fine moustaches have thin patterned cloths wrapped around their waists. The three of them give me no notice as they walk down the final steps and launch themselves under the water. The cloths resisting the pull and floating above the men, three fabric lily pads marking these divers.

I want to get in with them but I'm fearful of the water. I'm not there yet wherever there is. I don't want to get sick. I put health before experience.

But I stay, and watch them, and stare at the lake. Small boat taxis ferrying guests to the Octopussy hotel, I can see the hill across the lake where my guesthouse is. Then up and around there are more hills, topped with small temples I can just make out.

I'm enjoying myself. And I feel bad for a moment.

Johno,
Izzy,
Diana,
Jonathan – the kid.

Got to remember why I'm here.

The men are out of the water. They could be a hundred years old. They dry off quickly in the sun. Serious about their bathing but happy, three old friends by a beautiful lake in the sun.

One of them turns to look at me.

"Is it good" I ask and make and embarrassing swimming gesture.

"Very nice"

But I'm too wrought still to get in.

-

The room has been rearranged. The incense now burns in the centre of the space. The mats are gone. The lights are off and instead candle lit lanterns are placed by the incense. It isn't all dark.

We stand around shuffling. Mathilde is chatting to an Israeli looking guy, sinew in a singlet.

Archer's assistant comes in.

"Make a circle"

Having spent the afternoon flexing we limberly form a rough circle surrounding the incense. He takes out his bell chime.

"Now, you will say your name, where you are from and then just three words why you are hear. Nothing more, nothing less. When the bell chimes the next person in the group must speak whether you are finished or not. Please no clapping. Just understanding why your fellow classmates are here"

Nodding.

"I will begin. Kavi, New Jailaburgh. Psychical, Yogic, Instruction"

He walks up to the woman three to my left.

"Now you will start, we will move clockwise around the circle."

I wouldn't be last. But almost. Kavi hits the chime.

"Laura, Ontario, Eat, Pray, Love"

"Mario, Sicily, Food, Culture, Yoga"

"Sarah, Wales, Harmony, Cleansing, Personal..."

The bell cuts her off.

"Daniel, Tel Aviv, Freedom, Peace, Adventure"

"Kirsty, London, Divorce, Self-sufficiency, Newness."

Mathilde, Paris, escape, fear, mindfulness"

"Abi, Miami, Curiosity, Loneliness, Obesity"

"Peter, arthritis, sybarite, twitcher"

"Lulu, Madrid, Buddhism, Hinduism, Animism"

"John, Sydney, ganja, motorbikes, girls"

John is smiling for a brief second. Kavi stops. He leans in to John from Sydney's ear. He whispers to him and stands back. John is surf cliché, various shades of blonde, part bear, patterned clam diggers, faded pink surf brand tee. John smirks.

"Your all cunts" says John, then eyeballs Kavi, "And you, who are you you jumped up little dickhead"

Kavi has already moved on.

The next girl, brunette, red lipstick, hi-tech yoga outfit isn't sure if she should start. The boy next to her nudges her.

"K, K, … Kara, New York, Physical, Mental, Spiritual"

"Brad, New York, Kara, Holiday, Proposal"

The atmosphere in the room is lifted.

"Neil, Birmingham, Archer, Darkness, Enlightenment"

"Pasha, Munich, Family, Heritage, Culture"

"Ingrid, Copenhagen, Tea, Cookery, Yoga"

"Johno, Chamonix, Archer, Tantra, Mantra"

"Louise, London, retired, holiday, peacefulness"

"Dave, Croydon, Octopussy, Research, Bond"

"Jenny, London, travel, seeing, tasting"

And then it was my turn.

"Matthew, Johno, Izzy, Diana, … no wait"

Kavi hits the bell.

"Alice, Jerusalem, quiet, meditation, cleansing"

"Olaf, Berlin, meditation, yoga, sex"

Kavi walks back to the centre of the room. He puts the bell on the floor.

"Many of us are here for the same reasons. But none of us where very honest today. And one person left us because in his dishonesty we could no longer trust him to be part of our group. I'm interested in you" he looks at me and continues "You give three names, this is more honest, tomorrow we will continue this exercise, but for now the day is finished. Any questions?

Neil puts his hand up, he's bespectacled, bearded, he is the first real hippie, must've been young in the 60s and 70s, and now he could be 70 himself.

"When will we see Archer?" – Neil asks.

"Archer will teach only the advanced classes, I am fully trained by him to teach you. Should you like to take those classes you first need to graduate from this class."

Neil doesn't seem happy with the answer but after the surf bum got kicked out he's not going to push his luck.

"Get some sleep tonight, tomorrow will be a longer day, we will be meditating, I will perform a bell washing ceremony and we will take a look at some traditional Indian drone instruments."

I didn't know what to expect. I was expecting more. But having heard everyone's reasons for being here its clear most want some exercise that's backed up by thousands of years of practice. But Neil is here for other reasons.

-

Mathilde is waiting for me outside. She takes my arm and walks with me part way down the street. Neil is outside too, he has his mobile phone out and is scrolling through it.

"What did you think of today?" Mathilde asks

"Have you heard from Juli?"

"Who's Juli" and she smiles.

"Isn't he worried"

"Spoilsport, come on, we go back to the hostel, later Daniel is going to take us to a café where they do the best bang lassi.

"I'll see you back at the hostel, I just want to catch up with someone"

I turn back to Neil. He is walking up the street away from us.

"Matthew" I reach out my hand

"Neil"

"Good to meet you"

"I'm going for some food – if you want to join?"

-

At a chaotic crossroads of full-beam motorbike lights, horns, cattle and hawkers Neil leads me into a small hole-in-the-wall café. Its painted in a sickly lime green and there's too tables. Neil smiles at the owner who fans his cattle shit stove with a piece of cardboard.

"You alright?" Neil drawls, Ozzy Osbourne Brum voice.

Neil sits us down.

"Two please" he orders.

At the next table there's two Indian guys tucking into the food, looks like a thin curry with chapatis.

"Its 50 cents"

"Looks good"

"Its very tasty. So…"

"What did you think of today" I ask.

"Dull. Just another hocus pocus course for mid-lifers having a breakdown"

"Does that include me"

"I don't know"

"In your three words you said you were here for Archer? I'm wanting to speak to him more too. I think my friend spent some time with him, I'm eager to understand what happened."

"Archer is a genius, he's an Englishman, Oxford educated, smarter than I'll ever be.

He laughs. "My late wife came out here a few years ago, when Archer was at his peak, met him , it changed her, helped her cope with her cancer, now she's gone I want to meet him, to help remember her, to understand what he told her that let her die calmly."

"I'm sorry for your loss."

"Thank you"

"I'd never heard of him."

"You wouldn't have, unless you are into alternative thinking. It's all closed up now but a ten years ago he had a complex, two thousand permanent residents, a meditation chamber shaped like a giant bell. But there was some kind of scandal, people stopped going or something, and then he disappeared for a couple years, 'til he started doing these short courses. Psychical Yoga Course I didn't expect him to teach them personally. He's pretty much a god in alternative health and thinking circles"

"Is he?"

"What"

"A god?"

"Well, you know."

The food arrives, prickly aubergine curry, thin buttery sauce, and chapattis.

"I've been in India for three months trying to get to him. I don't have much time either. I'm a drinker. I've done my liver in. After the missus died I stopped caring, now I want Archer to make it easier for me."

"Dying?"

He looks at me like I'm an asshole.

"More chapattis?" He asks the owner.

"I've been asked to find an old friend, I think they got mixed up with Archer, don't know for sure, they've gone missing."

"Is she beautiful? If she is there's every chance he couldn't resist her, he's very open about his relationships."

"It's a man, he's a man, Johno, my age…"

"Well not that open." The chapattis arrive.

"Whereabouts was the compound?"

"Complex… yeah it was near Varanasi. You know Varanasi?"

I shake my head.

"Its where they burn the bodies."

"Who does?"
"The Indians"

-

Back at the hostel I start to smell myself. Away from the thick scent of the auditorium or the food stalls and petrol fume filled roads my own thick musk is all I can taste and smell. I wash in cold water. I have no towel or soap.

I'm drying myself with a t-shirt when there's a knock at the door. Mathilde. Her hair is damp, she's in a smock and ethnic skirt.

"I was going to say you know you need a shower, so good" she says. "Also, you are late."

"I went for supper with Neil."

"Supper, supper?"

"You know dinner?"

"Yes I know but I thought you wanted to come and get high?"

"I don't know, it's not why I'm here."

"Yes I know, blah blah blah you say right? Well I think you need to live a bit Matthew"

"Maybe I do."

-

Lights burn around the lake. The hotel still a centre point. We are in another rooftop café getting high on lassi.

The American from the bridge is back.

"Indian hash is the best hash" he says.

"That's the law" says his friend, marine grade haircut, all muscles stuffed in a vest.

"It's funny, 'cause it's a desert, but they have such amazing fruit here too" – the American again.

Mathilde is hit by the bang and reclines on the thin faded mat.

It's got a Moroccan rihad design and wall paintings of surfers, expressionist almost, the fresco-faced chillum puffers smoke turning into vaginal wave troughs with spermy dolphins. And then the American's friend pulls out a guitar. Mathilde leans forwards, her braless breasts hang loose in her cotton top. We men all notice.

"Well I hope you all like Neil Young" says the friend before starting on a passionless version of Heart of Gold.

Mathilde is enraptured. He sings and plays note perfect but I'm bored. I'm too old for this, too old to want to compete with this, perhaps too old to be backpacking around India getting high. Or maybe it's just the bang.

-

Back in the hostel we go to her room. She plugs in her phone and balances it in a deep ashtray and hits play. I try and get her fan working. Then the Red Hot Chilli Peppers starts playing

"Sometimes I feel Like I don't have a partner..."

Mathilde is singing along. I open a bottle of water – she snatches it from me and drinks heavily.

"I'm so wasted"

The music is still playing. It isn't loud but someone bangs on the wall from the room next door. But Mathilde doesn't care. She's lost the words but half mimes to the lyrics. I sit on the edge of her bed and then let myself fall backwards.

"What did you think of the American?" I ask

"Which one, the guitarist was cute, his friend is a bit irritating."

"He's cute?"

"And he plays the guitar, I think I'm in love with music again." I sit up.

"You're jealous?"

"No, I should go" I say, she puts her hand on my arm.

"Oh come on, he's a boy with a guitar. He intimidates you? Oh please!"

She moves her hand up to my face.

"What's wrong with you?"

The track is now an upbeat bass jam.

"Nothing"

We kiss and I move my arm up her side, meet her coarse underarm hair.

"Bon"

We kiss again. She forces her tongue deep into the back of my mouth. We both have the same smell, mostly spice and sweat. They say westerners smell of milk, well even the lassi is wiped out by whatever it is we've been eating. It's in every pore. I don't know why I'm thinking this as we're kissing. She pulls away.

"Do you think I'm pretty?"

"Yes"

"You worry about Juli?"

"No." – and that was the truth, I had started to see how casual relationship were out here. Best friends one night, lovers the next, we'd be strangers by morning, I knew it already, I had no problem with this.

"Good"

I pull her top over her head and take off my shirt. She is super skinny. I lean her onto her back. And at that moment the fan starts whirring loudly and slowly the blades start turning.

Thrum, Thrum, Thrum, Thrum.

We stop kissing to smile at the fan coming to life on cue. She's the first person since the last, my mind wanders for a moment. Then I'm back to making out like a teenager, and it feels good. We're quickly out of the rest of our clothes, the Red Hot Chilli Peppers comes to an end and some horrible dance track with Indian instrumentation starts to drone. Neither of us are shaved, and both our stomachs taut with yoga and change of diet and maybe it's the bang but I'm starting to lose where I start and she begins. I move my kisses from her mouth to her neck, her breasts, I taste the salt in the line from her ribs to her belly button.

She turns around on the bed and arches her back and looks back at me. I look down at my penis, sweat dripping from my stomach down over pubes, and the fan is still going Thrum Thrum Thrum.

There is more banging at the door, I hesitate and she claws back at me.

"Oh come on!" she says tired of my hesitation.

I thrust, Thrum Thrum Thrum, Thrum Thrum Thrum, Thrum Thrum Thrum, Thrum Thrum Thrum, Thrum Thrum Thrum and cum inside her.

She's dribbling out my cum onto the floor and we're both hoping gravity is a birth control. She goes into her ensuite toilet and the shower goes on, the toilet is flushed, she comes out wrapped in a towel.

I move to kiss her.

"I can't sleep with you, you should go"

I look at her, not sure what I'm supposed to feel.

"Please go" she asks "I just wanted to have sex, now please go"

CHAPTER **THIRTEEN** - HARRY

Kavi had taken Neil and myself aside before class and asked to prepare our things and to meet Archer at sunset at the Monsoon palace. We would not be needed at that days workshops. I walked into the entrance to wave goodbye to the other students, Mathilde wasn't there.

Neil and I walked back down through town. He was smiling a lot.
"This is it" he said.
"You're excited?"
"Yes."

-

She wasn't at the hostel either. I wrote her a note. In trying to guess how she felt I didn't write that I was sorry but that I was pleased to have met her and I wished her good luck with her trip.
It took me moments to pack my bag, I paid the 900 rupees I owed for the room and sat briefly in their marbled reception area tapping out a message to Isabel and Diana.

Dear Diana,
I am now increasingly certain I have met a man who knew of Johno
when he was here an• at the time of his •isappearance. He is taking
me an• another tourist...

I delete tourist, can't think what else to write.

Me an• Neil, a man from Birmingham.

That doesn't sound right either.
"Please, once you check out, you check out, if you want to use internet, you pay for another night." Says the receptionist.

Taking me with him to the next city where I hope to fin• out some
more answers. Please sen• my love to the family.
Best
Matthew

I stand up, wave goodbye to the hostel and head outside.

-

Without the laptop I haven't much to carry but it's still too much in this heat. Walking quickly gets to be too much. A few shouty rickshaws try and get me onboard and I relent at the fourth. A young wiry man in fashion-ripped jeans and a polo shirt. I ask him if there's anywhere with air con.
"yessir, yessir, the cinema"
-

We drive through downtown Udaipur, Indian Udaipur, the lake is a trap, and this is where the Indians are. He points out the castle.

"Did you visit yet?" he asks

"No"

"Very beautiful"

"Perhaps next time?"

"No next time, today."

"Maybe cinema and then castle?"

"I know you won't come back" he says.

-

The cinema has two films on. The first has a Harry Potter style poster but is in fact a retelling of Hindu mythology. The second poster shows a well-groomed man with leather jacket carries a pistol in one hand and shades in the other. A love interest and side kick stand behind him. Neither appeals. I have hours left here. The rickshaw driver shares my disappointment.

"I think you will go to the castle, much better" he says.

-

After a couple of hours spent walking through the cool corridors and airy battlement-top gardens my patient rickshaw driver drops me at the monsoon palace gates. I tip him and then ask around if anyone has seen Archer. I describe him and then Neil to the ticket seller. There is only disinterest and nonchalance and pointing up the hill. A taxi is leaving to the top, the driver takes my bag and throws it on a rack on the roof and I jump in with an Indian family.

The radio is playing upbeat music, I guess it's Indian pop but to my untrained ear it sounds like Bollywood meets hip hop. It gets turned up uncomfortably loud as we scream up the hillside.

-

Neil looks glum. He looks like he'd sooner be in a clinic in Switzerland than watching the sunset in Rajasthan. I guess he's remembering his dead wife. All that she saw that she couldn't share with him. All that he sees now that he can't share with her.

The palace is nothing like the castle in town. It is rudimentary, unfinished, empty. But from where Neil and I stand we can see the sun slowly going down for miles and miles behind range after range of mountains.

"They built this place to watch the rains come in" says Neil.

"Why?"

"Oh, I don't know." Says Neil, he seems frustrated. "I mean, how would I know." He adds.

"Do you think he's coming?" I ask.

He tuts at me and then" I don't know, I think I'm ready to go home" he says.

Neither Neil nor I have very much luggage with us. But Neil looks like he's giving up.

"I'm going for a wander" he says and steps back into the palace itself. He appears on the floor above and waves at me, he seems unsure what he's supposed to be doing here. His time in India as worn out as his sports-sandals.

There's a bench at the back of the terrace and a middle aged English couple and their guide are sat there. The guide disappears for a few minutes. When he returns he brings them two large bottles of beer. No one seems to care but it seems sad when presented with such natural beauty that you'd have to have a drink to take it in.

Suddenly a few young kids start talking to me, they want me in their photograph. We take a half dozen pictures and then they ask me to take their photo on my camera.

"No camera" I say. They point at my pocket. We repeat the photography session on my phone. I look quickly at the pictures, I'm a little sunburnt, stubble turning into beard, hair a mess, clothes dusty and stained, the kids show me up in their pristine ripped jeans and smart shirts. There's no one that I can send one of these photos to that would care.

I look up, Neil is sat on the bench drinking beer with the couple. Their guide is crouched on the floor.

There are about thirty people watching the sun go down. A mix of Indian families, backpacking teens, a couple more middle aged Europeans and me and Neil. No Archer.

After the sun fully sets behind the mountains the light still hangs in the air for a moment. Slowly people start to drift back through the palace. A group of backpackers take a final photo using a selfie stick. Neil is now deep in conversation with the English couple and their guide.

"Hey Neil, any sign?" I ask.

"This is Julia and Andrew" he says.

I reach out a hand.

"Oh I'm sorry, not used to a handshake after all the bowing!"

"What shall we do Neil?"

He shrugs, then "I'm happy, I think I've seen it"

"Really, you're done?"

"Yes."

"We're going to the pizza restaurant in the hotel tonight, they have real mozzarella" adds Andrew.

"Neil?" I ask again, he can't be backing out now.

"Doesn't that sound good" says Neil.

The guide collects their empties and gestures to the car park.

"Your carriages await madam and sirs"

"You sure Neil?"

"Yes" he says. He necks the end of his beer and passes the bottle to the guide.

There's a man with a large number of keys walking towards

me, I guess he's the caretaker. Neil and the couple set off for the car park.

"See you Neil" I shout. He runs back. Shakes my hand.

"Good luck Matt, I hope you find your friend. Or at least… Well, good luck" and he's gone.

The caretaker looks at me.

"I'm leaving, it's okay." I turn.

"Matthew?" he says

"Yes."

"Archer says you are to come with me, I will take you to him. But he says if you want to follow him you must leave behind all of your bag here."

"Why?"

"That is what he says"

"Why the bag?"

"You will only need what you can carry, your belongings are about your past. Your future is with Archer."

"What about my phone."

The caretaker shakes his head.

"You cannot bring this."

I look at the caretaker. He seems serious. I quickly open the phone and send an email to Isabel and Diana. I tell them that I won't be contactable for a week. That should be long enough. I then hand the phone over to the caretaker. I pull a waterproof from my bag and a shirt and put both on over my t-shirt; then a pair of sunglasses and a hat. The caretaker smiles at me and then he shrugs. I pass him the bag.

"Okay, you follow me."

Neil stares at me from the back of the taxi. He waves slowly. Saying goodbye to me, but also I guess goodbye to India. He'd seen all he needed to, I was envious of him, I was giving myself to Archer, handing myself over, willingly letting myself be kidnapped by him, and for what, to find Johno?

I knew myself better than to know that to be the whole truth, I'd given over my phone with the same quiet joy as giving up work, I didn't long for a year zero, I longed for more meaning, I longed for reason, I was looking for many answers, Johno's disappearance was definitely one of them, but there where others.

I hoped wherever the phone ended up that those pictures of me and the kids at sunset where enjoyed, that whoever found them appreciated the draft text messages that I wrote you to explain myself or for you to explain yourself, I hoped that whoever found that phone looked through the few pictures from London and struggled to understand how a guy who ate so well and who logged so many miles could look so unwell.

I hoped whoever dredged the depths of that phone found the late night messages to exes both sent and unsent, the half-deleted data from lonely hearts and sex chat apps. That they liked the four songs I'd been forced to download by work to get them into the Christmas charts for clients and I'd never been able to delete since.

Most of all I hoped that after laughing or crying through the last 18months of my life that they deleted all of it.

CHAPTER FOURTEEN - INTO THE DESERT PART ONE

I'm sweating hard, and pause to scrape out the dusty rheum that's stopping my eyes from crying as another sand filled desert wind passes us by.

I'm unloading a truck on the outskirts of Pushkar. It is camel fair season and Archer, for all his talk of inner peace and self-love, the value of kindness and the weight of true happiness has been pushing hard on the idea that this camel fair, with its tourist boomtown is a means for us to make as much money as possible in the next few days.

My shoes are starting to tear, this is the third day of loading and unloading and my trainers weren't meant for this. Archer oversees us workers. A box tumbles out, mishandled by a Berliner called Alec, tie-dye smocks fall out onto the street. I work with Alec to box them up again and carry them into the shade of the warehouse.

I pause for a moment to drink a cup of water from the steel tank. Having learnt from the Indians not to let the cup touch my lips and also not spill any. Archer is shouting at the driver to wait. He looks back at me and I run back out and start unloading again. It is 6pm, we've been unloading trucks for twelve hours now.

-

Alec and I eat some chapattis and lentils. We sit in our boxer shorts, our clothes drying on lines around us. He's skinnier than me and I worry he's not eating enough. But there's always his dreadlocks if he gets stuck, they're a gross crawling mass on his head. If he lasts another week of labouring I'm going to cut them off in his sleep. He'll thank me for it.

We don't talk to each other. We had a disagreement on day one of working with the trucks and now he keeps himself to himself. He's also had the shits since I've met him and I kind of figure the more he keeps shut the less chance I have of getting sick too.

We eat off our steel plates with our hands, wrapping the lentils in bread. Both sipping from our water bottles filled from the water tap. His, cloudy with salt powders he was given by tourists.

Our hostel is at the far edge of town. We are not the only westerners staying there but all the westerners there are working for archer. Everyone else is Indian. This I've learnt quickly is uncommon. Indians and Westerners don't share hostels but they do share hotels. The reason being is that even at 300rupees a night the cheapest western oriented hostel is too much for travelling Indians.

Alec suddenly throws his plate against the wall. He stands and rushes for the latrine. A bucket behind a shower curtain. I can't stand to hear him shitting himself.

The things I miss the most from my bag are the books. I hadn't needed to read them before but in the downtime between working the lorries I need to escape. I need to drown out the sound of the poor roommate turning himself inside out. The other hostels I'd passed through up until this point had a small book collection, you'd see Siddhartha. White Tiger. The Beach. Dharma Bums. In this place there was nothing.

-

Alec sounded worse so I'd left. It took me twenty minutes to walk to the lake. If it seems like the sun is always setting here that is because, in Rajasthan at least, it gets up lazily and then slowly starts to go back to sleep. The sun never gets much further than breakfast in bed, or propped on its shoulders here.

Bats fly low over the lake. It is glassy. A fish surfaces sensing bugs, it unsettles the surface in its search, then it dives, and the mirror returns.

-

I was starved, tired and had no way to escape what I'd brought on myself and I'd started to believe, if only a little. The lake did have a heavy resonance. It was more than the profundity of this lake in the desert, the glassiness seemed otherworldly, the Ghats around it out of 60s science fiction, the holy men and charlatans who ran the Ghats added an extra layer of complexity, mixing Hinduism with capitalism in a complex pay for prayers, pray for money cycle.

I was too scruffy for them to bother me but as tourists drifted down to chance a look at the water's edge they were set upon one by one by these holy men and chancers alike. Groups looking like office away days were chanting over coconuts and ribbons, tying friendship bracelets on one another's wrists whilst holding in dihoarrea and praying more that their coach didn't leave without them than for a happy long life.

He must be dead by now or finished, I thought about Alec. I'd have loved to stay out, see the town come to life at night but I was dog-tired and needed my sleep. I chose a different way through the streets and chanced upon a small tattoo parlour.

I was here of my own will but this wasn't a place I'd ever choose for myself but some westerners had really made a life here. From the cracks in the doorway drifted a strong smell of marijuana, whatever got you through right? I knocked on the door.

-

Alec looked really sick. He was lain out on the ground between our two bunks. His face and chest was slick with sweat and he'd stripped to his underwear, which was soaked through, and dirty with piss stains. In the kitchen I had a coconut I'd bought earlier that day. I cut open the top with a kitchen knife and woke Alec to give it to him.
"I don't feel so good"
"You're going to be fine, drink this"
"I feel really bad"
"You look bad but you need to drink, tomorrow you'll feel fine, we can see the camels arriving"
"I don't want to see the camels arriving, I want to go home."
I forced him forward and helped him drink from the coconut.
"It's good" he said,
"finish it"

A couple of hours later I wake up again. He's standing in his underwear, shit dripping down his legs. I walk him out into the shower and hold him upright and try and get him clean.
"Is it bad?" he asks
"You'll be fine"
He vomits into the shower drain. I keep the water flowing. It's a pithy slurry that he manages to get out.
"I don't feel well"
I drag him out of the shower block. The owner of the hostel

is standing there in a heavy fleece and with a club.

"You are very late" says the owner "There is a curfew" he adds.

"I'm sorry, my friend is very sick" I say.

"Sickness not good here, everyone get sick" he says, cross with Alex and me.

"I know" I say.

He looks Alex over, then "You take him hospital?"

"He'll be fine" I say, but I don't believe it.

The owner lets the club drop, it hangs on a lanyard on his arm.

"You work for Archer?" he asks

"Yes."

"Tell him he needs to pay for the rooms"

"I'll tell him"

"This man needs medicine, now" Says the owner.

"Okay"

"Not okay, you don't know what you do, how will you get a doctor?"

"I don't know"

Alec is groaning in German, I don't understand him. I let him slip onto the ground.

"I will get you a doctor, it will be five thousand rupees."

I look at Alec. He's just ruined his one pair of underpants. He can't afford decent soap or food. He doesn't have the money. But me, I'm a charlatan, I still kept my wallet after Udaipur. I have the money.

"Okay."

"Okay, first you give me the money, then I will find the doctor."

-

We're downstairs in the street. We've got Alec into his shorts and t-shirt and he's propped upright against a wall –

there's nothing more to come out of him. I give the owner
the 5000rupees and then have pay for Alec's room too. I have
written Alec's first name and the name of the hostel onto his
arm – it's all I could think to do.

A tired old taxi pulls up and I see the owner take a thousand
off the five. He hands the four to the taxi driver and in a flurry
of Hindi I think he's telling him to take him to the hospital in a
nearby city Ajmer.

"He's going to the doctor?"

"Hospital, it is better" says the owner

"But I've just given you the money for a doctor"

"Many doctors at the hospital, very good ones"

"I don't know"

"Please…" he says and gestures for me to go back into the
hostel.

The taxi driver looks back at Alec lying across all the back
seats and shakes his head.

"You sure?" I ask.

"Ajmer, it has a very fine hospital"

"You hold in there Alec"

The taxi leaves. I don't feel good, I feel like I've abandoned
him.

"I should go with him"

I start to run after the taxi. I'm screaming "wait, wait, wait"
but the taxi doesn't slow down. I try to cross up through the
streets towards the road the leads out of town, try to get ahead
of the taxi but I can't, I don't know this place at all.

I can hear the taxi getting further and further away from me.
I stop. I catch my breath, a cow stares straight at me.

-

I'm chatting to some Nepalese guys who are here on holiday

from working the kitchens in some hotel in Bombay. We are watching the tents, camels, pens and hawkers filling up this camped caravan at the edge of the city. It's a dusty bowl that shimmers and shakes as the camels move about in the heat.

-

Back down in the tents things are readying for the fair. We've a stall all ready for the tourists, packed with the latest Chinese repros of western-Indian ethnic tie die wear. And as the afternoon cools off people start to trudge the short way out of town to come and visit the camp. There's still a couple weeks to go before it gets fully set in motion but already they are here, with their massive zoom lenses so they don't have to get too close to the animals or the people.

I'm working on the stall with a young Indian boy called Ilad. He's a good salesman – Archer pays him per sale, whereas I'm a volunteer, one of Archer's group. An intern I guess.

Ilad makes a few sales. Ornately costumed camels start to be led out with their little buggies behind them for evening tours of the desert. The desert here is more scrappy arid ground than Lawrence of Arabia and over the last few days I've watched as mainly Indian tourists pay for a half hour tour of a figure of eight through dusty tracks that lead away from the camp. Ilad is shouting at me. He's bought us some tea. It might be my tenth cup of the day, after Alec left I didn't get back to sleep.

-

The camp's activity slows down for the evening. One by one the buggy camels have their tackle removed and cleaned. They are fed and led back and tied to their wrought iron posts. I take the tally of clothes sold and we pack up the stall. Pull down the tarpaulin and clips that hold it together and put it all on the back of a handcart and then wheel it back to the store on the edge of town. I leave Ilad to lock up.

There's a small queue of backpackers at the ATM. I wait and smile at them and they smile back. They've probably been out here longer than me but I know that in the last week I've accumulated as much muck as is possible. I'm fine for money. I feel like I'm playing a game here. Archer wants me to give up everything but I've still more than enough to get a flight back home should I need to.

-

The owner is smoking outside the hostel. He looks at me. Something in the way he smokes, something in the way he stares. And I know it.

"You're friend, Mr Alec, you know, I am so sorry, he, he is passed on."

CHAPTER FIFTEEN - INTO THE DESERT PART TWO

Archer drives a van.

Ilad and I had sold the bulk of the stock over the course of the fair. I'd gotten stoned in my hostel alone every night and on the last day of the fair Archer had arrived, paid Ilad, made a gift of some money to the Rama temple and then given me an address to write to in Germany. It had turned out that Alec's appendix had burst inside him some days before the shower incident. The taxi driver had pulled a corpse out at Ajmer. I wrote to his family, told them I had met him travelling, that he was an inspiration, some more lies and then some well wishing. It was the best I could do.

I thought a lot about Johno, had he died like that, his body imploding in the back of a taxi in a city where not one person knew his name.

Archer had asked where I'd gotten the money for the taxi to the hospital. I explained that I'd kept my wallet. He seemed okay with that but asked that I give him some money to pay for my keep and a new uniform that I would need when we got to his camp.

-

After eight hours of hardly talking and me jumping out at three petrol stations to pay for Archer's fuel and pick up samosas and cokes we arrive at our stop off for the night. Archer smiles at the sign post Orcha.

"This is us for the night, you'll sleep in the van tonight, I have to meet some friends in the hotel so I'll stay there."

There are soldiers running the roads in and out of the town here. And passing us in a constant stream in the other direction are tractors with trailers each filled to every corner with women in bright floral saris, each woman carrying a copper coloured pot, they smile and sing to one another as the tractors grind past the military control.

"Who are they?"

"Pilgrims, they come here for the special holiday – wash in the river, collect the water and make an offering at the temple."

"How far are we?"

"We're a long way from where we are going."

"And were are we going?"

"A faraway place." He pauses, "look at the junction take a left towards the hotel – it's in that big palace over there." He points to a big palace set back from the road. "You're time is your own until the morning. There's nothing here. Stay away from the river at night. I need your wallet and your credit cards"

I take 500 rupees out of my wallet and hand it over to him.

"What's the code?"

"2221" I tell him.

"You're unsure you want to give me the wallet?"

"It's fine"

"You don't need this money anymore do you?"

"No" I didn't know how to answer that.

"You think I'm stealing from you?"

"No, no it's fine, I'll see you in the morning"

"You want something from me the money can't buy, and I'm

willing to share my learning's with you, but in return I need your trust Matthew."

"I know"

"Are you still upset about Alec?"

"No" Although I felt responsible.

"He'd have died with or without you, he wasn't strong enough for all of this, he had a weakness he hadn't addressed, he was dishonest. He was lying to himself"

"Sure"

"You're not sure."

There's a soldier rapping on the side of the van. Archer leans across me and passes the soldier a 100 rupee note.

I turn off the road and down towards the palace. Coloured lights illuminate it from below. The road towards it is typical half finished shops and a couple of cafes. I don't so much park as just stop the van. Archer gets out.

"Look I know we haven't had a chance to talk properly yet, I know you've a lot of questions yet but all in good time" I want to tell him that we've just had 12hours in a van to talk, he spent most of the time asleep except when he was asking me to ask me to pay his way.

"Sure" I say.

Archer walks off over a small bridge towards the lit up palace. I turn back to the town. Sit down at a café. I'm about to order another marsala pancake but I order eggs on toast and coffee not tea. I wish Neil was here, someone to talk to. Someone to talk to about archer. Its 7pm, I'm eating breakfast in a strange town, pilgrims still rolling by on tractors singing.

-

The Betwa river curls across the east of town and on the western banks sit the proud cenotaphs of kings of old. I know this because I'm reading a bronze plaque. Monkeys are playing in the waters alongside kids and the last of the pilgrims. One of the women drops her copper pot in the river and the current carries it away, she looks completely lost without it. She carries herself back up the side of the banks and trudges away from her group.

From the tops of the cenotaphs large birds of prey occasionally hop across from roof to roof, they look like vultures or eagles. I know nothing about birds but these guys are bigger than any bird I've seen back home.

I'm pissed off and confused. I'm weak but I'm trying. I'm definitely lost although I know roughly where I am in India and thanks to the tourist map in front of me exactly where I am in Orcha.

"It means hidden place" says a teenage boy. "Now we take a photo"

Another selfie with a stranger – he shows it back to me. I am less and less myself these days.

-

More pilgrims walk through the markets by the town's half-modern temple. They also fill the square before it. Sat sharing chapattis, rice and lentils, water from the square's tap. The market seemingly sells only two things – fake looking copper trinkets, bangle and pots and weirdly fudge. I try to buy some fudge, I just want one piece, the pilgrims in the queue are buying whole boxes, and I see others carrying their fudge towards the temple entrance. I can't buy one piece but the man in the stall gives it to me for nothing. It comes with a couple of ratty looking wasps that chase me as I pick my way through the squares pilgrims.

The pilgrims are universally poor looking, for all their bright clothing and glittery bangles they just look dead broke. There's a cheapness to everything new in this place, set against the old grand tombs the thinly coated jewels and the rope lights that illuminate the temple seem out of place. But everyone looks happy and content.

I hate Archer for making me give him my wallet, but why do I hate him, I have more money in my pocket probably than half of these people but still I want more. I want it all.

And then the power gives out. Total blackout.

Only the fires of the men boiling fudge and tea light the way between the pilgrims now. I slowly make my way through them, walk straight into some deep cow shit and I'm back where I started at the café. In the dark I order tea. The lights come back on. The palace has never been without light though.

-

It's too early to try and sleep. I walk over the bridge towards the palace. It's a massive fucking palace. On one side of the courtyard is a glass-fronted hotel. I look back across the bridge at the pilgrims in the dark. The police still moving people on. Five hundred metres can make all the difference in life.

I peer in at the reception to the hotel. Archer is sat on a sofa by what looks like an open fire. It still must be over 25 degrees outside. He's in a clean white shirt, jeans and smart shoes. He'd not look out of place at most of London's dull work-in-media-arts private clubs.

There's a beautiful Indian woman sat next to him, the two of them look to have long glasses of fizzing wine, a bearded Indian man leans in to the two of them talking at pace with his hands. The three of them laugh. The girl leans in to Archer and whispers something. He and the girl stand. The man nods and shakes Archer's hand with his two, holding on for a moment to the great man. The girl takes Archer's other hand and pulls him away, the receptionist looks up as they cross the foyer and disappear.

The lights change outside the building and suddenly I'm fully lit in a deep purple hue. The bearded man inside the building looks at me. He walks towards the door.

I start walking back towards the van. The bearded man runs after me.

"Hey, hey you, can I help you?"

I keep walking and without turning around say "No thank you"

He stops his pursuit.

-

Your parents' house didn't scare me, but waiting around it whilst you went in to borrow their car keys humiliated me. I felt as if the furrowed lintels of the first floor projected the same disappointment you'd come to feel in me, the house loomed and judged because the parents I'd never meet would've done the same, the trees wet with a recent downpour from those humid weeks before our going our own ways wept for the time you'd come to waste with me. And the driveway crunched glacially telling me that I would never be able to walk back up it. You'd insisted on starting the car without me and I'd watched from behind the neighbour's car as you said goodbye to your mother. I had our bags just out of sight.

It had taken us 3 hours to get an hour out of London and to the coast. We were later than we hoped in arriving at the boutique bed and breakfast cum hotel. The owners quickly rattled off their own escape from the city some twenty years earlier and sure enough their daughter in her late teens was trotted out as proof-of-life that coastal air offers.

It had looked great on the website. Their partner site hummed with subtle ads I'd written which I should've known was a sign this was a terrible idea.

You unpacked excitedly, underwear we'd ordered together, that book you'd been meaning to finish, and what you described as your festival hip-flask full of gin that tasted of fairy liquid.

We'd laid back on the bed and sipped the soapy gin. Both pleased at least to have finished work for the week. The bed creaked as we made love for the first time that week and we both grew sensitive which helped the love if not the making. Then the neighbouring couple's bed started creaking like a wooden fart. Someone in the corridor skulked around and so we'd put the TV on to drown out the others. We were meant to be escaping, not camping out in another family's holiday.

On the TV there'd been a bombing in Iraq, pixelated bodies filled the screen. I asked you what you'd said to your mother. You told me she was too old to have to hear about your boyfriends and it was better that you were off to visit friends in Brighton. You drank some more gin and cried. You said you were crying for the kids on the TV but we both knew that wasn't true.

Then it really started to rain and grew cold. The single glazed windows rattled, a knock at the door and the owner's son in penis hugging jogging bottoms asked if we needed a taxi. I didn't know where we were supposed to be going but agreed to one.

We'd gone out in the taxi and drove in a large circle for a half hour in the rain before stopping back at a pub a few hundred metres from the b&b. There we'd meant to order food but neither of us ever really had eaten in front of each other and we weren't about to start it now.

So we'd gotten slowly drunk, hugging each other against the strangers in this small town. Then the landlord lit a fire and we'd moved closer to it. We'd moved from lager and gin to port and whisky. Neither of us cared for the quality of the drink, only that it would get us drunk. We ate packets of lemony scampi fries and kissed.

Back at the b&b in the reception area the son was watching an update on the Iraqi bombings with his hand down his joggers and the other hand on the remote. We'd gone up to bed and you went in the bathroom and tried on the lingerie. You said through the door that you looked silly and you came back into the bedroom and packed it away along with the vibrator. I held on to you for hours as you cried and you said you didn't know what was wrong.

The next morning we got up early before the owner had even started on the full English and we drove back to London. I took the bags out and waited in the rain whilst you parked the car back in their driveway. Your dad shouting after you to give you money – you always were the independent type. We went straight from their to a hotel in Shoreditch.

Middle range anonymity. With our cases we looked like tourists, and, with complex automation, once the door to the hotel room slammed shut and the bags dropped to the silent concrete floor we showered together and started to screw.

We got up that evening to go and drink in a bar and you recognised some of friends who must've been out that night. She was with a man in a crisp white shirt and brogues, you said you didn't understand what a real girl like her was doing with such a dry old man such as him, but he looked rich and confident and together and she looked like she was enjoying his company. They were laughing a lot and then they left in a lift.

We got drunk again and walked around the corner to an off licence for a bottle of gin to take back to the room.

We spent the night in and out of the bed, screwing, kissing, had a bubble bath and watched a Michael Douglas movie on the TV. We caught the bus back to your street the next day and I said goodbye without thinking it strange I didn't come up. You smiled and made a joke about the Michael Douglas film. Neither of us mentioned the trip to the sea – it was a mistake.

-

I wake up early, its cold and the condensation has collected in the bottom of each plastic part of the van's interior. I'm wearing most of my clothes. I open up the window for some air. Then suddenly they hit me. Flies. Black flies dart into the van and start settling. I wind back up the window – they are everywhere.

Outside the van the whole town is crawling, flies on every surface, in every drain, all over the stalls, café's, plants and people. Animals bat their lids and flies drink the liquid from their eyes, cows flick their tails, monkeys pick at the flies and dogs roll in the dust.

Back to the café next to the van I order eggs and coffee again, and then tea, flies are here too – the owner bats them away with the menu and then brings out a large supply of incense to smoke them out. There's flies picking my food when it arrives, I scoop them away. The coffee has somehow survived the plague. The crossroads is already busy with pilgrims and market traders. The stores in the street beyond are hurriedly boiling up the fudge ready for another day and even further I can see through to the steps of the temple where the rope lights and led deities never stop blinking their paths to piety.

Archer taps me on the shoulder, he's back in his calf length tunic and sandals and carries a small cotton bag. And he passes me back my wallet – there's no cash in it but my credit card is still there.

"Can you get us breakfast" he asks and goes to the back of the van and slings his bag in. "We've got to make good time today. Have you filled up the tank yet?" He asks. I shake my head. "Well what have you been doing?".

"Sleeping" I say.

"No time for that, you can sleep tomorrow, come on."

-

We are on the road an hour later. Archer had forgotten something at the hotel but he smelt of roses when he returned. She was beautiful, this was the part of Archer I understood. The cad, the bully, the difficult businessman. But the part I didn't understand yet was what made him great. But I was paying to find out.

CHAPTER 17 - THE COMPOUND

I know that we are getting closer to our destination when a couple of motorbikes pull along side us on the road and wave at Archer. He speaks to them in Hindi and they drive off. They return with more bikes and horns start firing.

One of the rider's pulls down the scarf used to keep the dust from their face and I see she's a westerner, but she and Archer speak in perfect Hindi together, again the riders pull away from the van and I'm told by Archer to pull over at the edge of town.

There are a few dumpy looking soldiers or senior police, I'm not sure which. They greet Archer with hugs and look at his van. This small group walks around the van and shares a joke and then Archer points at me and they all laugh again, I'm not sure what's happening.

Archer gets on the back of a soldier's bike and a young teenage boy gets inside the van and beckons me back in to start driving again. I crunch through the now worn out clutch and follow the kids rough directions through this new town.

I can't understand the pronunciation but then I see a sign. It is some kind of special site but from my view through the windscreen it's just another dusty and fly ridden town.

Unesco World Heritage Site: Khajurahao

-

We continue through town, and I get a glimpse of what I would later learn are the erotic temples of Khajurahao.

We pass out through the eastern end of town. There are kids playing cricket surrounded by cows, a dried up lake, more police.

Keep going, keep driving. The kid smiles at me then taps on the dashboard. I pull over and he hops out and runs off into a field.

"hey, where am I supposed to go"

The kid turns and laughs at me and carries on running.

I start back up the road and there ahead of me are a few motorcycles at the side and a man in a shell suit and a t-shirt with a picture of George Michael waving me into a compound of some sort.

-

This is it.

It is massive.

It was never the hotel that the original owner must have planned it to be. Like those Iraqi palaces that get looted and squatted this hotel has been reworked from the ground up. From parking the van to being led to my dorm I get a sense of what I've walked into but it is a lot to understand in the quick backstage walk I've taken.

Fruit trees, vegetable gardens, ripe guavas. Tiles and steel decked kitchen, westerners, far east Asians and Indians are working together, no one looks up from their preparation. All are dressed similarly in various shades of brown, grey, white and that mild ochre orange of the Hindus.

The rear of the building is lower than the front, so the kitchens are below the ground floor, and there's a stairway down to what must be the stores as a Japanese looking girl drags a sack of rice up onto basement level, I go to give her a hand but she pushes me away and carries on dragging the sack towards the kitchen.

After this I'm in a laundry, hand washed, beaten and boxed up to presumably be hung outside. The clothes are again those uniform colours, earthy tones, muddied, perhaps all colours run together in these vats bring on these mid hues.

There are windows missing from the side of the building here and a lean to of tarpaulin and wood has been formed. There are stacks of stainless steel trays, cups and cutlery, unwashed next to two large plastic oil drums. A young Indian boy runs past me on his iphone.

A wide flight of unfinished steps takes me up onto the ground floor where what could've been an impressive courtyard garden has been concreted over. There is a flurry of birds and suddenly I am reminded of the mosque back in Delhi.

Arranged at the edges of the courtyard are various speakers and wires. It takes a couple of minutes to cross the courtyard, I can't imagine this place ever being full of breakfasting tourists but what do I know.

Someone is staring at me from a first floor window, they don't take their eyes away from me even as I hold their stare back. It is a woman, olive skinned.

I duck into the shade of the covered walkway at the edge of the courtyard and turn back to the main building. It is strangely empty.

The Field: A man in a plaid shirt with a fine Indian 'tache and smart belted levis is shouting at me. He has a walkie-talkie and points with the aerial towards a door at the side of the ground floor. I don't know what he's yelling about but I follow.

Outside the back door of the compound the concrete gives way to an incredible gardens. Railway sleepers raise the bedded gardens off the ground, to each side the compounds walls are mirrored deep into the dust wastelands beyond by tall acacia trees or perhaps they are eucalyptus, I don't know. It's about 500metres across between rows of trees and lined up like busying bees between all of this are the occupiers of the compound. Long spaced out lines of workers all again in those hues tend to the gardens.

There must be a hundred or more people here. Vegetables, fruit trees, decorative flowers. All these things seem to grow abundantly out here, somehow although surrounded by dust and other abandoned buildings this earth thrives.

A Chinese looking guy taps me on the shoulder and passes me a mattock. He speaks with a north American twang.

"Cow shit is a sacred and beautiful thing isn't it?" He reaches out his hand "Tim, from Vancouver"

I shake his hand.

"Matthew, London, I think I've seen enough crap to last me a lifetime. But..." I say, but he interrupts.

"It's nature's fertiliser, gods gift to tomatoes – did you know that? Did you know human faeces is even more rich, we're just scared of it, but it's the best, often you'll see us squatting out here in the mornings, its because those that know can't bear to see it go to waste. Anyway, we need to get those guava trees in before sunset so they can make the most of the watering tonight, can I trust you get on with that." He says.

I now regret shaking his hand.

"Yes, I just arrived, I don't know what's going on, I came with Archer"

"We all came with Archer, he's found all of us, brought us all home" he says.

"The guavas?"

"You need to clear that low bed there, add water to those dried shits and then turn the soil over, then re-plant those twelve trees. Think you can handle that?"

"What happens here?"

"This is food for the group, supper is at 7, curfew is at 11, there's a cricket match at 8 but its back in town so you'll need a scooter."

"I just have what I'm wearing"

"Course, did you give everything away?"

"it was taken" I say and Tim chuckles.

"Well get on with the soil, we can see about getting you a lift to the cricket, you British are good at cricket?"

I think back to days of school cricket, then Johno, I hadn't thought about him for a few days now, hadn't thought about why I was here at all.

"I haven't played since I was a kid"

Tim swings at me with a spade, I take a step backwards and lift the mattock as though to defend myself.

"Just practicing my swing" he says.

He looks at me, I must look lost, scared, I feel suddenly more out of place talking to a Canadian in a vegetable patch than in any place I'd visited so far. I look at the other workers here, all of them look to be western or Asian, a few blacks, no Indians. If this seems like I'm dwelling on race I'm not, its just that everyone here is from somewhere except the Indians. And even they have come to this compound for a reason. All of us are here for a reason, brought, lured, sucked towards it, drawn, entranced, led here, like Johno was? Like other have been?

And what happened at his previous place that Neil told me about, what was the scandal there, what closed it, what am I doing digging out soil and breaking apart dried cow shit when I could be back in the office flirting with Lottie and dodging work by cruising forums on the best way to make real changes to your work life balance or whatever other rabbit hole I fancy. I'm not a manual labourer and I'm certainly proving myself not to be a detective, I've sort of lost count of the days and as I tell this story back to you I know that its losing clarity. It's coming up to a month, but it feels much longer than that.

Tim is staring at me.

"You got a couple of hours to get them trees in, then you need to wash, you kind of smell. I'm only telling you because here we try to be honest with each other. I'll see you at supper, if you want to squat do it by the lentils"

I smell myself. I can't tell anymore. I walk over to the group of twelve saplings and look across at where another dreaded surf bum type is putting his own trees in the ground, I look at the mattock, then the earth, and I start to dig.

-

Although I think Tim saw me as some kind of snake in the grass he offered to take me in to own afterwards for cricket. At the table earlier I'd met a half dozen other people newly arrived, like first day at school we'd picked an uncrowded table where no one seemed to talk.

Each of those people had paid $1500 for a two week stay here and they'd flown straight here, the only India they'd seen so far was between the airport and the compound, a couple of kilometres at most. But still they buzzed, I guess like all of us did, they buzzed with the simple newness and excitement of being away, of the other.

There is little to say about them as individuals, they could easily have been back there at that workshop in Udaipur, or even at that bar on the first night in Delhi. They probably felt the same way about me but I saw them straight up as tourists.

The only thing I thought about whilst I was there was that I might also be asked for the $1500 donation. I'd already subbed Archer petrol money across half of India, my slush fund from Diana was down a few hundred for that, and then there was Alec's doctor and taxi costs and that hostel. I was on my way to making a decent enough donation.

So Tim drives me back in to Khajurahao.

He is more nervous away from the camp. Maybe he doesn't know so well what to do out here. The camps scares me more than these streets do, in fact I'm starting to feel at home out here, the thing I'm most terrified of is what happens when we get off the bike, will Tim prove to be a total wreck and collapse at the first site of an Indian?

He's getting more and more wound-up the closer we get to town. Indeed as we got to a crossroads a relaxed policeman gives us a wave, I guess although the novelty of the westerner is limited there's still a healthy excitement at the sight of us tourists. I wave back but Tim doesn't he pulls over and looks back at the policeman. He takes out his wallet and shouts back at the policeman.

"ID, I've got ID"

"he doesn't want your ID" I tell him "he's waving at us."

"Why's he doing that " Tim asks.

"He's being polite"

"Oh"

I wave at the policeman, again he waves back. And we continue on our trip.

Tim drives past the cricketers. He's not great on the bike and as we slow down for a series of sharp turns in a guttered alleyway the tyres are churned against the roadside as he loses control a little. He stalls the bike. An elderly man, shirtless and drinking tea on his front chuckles at our ineptitude.

"We've passed the cricket"

"I know"

"Do you need help"

"I got it, its fine" he says.

He starts up the bike again and over accelerates almost knocking down a pole that serves as a washing line.

Tim stops the bike at a small square in the centre of town and points to the cash machine.

"Archer says you need to pay for your lodging like all the rest of us."

"Today?" I ask.

"What can you take out?" he turns off the bike

"I don't know" I say. But I do know.

"Take out what you can then."

"I haven't much left" I lie.

"Archer says you do, he says you're an advertising big shot, he says you can pay."

Tim and I would be evenly matched in a fight. I'm not a fighter though, and I suspect Tim isn't either. I don't want to pay the money. I just want to find out what's going on here. Suddenly I just want answers. Its fine until you're challenged, and then you got to make up your mind, what do you want, what decision are you going to make.

"Come on" he says "We'll miss the cricket"

I get off the bike. The cash machine is a mess of zeros. I do quick calculations. Then look back at Tim, mime being pissed off and then withdraw about £200 in rupees.

I hand Tim the rupees.

"It's all it would give me"

"We can come back tomorrow" he says as he takes the money and lifts his shirt to put it in a pouch he's wearing underneath.

"Sure"

I get on the back of the bike. I hate Tim, I don't know why but I do. I don't even hate Archer. Archer seems incredible happy in his ability to take money from us dupes who are willing to pay him. But Tim, in acting as Archer's "bag man" lacks the charisma to pull off this role he is making for himself.

-

The group playing cricket are a little older than they first appeared. They are all about the same age as Tim & I and exclusively male. Tim immediately sits down and starts rolling up a cigarette and shows no more interest in playing cricket, I guess he was just tasked with extortion and now that's done he's going to have a post extortion smoke.

So it's down to me to prove that as a Brit I have what it takes to beat the Indians at our own game.

Except I've no idea what I'm doing. If this was football I'd have more of an idea but as the first ball slams into my shins and I'm immediately out I remember that I hate this game and that the kid version of me would have faked any illness to avoid the indignity of the cricket field.

I sit next to Tim and he offers me a smoke. I refuse it. Other boys come and sit with us. We small talk about London, about Canada, about "American Indians" about the temples that loom behind us. They ask if I've seen the temples close up yet and then laugh. I haven't. Tim sniggers too. There's still some tourists the other side of the fence where the temples are and they lean over onto our side to take photographs of the cricketers.

-

The dorm holds six people in it. I'm last in so I don't get a bed by a window, instead I'm jammed underneath an overhanging bookshelf where Zen and the art of Motorcycle Maintenance sits alongside a Donald Trump biography.

I really wish I had those books with me.

Tim tries to introduce me quickly but he keeps touching his belly where the pouch is – he's nervous about a couple of hundred quid. What a tosser.

I'm introduced to a girl who I think is called Anke from Germany. There are a couple of older men from somewhere in Spain – the north I think. Then a girl from Hull – she's immediately distrustful of me and wraps herself up in a heavy parka, Virgin planes branded eye mask and earplugs.

A strip light has been covered in a peeling orange film to take the edge off the stark brightness.

We all busy ourselves with getting ready. Washing teeth out in the hall. The sound of each of us pissing and shitting in the shared toilet in the stairwell outside the door. Some listen to their iphones they've somehow got to keep. Why do they have these things when I don't.

-

The next morning I see Archer at breakfast.
"How are you getting on?" he asks
"I have a lot of questions"
"I'm sure you do." He says knowingly.

But instead of asking about Johno or about the money I gave Tim or about what they are doing here in this defunct hotel at the edge of a Unesco site I choose to ask about my books.
"In Udaipur I gave a man my bag with my books and phone in it. Here the others seem to have smart phones, books, clothes"
"Who did you give your phone to?" He's smiling too.
"The caretaker, who led me to the car, at the monsoon palace."

149

"Why did you give your things to this man?" asks Archer

"Because he said you required it of me."

"Did you think it was strange?"

"I didn't know" I say.

"I will ask after your books" he says, holds my hands in his and then walks away.

-

Now the story takes a stranger turn.

You see, these events took time to unfold.

Daily life seemed without particular interest.

Except for this.

The groups where split into two. The farmers and the others.

And it took me a while to find out what the others did.

But that wouldn't be the strange part of this tale.

You see this is hard to tell you in a way that rings true.

I've tried so far up to this point not to leave anything out, not even the inconsequential. Because without those details I think maybe you wouldn't believe me, so it's all in there. If you got this far you'll see I've tried to tell it honestly. And I hope you didn't get too bogged down in it. Some stuff I guess I have left out like changing the tyre on the van twice as we drove from Pushkar to Khajurhao.

And maybe time has started to make less sense, maybe Alec took a few days to die in that hospital and maybe I went down to that city to see him.

And perhaps I stood over him telling him that he was going to be fine as the doctors struggled to understand what was wrong with him, and how too late they realise that something was really wrong inside him, and that he knew when he looked up at them that they didn't know what was wrong, and so after he died when they finally opened him all up to find the exploded appendix it was all too late, and I'd spent the three nights after the hospital visits sleeping at the station in a 150rupee blanket right there on the platform with the 'unfortunates' or whatever you want to call them.

And then I'd paid my way back up to Pushkar to collect my stuff and then been ripped off by the hostel owner and only after I prayed at the lake and committed a day to walking between the two highest temples around did I start to feel better. I'd ridden a motorbike at speed into the desert and hadn't thought about coming back and I'd run out of petrol and pushed it a mile before a goat farmer came to my aid and collected petrol and water for me and I'd gone back. You see I've started to lose track of time.

And this is what happens, and I was warned that this would happen. And I feel lost, and I keep forgetting why I'm here. At the beginning I'd forgotten about Johno when I was having a good time. Now I was no longer having a good time but I forgot about Johno even more now.

I had been at the compound a week. Farming during the day, playing cricket in the evening, taking cash out for Archer in between. I'd made no friends really, and although Tim had slowly warmed to me he remained suspicious and changed personality heavily when he was called on to take me to the cash point. On the 6th day I'd paid all I needed to.

-

On the 7th day I rose early.

There was some commotion out in the front of the building. I peed and grabbed my t-shirt. At least I hoped it was mine because by now all of my clothes had taken on that same earthy tone as everyone else's.

Tim had come off his bike and crashed into what looked like some sort of electrical conduit that was now on fire, people where kicking sand at this squat metal cabinet in the street. Tim was lain on his back holding his arm that looked very broken, he was staring at the sun. Quickly about thirty of forty men where all trying to put out the fire, getting in one another's way and making things much worse.

And then a woman came rushing out of the compound's entrance and started shouting at Tim in French. Cursing him, a girl I hadn't seen before, she wasn't European, perhaps middle eastern. Confident, seemingly in charge of something. But, most curiously what I first thought to be a black metal hair band holding back her thick curly hair was in fact a phone handset, and sure enough dangling down her ochre coloured vest top was a long cable.

The men turn to look at this woman and Archer suddenly appeared too. The woman pulls the handset from her head and stuffs it in Archer's hands. Archer shouts at the forty strong throng of Indians making matters worse and they all stop with the sand kicking. I go to pick Tim off the floor and his loose arm dangles and makes a "cricking" sound. He's in pain.

"Who was that" I ask him.

"She's not a farmer" says time

"I know that " I say, "But who is she?"

"She works upstairs, she's on the phones" and he stares at me, he smiles "You really don't know what's going on here do you?"

"Expensive yoga?"

Tim laughs and then his arm makes another horrific sound. He starts crying.

"Tell me, please Tim, be a, be good sport?"

The pain really got to Tim, he passed out in my arms and I fell back with his weight onto the floor. I'm recognised by some of the boys that play cricket and me and Tim are bundled into a rickshaw and driven to the hospital.

I stay with him until he comes to.

When he wakes up I press him to tell me a little more but he doesn't want to talk. He wants to go home. He asks me to fetch his belongings from the compound, he's done here he thinks. But I'm not done with Tim, I need him to tell me, but then I think back to Alec, how I wish he'd just gotten better. So I do what Tim asks, I walk back to the compound.

-

It takes me an hour to cross through Khajurahao and to get back to the compound. Afternoon turns to evening.

Outside the electrical box is still smouldering. Tim's bike has been moved out of the road and is leant against the wall. Somehow it's come off okay. Hard to tell.

Inside the compound a whole group of people I haven't seen before are sat around the main courtyard on mats – they're about to get on with some exercises, I skirt around them as I don't want to get caught up in any group work – Tim's going to tell me, I just need to help him and he'll help me.

I look back at the crowd, one of Archer's seconds starts to lead them through the asanas. The girl from earlier is there, an elastic band has replaced the handset. This group look paler than the farmers. She sees me staring at her and seems to shake her head a little.

-

As I put Tim on a night bus to Lucknow airport he said "All you need to understand is on the top floor." He smiled and then. "It's no big secret, not the horror you're looking for" And then the conductor shouted at us both to get on with it.

I watch Tim leave and wished I was going with him.

Tim got out. It took a broken arm but he got away clean. And me helping him hadn't gone unnoticed.

-

I got back too late to eat, and too late to play cricket. Besides I didn't feel like eating or playing. I felt like going home, this had been fun up 'til now. Playing detective, looking for a friend. Spending his family's money on my make your own adventure. But it was no longer fun. Falling through the cities, meeting the Indians in the street, tumbling down streets in the rickshaws – that was all fun, but being locked in at night with hundred other westerners in a trumped up hostel waiting for the quasi spiritual daily exercises if only because they interrupted the actual hard labour of working in the gardens had started to lose all of the charm that it never had to begin with.

Instead of going back to my dorm I walk to the other wing of the hotel and to the second dormitory. Here people stare at me when I walk in. They seem to have a greater sense of privacy here. Above each bed hangs a mosquito net – missing from my dorm. Also they have more belongings, paperbacks, stereos, ipods, magazines, the occasional bottle of gin, whisky, some mixers warming in the shade away from the windows. There's even a small bookshelf at the end.

One by one the men and women in this dorm sit up from their post supper slumbering and stare at me. Then the middle eastern girl appears in front of me.

"You shouldn't be here, this isn't your dorm"

"This isn't my dorm."

"The farmers sleep at the other end."

"And you aren't a farmer?"

"The farmers have another dorm, you know that, you shouldn't be here"

I look over at the bookshelf. And impossibly I spot the word

Slocum on the spine of a book.

"I was looking for a book" I say
"Well take it and leave" she says.
I reach for the book and walk back the way I came.
Out in the corridor I open the book to the title page.

Sailing Around the World
I smile. It's a sign of some sort. I'm not spiritual but it's a
boost. It's a one over.
I notice I'm being followed. I turn and my follower ducks out
of the light and behind a pillar.
I continue back towards my dorm.
I fall asleep that night thinking about this girl and Tim's bike.
My head fills with tales of voyages across oceans I have never
seen.

-

I'm up early on wash duty, boiling up the vats and adding the
clothes. Helping a young Indian boy with his English, he brings
out his phone and shows me pictures of London, of Chelsea
football players and Lamborghinis. In return he helps me wash
the clothes quicker, explains how to avoid the blisters when
wringing out, how to split three pegs on two sheets and so on.
He's a good kid.

-

I go out to the street. Overnight the electrical box has been
replaced. Tim's motorbike is still there. I decide that he'd have
wanted me to have it so I wheel it back to the compound and
out through the back.
There's no one here yet, the garden is peaceful. I see a guava

and pick it, cut it open with a cutting blade from the tools. I eat its fresh flesh as I stare at the bike and think what needs to be done to it. I need a mechanic. I'll need money for the mechanic, tonight I'll go into town with it – get it fixed up.

-

The farmers start work a half hour later.

We just get on with picking, pruning, watering, bedding in. All useful skills for sure. Then the sun comes up full and everyone slows down.

It's only eleven o'clock but I'm already exhausted. We're expected to work another couple hours but I'm not into it, not feeling anything today. I wander away.

I walk back to the compound and onto the dormitory floor. It is empty in my dorm. I cross to the other end and into the other dormitory. Also empty. From the second dorm there is another staircase leading directly on to the top floor. I look down the stairs and it seems to lead down to the kitchens again.

I walk up.

On the top floor an airy rooftop courtyard is flagged off on all sides with western clothing drying in the sun, they avoid the muddied look of the farmers by washing their stuff separately.

Off the courtyard are low looking rooms at each corner of the roof. On top of each of these rooms is a massive AC unit bleating out under India's sky.

I scuttle between German army surplus shirts and floral yoga pants, No Fear surf t-shirts and three quarter chinos. Another world up here above the world.

Outside one of the rooms a couple of men in smoke. They both wear headsets.

They stub out their cigarettes and pick fleece jackets off the floor go back inside.

A hand touches me on the shoulder through a linen shirt and

I almost fall off the roof. It pulls me back through and the shirt
falls on to my head turning me into a ghoul.

It is the girl.

"I shouldn't be here either" I say quietly.

She shakes her head.

I nod to her and start walking away.

I push through the clotheslines.

And there he is: Archer.

"How are you Matthew?"

-

So this was it. This is what I found out so far. This is what I
wrote you first and Diana second. I never sent you that letter.
And it would take me a few days to get to an internet café to
write to Diana, and you'll learn why that's ironic.

-

Archer introduced me to Fani, I don't think that was her real
name but later when we were alone she would always refer to
herself as that.

Then he took me to one of the rooms.

Maybe they were intended as rooftop lounges or deluxe
suites. But that was then and this is now. Now the AC unit ran
straight into the roof, a Mitsubishi AC fan inside dispersed air
at a pace across the room.

There are a dozen men and women on the phones. In front
of them beige PCs are fizzing away with onscreen information.
The men and women talk in a lot of different languages
but I pick up on English, French, Spanish, Japanese some
Scandinavian language, Russian, Italian and a couple of other

European languages I can't place, or perhaps one of them is Yiddish.

On the table by each computer is a written script of similar length printed and laminated – large comic sand lettering. And I watch at the operators operate. The headsets seem to dial and hang up for them. It's a neat operation, and it takes me a while to tune in on what they are saying.

"Is it what you were expecting?" asks Archer

"I wasn't expecting anything." I say

Then I start to hear what they are saying, it's a well-prepared script asking for payment on their electric bill. From their intonation it seems to be the same script across every language. There's a quiet ticking sound as the headsets redial automatically. They cycle at a pace through the numbers on screen.

"So?" he asks me.

I want to be shocked, I want to be angry, I wanted Johno to be here sat in a chair wearing a white Nero collared suit stroking a cat. I wanted Archer to drag me up the jungle and sacrifice me to cannibals. I wanted lots of things. What I got was some ISDN lines and well-trained gap year con men and women. And now I was being made to feel like a schmuck because I'd sneaked around and gotten caught.

Is this all there is. Stealing. He's a thief.

"I saw you, " he says "in the garden this morning, you took a guava from the tree, without asking, ate it up. Was it yours to take?" I look at Fani.

"I best get back to gardening" I say.

"You're a little too nervous for this work Matthew, aren't you?" asks Archer.

Fani sits at the desk, headset goes on and she starts talking away in what I'm guessing is Arabic.

"I guess I am" I say. And I walk away.

-

Dear Diana,

Although I cannot be certain I think that Johno would've worked here in India for the man named Archer. I think that he worked as in telephone sales but not of the entirely legal kind. It seems that the ashram I am staying in, if that is how to describe it, is run as a sort of modern day Fagin's den.

We westerners are the lost boys, turned to India for streets paved with meaning in place of gold. I think certainly Johno would've come through here, but I do not think he fell foul of any violent act here. This is a place where people come and go, and of those that were here at the same time as Johno few are open to talking to me. I feel certain that he might have left here with some money and moved on, to where I'm not certain.

I am not sure where to turn to next, however, if it is alright with you I should like to have another thousand pounds in case I need it.

Please send my love to Isabella.

Johno

I wanted her to still believe that I was taking my duties seriously.

I hit send and leave the dusty internet café – twenty or thirty years behind the hi-tech equipment Archer is running.

Outside the café Fani is waiting for me by Tim's bike. She wants to show me a nearby waterfall.

She puts it into second, doesn't give a fuck. I cling onto the rails on the back and off we go.

-

There's a long and winding road, actually yellow bricks and only slightly wider than a car and it takes us all the way to the waterfalls. We pass tumbled temples, monkeys and farms. The road undulates. The rails slip under my hands so I hold on to Fani. We pass guys trying to get their tuk tuk out of a hedgerow, if I was alone I'd stop to help but Fani is in charge and she doesn't care. Maybe she's been here too long.

-

Arriving at the falls entrance we pay the white person fee as normal. No matter how ingratiated you might become and how long you stay here your skin is always going to give you away. Still an outsider of sorts, still someone with more money than anyone else here. So we pay our tourist tax and walk to the falls.
They are impressive.
I'd imagine the canyons on mars look pretty similar. Arid rocks bare of vegetation lead away from us into shadowed depths. A slow cataclysmic erosion has produced these deep ravines that look ravenous, about to swallow up the earth, sucking in life and leaving only barren rock.

It takes us both a moment to realise that there's no waterfall. It is dry season. There's no gushing, rushing of water. No gurgle. No cooling spray as the falls gets picked up in the afternoon breeze. Instead just the feeling that gravity behaves differently here, that this waterfall could eat you up but never spit you out. There's the geologic belly of whale deep underground where flutes and hand drums are played by those who have fallen in.

Fani looks disappointed.
"At least the ride out here was nice, and it is very, it is a very stunning landscape." I try.
"But where is all the water gone"
"It's dry season"
"But even so." She is really disappointed.
We walk around the railed viewpoints. Men with badges sit cross-legged in domed pagodas. Their radios and gardening implements at their sides. Fani takes my hand as we get closer to the edge of the waterfall. She looks over the rail. Shuts her eyes. She starts to cry.

-

Another concrete pagoda, a bottle of water she'd been carrying, sunglasses and sandals on the floor.
She's stopped crying now.
"We should go back soon" she says.
"I'm sorry about the waterfall" I say.
"I'm sorry about the water too, it was my idea."

She pauses. She looks around. From her bag she takes out a packet of cigarettes and goes to light one up. One of the gardening caretakers walks over to her. She pauses. Looks at him.
"Is it not okay?" she asks.

He takes a lighter out from his pocket and offers to light it for her. In return his hand comes out – Fani gives him a cigarette. He nods and makes the praying gesture with his hands and walks away.

"I'm waiting for someone, it seems silly now, I didn't care so much, but then you were acting all like what we are doing is suspicious and I suppose it broke me out of this, you know, this kind of a dream state I'd been in for a while."

"who are you waiting for" I ask.

"He's a photographer, I met him in Benares. He's very brilliant, he works for National Geographic, the New York Times – you know – very brilliant man, very beautiful mind. But he's a free spirit and you know when he makes a photo he needs to be there with the people, he needs to understand them, without a , how do you say, without a filter, you know."

I look at her. She smokes long and hard.

"He left you, to go and take photos?"

"Am I stupid?" she asks

"No but. When is he coming for you?"

"I don't know"

"You love him?"

"I think so…Archer says…"

"Go on"

"Archer says I shouldn't wait for this man, that there should be other people in my life, he says I am a free spirit too, that I should let myself wander, that I need to exercise the energy of my yoni, he thinks I should…"

I think for a moment she likes me.

"He wants me to go away with him"

"With Archer?"

"Yes…"

"Are you, and Archer?"

"Am I sleeping with him? Yes."

She starts sobbing again. The smoking gardener looks over. I hesitate and then put my arm around her. I feel bad for her, on behalf of men I want to apologise to her. I want to explain to her that most of us are bad. She probably knows that already.

"What should I do?" she asks.

"I think I'm leaving here soon, you can come with me, travel with me?"

"Where are you going?"

"I'm not sure"

"Okay."

"Okay?"

"Good, we will leave together."

"I'll get you to somewhere calm, where you can make some decisions."

"Away from Archer." She says.

"Yes"

"Away from Hello my name is Fani, I'm calling from behalf of your bank."

I laugh.

"Away from that too" and she laughs. The gardener stubs his cigarette out on a stone Buddha.

-

The following day I was upstairs.

Archer took me aside after that morning's yoga class. He wanted me to make some calls. He thought I should give it a go. Wanted to know, I think, that I was committed to his cause.

Before he would let me loose on the phones he wanted to run through the script with me. Archer stared long and hard as I read over and over the lines. When we'd gotten back from the waterfall the night before it hadn't gone unnoticed by him and indeed Fani had gone to stay with him rather than in the dormitory. As for the National Geographic photographer I guess he really had vanished.

First time on the phones.

"They can hear you, they can hear your face, they can sense you smiling, they will smile too." Archer whispers into my ear.

Fani is across the room already talking away.

We get halfway through the script, maybe I'm not smiling enough, I don't think it's going very well. There's a man called Sam from Winchester who's suspicious but as I ask him for his password he grows more at ease with me, then he challenges me and I really start to smile.

"Of course I know you aren't really called Matthew" he says.

"We are almost there sir, I just need to confirm the last three digits on the back of your Mastercard." I continue with the script.

"Probably a Sanjay or something aren't you?" he's getting to his point.

"All of you lot now do the work we used to do, good accent, almost couldn't tell."

"Those last three digits please sir." I say calmly leading him towards fraud.

"What's your real name then son? I know you're in some call centre in Bomb-bay" he says Bombay with a Peter Sellers Indian accent. Played as a hapless but kind simpleton, the same role I'm playing now.

"My real name sir, is Matthew, my parents were very fond of the English"

"I knew it!" and I can hear him smiling for sure. "So why do you need my details again, seems a bit unusual?".

I follow the script on the page – there's a workflow for this question.

"It's a reward account, you pay three pounds a month, for that you'll get phone insurance and great savings every time you pay by direct debit. It looks like you pay gas, electric, water – you're looking at about 5 pounds cashback a month" There, delivered the dull fake facts, so boring he won't suspect a thing.

"Righty, seems like a good deal. Three, three, five. There you go. When will I receive the details of the new account?" he asks.

"The new account will be ready for you immediately, you will receive the paperwork in the post shortly, thank you for your time this afternoon, what follows will be a short survey on how the call was for you, have a good day."

I'm rung off automatically and the survey plays.

The survey is one of Archer's little add ons – it's to buy some time – sometimes the electronic transactions take a little longer than real time and to keep the victims occupied for just long enough to use their credit cards to pay into Archer's spiritual slush fund.

-

It is tiring work. I get a headache after a couple of hours. I look around and people keep pushing through the phone calls, their computers autodialing number after number, the same script again and again. With each call a small discreet payment from credit card to Archer. Simple, small scale, effective.

I take a break at lunch. Look down at the gardens and the 'farmers' there – I wish I was down there, oblivious again to this rip off happening up here. I eat some chapatti and lentils for lunch with a little yoghurt, drink some tea and then get back on the phones.

I stick to the script, sometimes people ring off, sometimes people say this sounds like a scam to me and they ring off, you don't need to reassure them, you stick to the script, they make the decision, you never ever persuade them, the computer will never ever run out of numbers to call. Archer explained that there are millions of numbers, and more being added every day. Sometimes you get a kid, should they own phones – you hang up if it's a kid, there's no point, they wont have a credit card. So you race through the numbers, don't get caught up or caught out just stick to that script.

Later in the afternoon I'm done, the final call rings through, I can't check the number on my screen, so I can't be sure, but there was a voice on the end of the line that sounded like you, sounded like you answering the phone in your bag, or maybe you were running for the bus, I couldn't tell, but the woman on the other end of the line sounded exactly like you, and she realises that her phone has picked up, and she says 'hello, hello?' and I can't bring myself to introduce you to this lie, maybe it wasn't you, but that doesn't matter, like tapping a best friend on the shoulder only to see it isn't them, its just their haircut, their jacket.

You're a shadow. You're safe. You're alive.

I hang up.

"Another kid" I say to anybody listening in the room. "How can they all afford phones so young" I add to build on the lie, to sell the lie in to the liars all around me. But they aren't interested. Fani stands and takes out her cigarettes. I leave with her. AS we get outside I take off the pullover I found in the laundry and hang it on the line outside. Fani lights up and as we walk down the stairs I tell her I'm going. I'm taking Tim's bike and I'm getting out of here. I don't know where, I have a little money and there's more on the way. Come with me, leave him, he's bad news. She seems upset, and more so after I suggest we meet after supper.

"It will be okay" I tell her.

"he won't know where I am" she says

"The photographer?" I stare at her "Sure he'll know - can't you email him, call him?"

"Archer" she says. "He won't know, he won't understand"

"It'll be okay. I'll pick up some supplies and meet you out the front of the building at midnight. Bring something warm to wear in the night.

She smiles. "Sure"

-

I don't pack up my stuff, I don't want to attract suspicion. All I need is some clothes, wallet and Slocum's book, I'll steal a phone if I can find one plugged in. I've an hour between finishing work and supper, then there's cricket to go to as well. But today I'm taking a little of the money I've left and I'm going to look at the temples, do the tourist thing at sunset.

-

It is sobering to drink tea sunset in a 'tree house' restaurant overlooking the Unesco protected erotic temples of Khajurahao. Thick set Germanic safari suit porting couples with androgynous haircuts and man boobs squat on canvas chairs and compare the Indian beer with the 'much better beer' back in Bavaria. They start shouting at the waiter that their souvlaki is now taking too long to arrive at the table. I pay and leave.

Inside the temple compound I pay up and then go all-in and get the audio tour.

A calm Indian woman leads me through the temples reminding me at each staircase to remove my shoes before entering. Hers is a calming presence and I enjoy listening to the tales of ancient civilisations, wars fought over romance and the complexities of building these magnificent totems to love, sex and godliness. They are overwhelmingly beautiful and in the dying light of the day I smile at every turn as man fucks woman who eats out another woman who is getting fucked by an elephant who is watching another couple fucking and so on. Cheeky is lame. This shit is funny, its pornographic and its never ending. The friezes run high into the sky around every temple and like the coach parties of elderly and obese Europeans I gawp and laugh and think how nice it must be to find someone as beautiful as theses carvings, there stony perfect bodies curved and pert and rendered in a state of ecstatic sexual bliss for an eternity or until the rains eventually wash these rocks away.

For a half hour I just sit near the end of the audio tour. I talk to a guide who is watching over a giant Nandi statue. We just talk about cricket and the weather and he asks me about London and I'm so grateful that I'm just another tourist again that I want to fucking cry.

-

I'm late for supper and so I end up serving the rice. There's a queue already formed and I dish out. Fani is in the queue, doesn't say a word, "see you later" I say but she just smiles and moved on to the curries.

I take the vats of leftovers to the kitchens, sit and eat quickly on a bench before starting the washing up. I'm not really hungry. I'm just thinking about where to go and how to get there. I'll need petrol and I'll need to fill up before it gets dark. I don't know the range of the motorbike on a tank. I have no direction to go in but I know there's nothing here. For Fani, for me. I'll take a week long holiday in Goa. I'll go smoke pot in Rishikesh, a few afternoon cookery lessons in an upmarket Delhi hotel.

I finish my chores. I take my book and a jumper from my

room and say to the few early to the dorm that I'm off to
the cricket. Why I tell them that I don't know. They aren't
interested. I deviate on the way out and double back past the
kitchens where earlier I'd seen some iphones plugged in.

I take the first phone I see and pocket it.

I see Fani across the concourse as I leave. She is hanging out
laundry. I wink at her. She smiles back and nods.

-

I drive across to the town, weave past the temples and
purposefully carry on all the way out west until I reach the
petrol station by the motorway. I fill up the bike and then drain
a bottle of water and fill that up with petrol too and strap it
using a bungee to the back of the bike.

Then I stop for tea at the edge of town. I don't want anyone
to see me here, I avoid the usual spots. I avoid Archer's spots.

-

The cricket is starting and I bring the bike up over the dust
and bring it to a stop.

One of the boys is fishing the stumps and bat out from the
hollow under the tree that overhangs the crease.

They split into two groups, I'm called over and asked to play.

Fielding and not bowling as normal but its fun. There's
shouting, name calling, laughing. The scoring seems arbitrary.
I'm in to bat and am caught out straight away, the ball span off
a miss hit.

I take my queue and sit on the stone steps and watch.

It starts to get darker. I start to wonder how I'm going to
spend the next four hours until it gets dark. There's only so
much tea I can drink so reluctantly, and knowing that no one

from the compound would come looking for me there I go back to the tree house restaurant and order.

"How long you India" asks the waiter

"A couple of months" I say

"Why I've not seen you before?"

"I'm just passing through"

"Where are you from ?"

"London."

"London, Chelsea..."

"Camden Town" I interrupt.

"Camden Town" he replies.

I order food first, and then a beer, then another.

-

I haven't really drunk since I got to Delhi.

I felt really drunk.

I drank coffee not tea to try and sober up.

I paid my bill, about 5000 rupees of omelette, chips and beer.

I'm the last to leave. Someone from the kitchen of the tree house recognises me. Friend of Archers.

"Hey you, friend?" he's walking over to me.

"Hi" I try and leave

"You are Archer's friend? Then you are a friend of mine, please sit I will get whiskey"

He's a plump smiling man with a visible belly button, heavily stretched Ralph Lauren polo shirt and a fine moustache.

"I don't think I can but thank you." I say.

"Please, please? Is there something wrong?" He looks concerned.

I have an hour to get back to Fani, I only need twenty minutes to get to the gates of the compound. I'm a little loose on my feet.

"Great."

I sit back down.

"Saura" he offers his hand

"Matthew" I shake it.

"I know I know, very clever man, asks many questions, Mr Archer very praising"

"Thank you"

Then there's an alarm sound. I look around in horror.

Saura starts laughing and he leans towards me. He reaches into my pocket and brings out the Iphone.

"You don't know you own phone?"

"Ha-ha" I laugh it off.

"Go on, answer it, I will get the glasses"

He watches as I go to answer the phone.

I press answer and hold it to my head. A voice I recognise as Karl – one of the real yoga nuts.

"I know you took my phone" says Karl

I don't reply. I smile, Saura leaves.

"You've stolen my phone"

I hang up.

Saura comes back with glasses. They are dusty and we rinse them with whisky, pour it out and then refill.

-

It takes a couple of glasses of Whiskey for Saura to open up.

He has a hotel in the south of town towards the Jain temples he is saying. I've seen them from the bike but never explored them. He can't believe how many weeks I've been here and not seen all the temples. He reminds me how caught up I've been in the compound, in Archer, in Tim, in Fani.

We get on to Archer.

"You want to know about Mr Archer?"

I'm quite drunk, thinking about the bike, thinking about where I have to get to, what I have to do, what order I have to do it in.

"Sure, tell me" I reply.

"Okay, I tell you, but first you tell me, what you know?"

"He's a really a genuine modern day legend my friend, oh yes, he knows a lot about yoga, he knows a lot about people, he's, he's a guru?" I'm uncertain what I'm supposed to say here.

"Yes, he's a guru" is Saura's response, and then I see it in his eyes, the glee. He's a father at Christmas taking more delight in watching his kid open a present than opening a present himself. Saura's about to give me something, something good, I can feel it.

"But not always a guru." He stares at me, I pour whiskey, he smiles and strokes the moustache, he sips the whiskey and watches as I sip mine, then he laughs full bodied and snorts, then starts talking.

"Archer was born not far from here, on a small farm, it was the 1950s, very poor here, these temples, no one cared, maybe , I don't know, but it wasn't like this, this middle of India, no one come here, no one care, maybe some archaeologist, maybe some people who didn't leave after the war, you know, still no one."

I nod. I top him up, I top myself up.

"So Archer is born someplace near here, no one knows where"

"Not England?" I ask

"No no no no no, not England, near here" he points around, then continues:

"Someplace near here, someplace. Very poor, he's not at

school, he works the fields, growing crops, working for his father, working for his mother, bringing home the food with them, his mother selling some food at market, maybe he finds some water hyacinths for a little extra money, still very poor, very poor, then one day at market he sees some people he hasn't seen before, you know who these people are?" I shake my head, he goes on:

"These people were hippies, a man and a woman, who saw Archer or Ash as he was then, and they remembered him, took pity on him, but Ash was not a kid who needed to be pitied or remembered, he would have been just fine by himself, he had no need of these westerns sympathy nor charity. You see from a young age, working the fields Ash saw that through hard work he might free himself and his family from that hand to mouth life, he might free himself from the poverty he was born into, but for one thing that might have been true. Ash, in any other world, would have been able to rise and rise from those small beginnings to be who he is now, he should not have needed the help of these westerners, he should not have needed outside help but Ash was born a dalit. You know this thing?"

He drinks his whisky and then beckons a waiter over and orders water. I'd heard the word around, I think I knew but I'd let him continue the story.

"Born a dalit, an untouchable, a poor man, with no status, the lowest of the no, no caste, he is told at birth by this that he can never amount to nothing. So he is selling water hyacinth in the street, other days he is burning them to make sweeter, or he stays working in the fields. One, two, three years go by. And then the hippie couple come back, they are a little older, maybe it was more years I forget the exact telling of the story, but you understand."

"Many years go by, and the hippie couple come back, they looked different, older, grown up, but also sad. Sad because they could not have a child, they had tried but Parvati had not blessed this couple with the ability to have children. They stay a few nights and each day they go to the market. On the first day they drink tea for four hours, but they do not see Asha, on the second day they spend five hours choosing and blending spices for to take home, on the third day they spend six hours learning from a samosa seller how to package the most perfect of these pastries, but all the while they are looking out for Asha."

"Finally on the fourth day they see him, he carries with his mother sacks of water hyacinth, burnt on the outside, sweet in the middle. He is grown up, and at first the couple do not recognise him but Asha recognises them. He has learnt a little English in this time from being about traders, sneaking into movies and listening to the BBC through the back window at the barbers that is on our motorcycle avenue, in main town, not this tourist town of course."

I nod, sip the whiskey and check the time. I need to leave here in five minutes if I'm to get there exactly on time, would she wait for me if I was late. I drink some water to counter the alcohol. He continues:

"And so it was decided that Asha would be sponsored by the couple to learn English in England. Of course this is not what actually happened, for back in their small home by the fields, that Asha had worked all his life with mother and father, the hippie couple paid his parents a sum of money for Asha and they would adopt him, bring him up as their own. In many stories this is where the child runs away, this is where he curses his parents, makes a promise to come back to get revenge on the parents and so on, but not in this story, no. Indeed Asha, knowing from birth that with all the work in all the world that society would never allow him to prosper he accepted this fate as a fortunate intervention into his life that might give him a chance for things to work out a little differently.

"And, after a year of visa and adoption paper struggles he

flew for the first time across several continents before finally
journeying the last leg from Paris to London. Once in England
he moved with his new parents to the edges of Oxford where
his father worked as an academic teaching about ancient worlds
and in particular specialised in ancient Indian cities."

How does Saura know all this, I'd never seen him at the
compound.

"England at that time wasn't England as it is now. Then Asha
found himself in a country where racism happened everyday.
So one of the first things he did was to change his name to
Archer, the second thing he did was make a decision that
although he now lived better than he ever could have hoped
for being born a dalit in rural India this was not enough. He
needed to be better than the kids who taunted him, he needed
to be better than the unseen men who wrote racist graffiti
on the bus stop. Who stared at his blackness from across the
street. Who shouted paki in crowded streets. He wanted to
beat all of these people at life. And so he prayed to his gods
and he worked hard. And, under the tutelage of his new father
and the kindness of his hew mother, but also largely due to
his own application, young Asha, now Archer became a child
of academia. There was not a subject he did not excel in, a
philosophical point he could not argue, an old master whose
line and shadow he could not imitate to perfection. And so
Archer found himself at Oxford university studying philosophy."

"And, after graduating he kissed his mother and father
goodbye and with their blessing, having served as their much
needed child for all those years. He then returned here, to
Khajurahao and found that his mother had died and his father
long since left a lonely drunk to live at the railway station. But
there was one surprise in store for him at his old family hut by
the field where he used to farm with father and mother, a boy,
naked, working the fields, with nothing. The boy was...well..."

I look at Saura. He didn't want to tell me about Archer, he

wanted to tell me about himself. If I leave now I can make it. I go to stand but take the whole table with me. Saura reaches fast and grabs the heavy whiskey bottle but everything else goes flying. Glass smashes, shards cut at my legs, I hit my head on the floor. Someone from the kitchen rushes up to help us. Saura reaches down and offers me a hand.

"Don't cross my brother" he warns me. "He has more to lose than you will ever know, you are a bad man, you are a bad Englishman,"

And with that he walks away.

-

I can still start the bike, and after a jolty start I get it going. I have the spare gas, I have the book, its already cold and I have a jumper on, and I have a wallet, the stolen phone.

I can still drive the bike. But I'm late, but I can't hurry.

There's a guard in the street at the checkpoint edge of town. He sees me, flags me down.

He's pointing to the headlight, I turn it on. He smiles. I'm away.

-

The bike's engine is too small to roar, it goes "thup thup thup" as I accelerate. I'm going to make it, maybe a few minutes late. Rounding a corner the bike gives way a little on the gravel, and, half cut I struggle to keep the bike on the road but somehow I bring it back as the gravel rattles and chips at the bike.

The compound sits ahead in the gloom. At night, more than at any other time it has that haunted hotel feeling, a melancholic sight of a site intended for greater things than a phone line con. Stars help to pick out the building in the dead light of midnight.

She's waiting for me as agreed. I pick her out – at the corner of the compound. She hasn't anything with her, no bag visible as agreed. Why does this seem important, why does my heart fizz with excitement, this girl I just met seems suddenly like the future, she's the reason I'm here, she's going to make it all alright, she's going to help me to forget, she's going to tell me what love is, she's, she's she's…

She is Archer. Fifty metres away and I pick him out, his long hair, his linen shirt. I don't cut the bike. I walk it forward, keeping my distance. He holds a guava in his hand, bites into it.

"She isn't coming" he says.

Silence now except for the bike, bats or birds swoop low over Archer as he walks towards me. Forty metres, then thirty-five, thirty, twenty.

"We can speak from here" I say. But I'm shaking. Cold all over, freezing. This is what death is like when he comes for you and all you can do is ask him to hold back for a little longer whilst the cold wraps you up and you succumb. His hair hoods in his face, ghoulish, I'm in awe of him, always have been, and I'm scared of what he will say.

"Are you okay?" he asks.

"Sure"

"Where are you going?"

"I'm coming back, I was out, late, with.."

"With my brother." He says. It isn't a question.

"Yes."

"I know. He's a bad drinker. He's an alcoholic. But he's loyal brother."

Looking up and down the road it is clear she isn't here. Just uncertainty and a desire to run. I'm quitting my job again, he's all the employers I ever worked for, his phone hacks no worse than the screen filling click-schmaltz I wrote to get people to part ways with money.

I must look disappointed, "She isn't coming. She told me to give you this." He says. He throws what I think is a cricket ball at me. I catch it. It's a small hand painted orange Ganesh.

He continues, "We're in love you see" For some reason it is salt in the wound. "I've asked Fani to marry me." He says.

"What about her photographer, isn't he famous, wasn't she waiting here for him" I ask. It's all I have to taunt him with.

"He's dead, he stood on a mine in Afghanistan four months ago. Buy the latest National Geographic, his obituary is in there. Nice guy, thought too much of himself. Believed he was invincible"

"Isn't he in India?"

"Wouldn't it be nice if he was? But he isn't. Fani came to me when she needed help, when she needed to grieve. I've been there for her, I've coaxed her back from herself, from torturing herself. He was a beautiful man, he made some very beautiful pictures I told her, but now he's gone to another place, so we prayed together day and night for weeks, before I left for the camel fair, and when I left her she was in a good place, now she's in denial again, but my loving her will bring her back from the dead again. She needs me, she needs a bit of my power and I will give it to her."

I'm done with listening and distractedly I tuck the Ganesh between the dials on the bike and the fairing.

"Well, say goodbye from me."

I slowly start to turn the bike up the road.

"Your friend, Johno"

I look back at Archer.

"He's in Benares."

I nod. "thanks" though why he couldn't have told me weeks ago I don't know.

"He wasn't well last time I saw him, don't go looking for him"

I turn the bike in a circle on the clutch, I don't know whether to punch Archer or leave him be. But I'm still a coward, still a little London boy scared of an elderly yoga gurus shadowy strength, still not experienced enough to dismiss the mumbo jumbo surrounding him, still one of his subjects, still loyal, my rebellious running away is ruined by his blessing. And what of Fani, what does she see here apart from a life with a fraudster, charismatic though he may be. All this spins through my head.

Fuck it. I point the bike up the road heading East. Archer nods.

Ganesh seems to wink at me. Gone.

PART TWO - BENARES & BEYOND

CHAPTER EIGHTEEN - BENARES

With the help of the owner and a New Zealand couple called Elle and Bruce we'd slowly watched him live out his final moments.

We carried him out to the edge of the hostel and sat him in his favourite chair to watch the sun set one last time over the Ganges. He smiled but couldn't say a word, the once blue-painted concrete peeling and cracking to the Ghats below. He didn't seem to hear the dogs ripping each other to shreds in the streets behind us. Nor did he mind the mosquitoes that ate from him as sunset turned to night. They landed to eat from his blood, this dying man, so much ash and so much dust.

The deep warmth of the day still radiated off the hostel's balcony and the light bounced on the shallow sand bank opposite us. Boats ferried their passengers across the river and in that moment my thoughts filled immediately with stygian metaphor and I smiled knowing that if there was any place for him to die it was here.

More than all the quiet English villages, retirement communities and seaside resorts for the elderly; better than any Miami condominium development, a last-night-to-live-hotel with a bottle in Vegas; easier than a discreet Swiss clinic and the slide into death welcomed and encouraged here. Here, in Benares, death greeted man like a new best friend who has waited to say hello for your entire life.

On the banks opposite, children could just be made out running on the beach, horse rides downed tools for the day, and sandy cricket moved back to Ghat cricket.

Sure enough under the watch of the streetlights that bloomed with sunset we heard the crack of bats and balls although I could not move him close enough to see the game that had started on the steps of the river underneath the hostel.

Again he smiled. I'm not one for auras but he definitely emitted a strong sense of being at ease with himself, at ease with his death here. All peace until the daily Hindu songs blasted out ruining the calmative evening. He grew agitated and I held him. Between Bruce and I we carried him back to his room, put his fan on full and lit the incense to counter the smell of death that had started to fill his little room.

Earlier that day we'd tried washing his bed sheets, but it wasn't that, we'd changed and washed his clothes, but that wasn't the source either, then we'd scrubbed the floor, thrown out his backpack, opened the windows, banged out the drapes over the steps and finally gotten the hostel owner to look at the plumbing underneath the bucket and string arrangement that made up both his shower and toilet.

But the smell of a man about to die only came from that man. It came from each and every pore, every breath a little of his soul escaped into the air and told us, I am a dying man, look over me as I say goodbye.

Bruce left to go and find a beer. Difficult but not impossible in this town. He wouldn't be back for a few hours. I sat for a while by him as he struggled to keep breathing. He pointed at the door and I shut it for him. I knew what he wanted.

It wouldn't be the last act of charity for him. I took out his small handmade pouch – embroidered with elephants and paisleys. I unrolled it on the bedside table and lit the candle.

He directed me solely with his eyes, as he hadn't spoken now for two days. I transferred the heroin into a small tin bowl, back and forth 'til he nodded I had the right amount. I added a few drops of water from the bottle and he smiled at me. I heat it up for him, tried to disinfect the needle with a swab of alcohol , draw it up through a cotton ball, then apply the tourniquet and struggle for five minutes to find a vein. Finally he turns over onto his front and I see a few marks by his balls and penis, I see the vein, inject, draw back a little blood and then plunge.

He's gone, he'll be happy for the night. I tidy up. I offer up my hands in namaste. I put his roll away. I leave his room. I could do with that beer Bruce, I think to myself. Or a swim in the river.

I go for a walk.

-

Savage dogs rule Varanasi. What they know and that humans are loathe to admit is that in many ways the end product of all the Ghats, all the holiness and all the prayer is that vicious stray dogs get fed, chewing up what doesn't drift downstream or across the river from the burning Ghats.

There are two burning Ghats in Varanasi, and between them at night it pays to carry a rock, a cricket bat or wear your shoes loosely in case you need to chase off the dogs. Tearing into one another, large strips of hair and flesh are ripped from the backs of weaker dogs, the bone & muscle motors that have delivered them this far are exposed and the flies and diseases move in, further enabling the ruling dogs to lord it up. Those who are particularly ruthless get to retire early from all the fighting, lain out like the laundry wallahs' washing in the sun, no dog dare fight them, no human dare deny them scraps of pastries or dishes of rice.

And so at night humans give these dogs the widest of berths and try to forget what the inside of a dog looks like by distracting themselves with the daily festival of light down at the main Ghat. And you risk the dogs on the Ghats because the back streets have the dying dogs in them, and the cow shit, and Varanasi is medieval turned up all the way, and so the shit has no where to go so it builds and sure its holy but it squelches and claws at your shoes, feet and trousers, begging you to squat down to the level of shit yourself, asking you to lie with it, to bathe in it. This combined with the honeycombed layout of shops and ant mound streets only adds to the fever of this city, one of the most holy in India, and so one of the most holy on earth.

And it isn't that in the time that I've been here that I've not understood that, and that I haven't come to respect that completely, though all my time here so far I twisted and turned around the subject of faith but I've come to realise that it isn't an issue as long as I take my shoes off at temples and respect the rules of this holy land I'm doing okay.

But that faith doesn't mean slipping in a cow's sloppy crap is nice, and it doesn't prevent a stray foot ending up in the mouth of a dog. That's life, that's death and that is definitely Varanasi.

I'm getting closer to the daily light display that marks the centre of tourist town at night.

A few Korean kids are practicing unicycling on the ghat edge. A boatman hustles for custom in anticipation of tomorrow morning's dawn ride on the Ganges. Kids sell pastries. Men with severed limbs beg for coins. Tourists clutch at large Canon cameras for dear life as if that's a grand of electronics worth losing your life over.

The main Ghat's name is unpronounceable, unspellable, and I recognise it only when written down. Even in Sanskrit it's recognisable in its curiously Countdown conundrum mix of vowels and consonants: "Dashashwamedh".

There, like every night, three golden warrior sons of light perform an elaborately choreographed routine to Indian and foreign tourists. Stripped to the waist and with long slick black hair the men look straight off the front cover of romantic novels. Clouds of incense, burning oil and DEET fill the air. I take a seat on the steps to relax after braving the dogs and stare at the back of a foreign tourist – his thin shirt is crawling with mosquitoes – perhaps two dozen just drilling for blood, makes a change from dog I guess.

Everyone here is taking the same bad photograph of the event, hundreds of cameras flash but I can vouch no one will take a good photo, in the week I've been here I've seen endless people staring at the little screens on the backs of their cameras, trying to work out how to take a picture of the light show. And the truth is its impossible, sort of designed that way I want to tell them.

The best thing about the show is the MC, each night he drums up the crowd, brings people forward and organises who gets to sit on the front seats, unconsciously or perhaps not, it seems to me that the more devout looking Indian tourists get the best spots at the front.

Then after the show starts he sings along to each of the Casio heavy holy songs that soundtrack the show as he traipses up and down and up again with his compact discs for sale. In contrast to the chiselled muscle men on the podiums lighting the lamps and swinging incense the MC dresses in adidas tracksuit bottoms, 'slider' style flip flops and each night a Queen t-shirt from every tour they could ever have done. Brian May and Freddie vie for space on the man's chest beneath Buddy Holly specs and Pablo Escobar facial furniture.

This is light, this is darkness, and this is Varanasi.

Rested I walk up the last of the steps into the market place and look for a clean patch of concrete to come back to, I buy samosa, tea and fudge from three stores and then sit down and my thoughts turn to wondering when he's going to finally die. I thought it would be today, but it wasn't.

-

Jay is his name. He's a heroin addict, was first an addict in London but chose to be an addict out here, from what everyone said: everyone knew nothing, no one questioned nothing; no one gave a damn about the guy dying in the smallest room in the hostel. But I didn't stop asking questions and slowly people started to come out of the woodwork, expats, hostel owners, market traders, everyone had a little something to say about Jay or Jay-man as he'd come to be called.

Lining the main street between the backpacker hostel 'run' and the markets on either side of the alley-of-dung are cafes, lassi stops, restaurants, music lesson shops. In each of these shops by the door is a small rack of the same travellers books I've seen elsewhere. And for the most part in each of these books it seems to suggest that in India, Thailand, Laos, the Gold Coast, Inca Trail, Colombian Hill Farms and so on, there's some kind of travellers code. Some kind of backpacker's ethic that people stick to. But I hope by now you are starting to realise that this doesn't exist.

In the true travellers code people will come and go, people will rip each other off, one day they promise you rupees for petrol, dollars for that train ticket you walked across town to get them. You see them leave their best friend behind to shit themselves to death in the hostel, abandon their slow friend who can't run fast enough to catch the train already leaving the station. You look at travellers fake the dilemma they are going through when they're offered a ride and cant take that new travelling buddy on the bike with them.

Abandoned, left for dead, stolen from, ripped off, used as
conversation bait, chewed over and laughed at during a smoke,
the butt of jokes, the example of how not to travel, the woman
its okay to leave crying and alone after her wallet is stolen in
the market, the man struggling for breath in the hostel room as
he runs out of life and heroin – the only thing that's kept him
going these last months.

Heroin was the reason Jay was in India, for like everything,
and certainly compared to back home drugs were cheap and
they were openly available. But what had drawn Jay to Varanasi
was, I suspect, death. Death in all its romantic rock star heroin
glory. If you are going to see yourself out in a blaze of needles,
vomit and incense then maybe this is as good a place as any.
And if heroin was the reason Jay found himself dying on the
banks of mother ganga then Jay was the reason that Johno had
found himself here too.

But now Johno wasn't here, that much I knew. But I'd finish
what Johno couldn't. I'd help his old college friend die with
what grace he had left, I'd clean him, wrap him in gold and set
him off to wherever is next. The pharmacy over the way was
starting to close up, I finished the tea quickly and stuffed the
samosa down.

-

After leaving Archer at the side of the road I hadn't got a
plan. No plan at all. I rode the bike East in the dark and after a
couple of miles of swerving, the drunkenness making it almost
impossible to control the bike something in me decided not to
die. So I pulled over and slept off the whiskey wrapped in my
jumper at the edge of a field.

Before the sun came up I woke. Cold to the bone. I started
the bike and thought I'd ride to Varanasi. But it wasn't to be.

It had spluttered to a halt some way outside of Patna. I'd

gotten a lift from the bike to a service station. Bought a bottle of petrol, waited for a friend of the station owner to give me a paid lift back to the bike only to find that it had gone, vanished, the bike that wouldn't run had disappeared.

My 'taxi' driver offered to drive me back to the petrol station. From there I got to the nearest train depot, and found myself squatting on top of a luggage rack in unreserved class alongside children as we trundled slowly into Patna.

In Patna I had a forty-eight hour wait for a train to Varanasi and I busied myself with eating, visiting the site of an old opium factory from when the British were here. I blew ten dollars on a pizza and milkshake and espresso in the square I look from a distance at the coming and goings of people visiting Bharat. Everyone wanted to know if that's why I was here – I told them I was templed out and that I was meeting a friend in Varanasi and then going home.

Patna, one guy sat next to me in the "American style" café is struggling to restring his small guitar. He sees me staring and thinks it's an invite to talk.

"Oh how long have you been here" asks the backpacker

"A couple of months" I had replied.

"is that all, you really haven't seen anything then have you?" he says, now tuning the guitar.

"No, there's always next time" I say.

"Sure is" he says and rolls his eyes.

They walk away, not with the world on their shoulders but with their world on their shoulders. He's not here, he's inside his backpack, he's the guitar, the portable speakers I see poking out, the second backpack on his front, the laptop computer, the phone, the camera, the Cds of tribal disco pressed in Czechoslovakia.

He stops at the side of the square and starts playing Bob Dylan covers. Every time he hits that new string its way out of tune. Indians take pity and throw the guy rupees. A few

western tourists smile and clap. I hate him only marginally
less than I hate myself. Yeah yeah yeah, we're all tourists, but I
know it, some don't.

In a small internet café I emailed Isabel and Diana. I also sent
a message to my dad. I wanted him to know I was alive, I had
lost track of time but I felt I had already been here long enough
to be reported dead. It was the first upbeat email to Diana that
I'd sent in a while. I knew where her son was.

Dear Diana...

In my inbox I had a plenty of spam. I had a few messages
from friends that I batted away with a quick summary of the
last few weeks leaving out Archer and upping the temple count.
There was a pleading email from Rossie and Russell asking
me to go back "There's no one that writes click bait quite like
you Matthew" and a brief paragraph outlining the costs they'd
had to remove the 'adult' content from my laptop after it had
arrived back from India... Also Lottie had gotten pregnant at
some point before I left because there was a picture attached of
her pregnant – some inference in the email that If it was mine I
owed it to them to come back and work for them because since
I had left things had really been turned upside down.

I wrote a message to Lottie congratulating her. She was a
good person, she'd be a great mum. That's kind of what I wrote
anyways.

The first night I had collapsed in my bunk shared with
American Buddhism tourists. The second night I slept less well.
In the middle of the night I finally fell into a deeper sleep. And
during this sleep fell even further into a dream.

I hadn't wanted to share the dream. Dreams are the most
boring of things to share.   But I dreamt deeply about you. I was
sat in the window of a bar. Outside you were there with a new
man. You were both dressed head to toe in grey yoga outfits

– his was cropped and instead of a stomach he had a marble column that rose from his leggings into his shirt, a Parthenon in Nike, his face equally chiselled – a real hero. Your faces were green like broccoli, his beard was a thicket of flowering thorns. You kissed like we never did. Leaning together over a table stacked with coffee lids and grappling at each other's thighs as if scrabbling for the line of an escaped kite. All around you other drinkers spat out their coffee, they exploded into beery spray, erupted with cheap prosecco, a man with pissy wine stains ripped off his trousers and they floated away. But you and him were oblivious to it. Didn't care. Because you had each other. And when you finished kissing your face was bleeding, but you were smiling and I could see that you were happy.

This dumb dream and the abundance of Buddhism tourists transiting to Gaya are my overwhelming memories of those two days in Satna before I got an unreserved seat and crouched in the doorway next to an elderly couple who's belongings filled one bathroom meaning slowly the other flooded towards me so I stood and watched Varanasi crawling ever closer happy in the false promise that in just a few hours time all this would be over. I would arrive in Varanasi, find Johno somehow and put him on a plane back home. But we know now that didn't happen. We now know that Varanasi had become a very different kind of episode.

CHAPTER NINETEEN - DEATH ON THE NILE

Back at the hostel I pass Jay's door, he is wheezing heavily. I walk into his room, make sure the fan is still on. I pour water onto his travel towel and then wet his brow and chest and wipe away the crystals of salt that have built up since he's been out.

I leave the room and Elle walks past me crying. Bruce is there.

"She wants to see the sunrise on the Ganges, wants something happy to remember from this place"

"Good idea" I say. Though Jay's forthcoming death shouldn't weigh heavy on any of our minds, it's his life and his death, but I guess Elle is taking it badly.

"Would you come with us to share the cost of the boat?" he asks.

That's what was coming.

"Sure."

-

5:00 am – total quiet. Even the dogs aren't audibly savaging each other. I look in on Jay and he's sleeping but moved onto the floor – there's a fresh stain in his bed. I hope he has some money left for us to add to when it comes to paying the owner for 'no trouble'.

There's no sign of Elle and no sign of Bruce. I go to the hostel gate but it's all closed up. I walk back along the courtyard edge to the other entrance but that's also locked. We are locked in – there's a curfew a night but I didn't realise that we couldn't get out. I give it a few minutes and decide to go back to bed. Mother Ganges can wait.

"We went back to get jumpers" Elle
"It's cold" Bruce
"We are locked in" I say.
"The fucking manager, I told him last night we wanted to leave" Bruce says.
"Fuck" adds Bruce.
I turn around and walk back to the gate. Bruce tries it.
"It's locked" he says.
"Can we get over it" asks Elle.
There's rusty razor wire on top.
"I guess we will have to try tomorrow" I say.
Elle shrugs. Bruce starts pounding hard on the gate.
Then he moves back towards where the hostel owner and his family live. He hammers hard on the desiccated wooden door they live behind. The owner's teenage daughter appears, she looks glumly at the three of us. Gets the key, and silently opens the gate for us.
"I'm so excited" says Elle
I look back at the owner's daughter yawning. The gate creaks closed behind us.

-

We go back and forth between boat owners, boat agents and boat hustlers. They all promise a good deal but Elle wants none of it. Bruce neither.

194

"I don't want to feel threatened into choosing a boat" says Bruce.

The sun is starting to come up.

I seize the moment and run down to a real hustly looking guy, he goes to speak but I'm first.

"Hello, how are you, what a lovely boat, it rides well does it, beautiful tour, twenty dollars? Perfect" I get all this out before he can even respond. "I've found our man" I say to Bruce and Elle. "Lovely guy, used to row for India" Maybe that's too much. Then I notice a young Chinese man on the steps.

"That was my boat, I was paying five dollars" says the Chinese guy.

"We can share" I say

"I don't think we can" says Bruce. Fucking backpackers I think to myself.

"I'm sorry" I tell the Chinese guy

I clamber onto the boat. The boatman is smiling. He points at a single child's life vest and then points again at Elle. But Elle is struggling to get on the boat. She won't get on.

"It doesn't look safe" she says.

"It probably isn't, haha" I say trying to make light of it.

"It looks really bad mate" says Bruce.

"It's wobbling a lot" says Elle.

"It just isn't stable mate, it's a death trap" says Bruce.

I sit down on the bench furthest from them.

I look at the Chinese guy. "Come on" I say and beckon him on board "I'll pay, don't worry".

Bruce swears. Elle has got a flip flop stuck in the jetty. I don't care. He's good around Jay but a pain otherwise. They'd have ruined the sunrise for all of us, I'm please to be here with this stranger.

The boatman clambers across other moored up boats and eventually pushes us free before jumping on board as well.

Slowly he starts sculling us upriver. A motorboat overtakes us almost immediately, twenty or more tourists have their cameras trained on the Varanasi escarpments as the sun starts to take back the world from the night.

Turns out the Chinese guy is called Sam. He's been travelling around the world for a year. He doesn't carry a camera, he is super calm. He swam in the Ganges yesterday and tells me it's cleaner than it looks but I don't believe him.

"Where I am in China, there's a similar river, much dirtier than this. I work in a factory, we produce parts for motors that go inside turbines, they just let the dirt run out into the river, on one side of the river is China, on the other side of the River is North Korea – the distance is the same as here, people try swimming across it all the time, some get further than others. I wouldn't swim in that river, more bodies than in this one."

He pulls his jacket around him, and I notice how cold it is as we get further out. All around us more and more boats slowly drifting along the banks. On the Ghats men arrive in loincloths and bathe in the water, women wear saris and also bathe, though more gingerly.

There's an unspoken turnaround point, a hidden destination. Harischandra Ghat. One of the two points for cremation on the river in Varanasi. And unlike the main cremation ground with its stacks of timber and colourful surroundings this one is more obviously a place of burnings.

In the last few days I've walked up to it, walked through it, but never stared as I do now. The endless flame still burning.

196

A piece of cloth finally turns to ash where a person once was. Dogs pick at the shoreline. Two men work to clean ashes from the path to the cremation ground, hosing them down to the water's edge whilst a third carries logs down the steps above, the burnings are carried out day and night here, so very many people to cremate. And, I've learnt, this Ghat also differs to the main ground because here you don't need to be a good person, or a pure person, or an honourable person to be burnt here, you just need to have a family with enough money for some firewood and to pay the undertakers. So at this ghat they'll burn the diseased, they'll burn thieves, they'll burn prostitutes and they'll burn drug addicts. And as Sam & I stare at the Ghat, because its impossible not to, I know that this is where Jay will end his days. He's a Hindu convert, he's a good person deep down, he'll burn here, he'll be happy here I know it.

We hover for a moment, the large motorboat wobbles as its occupants rush to take photographs. Snapping away with Iphones and cameras, large video recorders too. Then this strange early morning flotilla heads back towards town. The sun is almost up now. A couple of ghats along a parade of children appears, their heads shorn, their clothes uniform, they are lead by a leader, he looks like Archer might have when he was younger. They line up on the banks of the river and crouch in a yoga position before the surprising part of this voyage.

They begin to laugh, thirty children and their master are laughing. And they are life itself. All of us in the boats move our attention to these laughing kids, immediately taken away from the ashes of death to the cries of hysterical yoga. On land men and women in safari waistcoats snap endlessly at these little laughing yogis.

We arrive back where we started. Sam shakes my hand and leaves me to pay the boatman.

197

On the steps Elle and Bruce are waiting with water bottles and mars bars.

"Thought you might be hungry" says Bruce and hands me a Mars Bar. "Sorry about that" says Elle. "Shall we go check in on the patient" asks Bruce and in his voice I sense an apology for the scene on the dock and an acknowledgement that we all share of the sadness we are about to deal with.

-

What I hadn't told you was that Jay had a phone number for Johno. A mobile telephone number, and also some texts. The other thing that I hadn't told you is that Jay is very very charismatic when he wants to be, to the point that he is persuasive. And it turns out that after Johno hauled himself across India looking for him, always a few steps behind, evaded getting stuck selling scams down the phonelines for Archer and finally caught up properly with his sick friend he'd travelled more than I had. Turns out Johno had gone looking for Jay in the desert between Rajasthan and Pakistan, can't work out how I missed that one but I guess it must've been after Udaipur. So anyway Johno eventually catches up with his friend, the guy he'd come to India to save. But the problem was his friend didn't want saving, Johno did.

So, and this is all third hand, Jay and Johno spent a couple of weeks in Varanasi together smoking opium, weed, drinking bang, moving from guest house to guest house, outstaying their welcome at each place. And by all accounts those around them avoided them, look on as the fuckups, barred from the cafes and hostels. Clocked up unpaid bills. Chased by owners, bankrolled by unsuspecting tourists. Feared by the beggars. Kick out of tuk tuks, pulled from cycle rickshaws, dumped drunk outside temples for falling asleep.

In a couple of weeks they'd made a real stink and the police had been called. And that's apparently when Johno wanted out, that's when Johno realised his being here was pointless. He'd found his Kurtz and made merry with him, but now it was now fun.

You see Johno was in as long as he thought he could persuade Jay to come home, fraternising with the drunk to get him onside enough to put in a car at the end of the night to ensure he gets home in one piece. But Jay didn't want saving, he wanted releasing into whatever's next, and when he realised his friend didn't want to go on that journey, that Johno didn't fancy that final ferry ride across the Ganges and Jay turned inward and more destructive. He and Johno had fought and Johno had left to 'go and sort himself out. Did I know Johno very well? I'd been asked, did I know he was into drugs?... It's hard to explain how little I knew of the man and how far I'd come looking for him, it didn't make sense to them and I suppose it didn't make sense to me.

And if my journeying this far could be excused as really a crisis of self-hatred, a momentary descent into a voyeuristic tour of the east then what was Johno's excuse. All I could really get out of Jay is that they'd been friends a long time but I'd never heard of him. Diana had never mentioned him either, so I wondered what it was that made him a friend worth saving, what did Johno see in him that was worth bringing back from the dead. Jay wasn't able to tell me, the hostel owner and other travellers didn't know either. All they were able to say is that they think Johno left on a train heading East in order to 'get clean' leaving Jay here to die.

Or at least that was what I understood then. That the truth will out is true. But all in good time.

"I don't want to judge a man,..." said Bruce on the first day that I had met him "but it seems to me that your friend Johno is a bit of a soft touch. A bit prone to a bad idea."

And I guess at that point Bruce knew as much as I did. Summed it up pretty good too. And after all of that finding out as I retraced now the footsteps of the man I'd come to find and also the man he'd come to find I discovered more and more. Like all the backpackers before me who'd come to tread the same well worn paths since the war; I'd come to feel that what I was experiencing was unique whereas the reality was even amongst Johno, Jay & I there were very few real new decisions made. And it was only after his death and in sorting through Jay's small collection of books he hadn't sold on that I found out whom he'd been following.

Back to Johno - I wouldn't know why he'd come all this way to save his friend for another month. All I could do now is be human. Follow what millions of other people came to Varanasi to do. To say goodbye to someone who is very very ill and help them in those last days. Jay needed his hand held and I would do what Johno couldn't, I'd stay clean as Jay dirtied himself, I'd keep my distance as Jay destructed, and when it was all over I'd walk away knowing I'd done all I could.

CHAPTER TWENTY- WOOD PILE

We gathered early in the morgue.

I'd gotten up well before dawn to wash. Bruce came with me to the cash point and I gave him half the money we'd need for the day in case anything should happen, or in case I couldn't cope. He stuffed the money into his well-worn surf-shorts pocket except for five hundred rupees he kept out "I want to buy a shirt and trousers for the funeral" – I nodded, that was okay by me.

Together we walked to the edge of the market and take a rickshaw through to the mortuary.

It's much like visiting a relative in hospital with some of the formalities and all of the smell of sickness and disinfectant. I sign forms and explain I'm not family. No one seems to care. To the best of anyone's knowledge Jay lived the last years of his life as a Hindu and died a Hindu. Hindu – it's there on the forms, as well as the cause of death – heart failure. The mortuary has helped Bruce & I meet with the Doms, the funeral directors, I should follow their instructions now. We give ourselves over to them, they will tell us what to do.

-

Women aren't banned from attending the cremation ceremony but they don't attend. It's thought that if a woman, overcome with grief, should see the ceremony they will fall into the fire themselves and be consumed by the flames. So Elle's got a decent enough reason not to attend which leaves just Bruce and the professional mourners, and I'm grateful for them. They know how to manhandle the stretchered body through the streets, they glide above the crap, bypass the queues of pilgrims and tourists vying for a glimpse of the central temple. The Doms know when to pause so that holy men in doorways can pay their respects and finally deliver, without dropping, the body to the cremation grounds. As we round corners the sun rises again. Amongst the streets of Varanasi the sun is always rising or setting for the tarpaulins, makeshift roofs, ad-hoc extensions and cool stone passageways don't allow for a midday sun. Sunrise and sunset, life a death. A sadhu sits cross legged surrounded by incense, the mourners slow their pace and let the sadhu say a few words for Jay. I drop a few hundred bills in his cup. I'm grateful for the words whatever they were. Looking back I wonder if I should have paid more to the sadhus, more for the wood, more for the mourners, more for the boys who sit and fake hawk the piles of wood. If I'd paid more would Jay have had an easier time going off to the next place?

They take the weight of the body and we are off again. The streets spit you out here whoever you are. There's no escaping the contrast between ghat and city and it's only made more profound by the His body is bound in white silk shrouds, he was taller than most and so his feet protrude.

No one here knows the man we are cremating. But all of us are somehow okay with that. It seems now as much my duty as theirs. And I'm grateful it isn't Johno that I'm saying goodbye to today. Not because this is a difficult moment. Not because see the body washed in the river, stiff with rigor is to confront the body for the first time outside of that sterile mortuary. Not because to see them secretly add oil to the cloth takes away any dignity of the moment, because it doesn't. But because burning Johno today would mean failing today. I hadn't and still don't expect to find Johno alive, it seems life is too weighted towards death for that. It's that to say goodbye to my old friend today would mean telling his mother, would mean telling his wife, would mean no more reason for being out here save for some paperwork in a mortuary, some counter signing of local dignitary papers, the collection of his few possessions and accounting for any repatriation costs. Not so with Jay, we don't know him, his phone contained few clues, the British embassy notified but not interested.

Bruce and I paid again and again and again for more wood from all that gathered around us. Great flat-bottomed boats heaving with wood were pointed at by the hawkers – "This is your boat" "You bought all this wood" "All of this is yours" they shout at us as we wait for the body. The boats of wood hang around just off the ghat, they shout and wave their arms at the Doms who in turn shout and point down river. At the edge of the ghat a body, only half burnt, is pushed into the river, their seems to be some disagreement about the state of the body, from the pointing, the state of the deceased and their relatives I'm guessing they ran out of money for wood.

Jay need not fear dismemberment down river by dogs, Bruce and I will make sure of that. Bruce returns from the top of the steps with two cups of tea and we sit on the steps and watch an elderly American couple paying to take photographs of Jay's body lying out in the sun.

We are at XXX ghat. This is the ghat for drug dealers, thieves ne'er do wells. And so it attracts a more morbid audience. These aren't just the dead, these are the dead that didn't live well.

"Shiva power twenty-four hour" says one of the Doms as suddenly I see Jay's body ignite. The logs between him burst into magnificent flame. I don't know what it was inside Jay, or perhaps it was the toxic plastic gold cloth he's wearing, but suddenly the quality of the fire changes. He burns purple, green gold and blue. Then the burns a deep rich pink tinged with azure. Bruce and I smile and then both start tearing up. This isn't what men should do and it's a possible sign that you'll fall into the flames yourself so we both consciously check the crying and Bruce is the first to smile.

"He burns good" says Bruce, his voice wobbling a little as he holds fast on his emotions.

-

It wasn't much of a wake. But Bruce and I had stayed with the body until it had all turned to ash. We then started to walk towards the hostel before deciding to take a rickshaw to the opposite bank. "I need to get away from here" I said. And Bruce understood. We collected Elle from the hostel, she'd been crying, said she'd prayed for Jay and cleaned out his room. Sure enough there outside his room where a couple of bin bags and a backpack.

Across the river by the old castle was a blue wooden painted box, just tall enough for a man to sit in and deep enough for his bowl of yoghurt, a wash bowl and some water. There he did a good business whilst seated with yogic complexity between all his utensils. Although far back in the queue we didn't have to wait long to be served and the three of us chewed animatedly on the gooey caramel topping on top of the lassis he produced for us. Elle looked at Bruce and then at me.

"So where next for you then?" she asked me. Then continues: "We've had a chat, we think you should go home." She holds my hand. Bruce looks away. There's more: "You've been through a lot here, you've done all you can." Bruce nods and finds his

204

voice. "Time to get back to London mate" he adds making it clear this is more her idea perhaps than his. He reaches into his board shorts and hands back the unspent money.

"Keep it." I tell him and smile "Today was hard. You might need it." Elle looks at him and Bruce passes me something else, a piece of cardboard, I unfold it – inside it is a train ticket to Calcutta. "You don't want to end up like him mate, you're better than that, nice guy but…well, you know."

CHAPTER TWENTY-ONE - NJP

The journey is over.
On the train to Calcutta.
I've bought a new bag for a few things I bought back in Varanasi. Eventually I succumbed to an evening sat drinking tea looking at scarves and bought two for Isabel and Diana, now I'm looking at them again on the train I think I'd better give them to family instead.

-

The day after the roof, all the way back then. I'd gotten you a present, not a scarf. Not really a present I guess. I'd wanted to say sorry, I'd wanted to make it alright because it was ugly, and I wanted forgiveness. I'd stopped at a garage, one of the cheap ones with the chain you don't recognise, that does a good line in motorbike oil, pornography and flowers. I hadn't known what I was doing that day, and I'd vomited immediately on the forecourt after buying them, as if I needed punishing any more for my own bad decisions. And then I'd started walking back to were the party had been still raging just a few hours earlier.

Except now I couldn't find it.

I'd started walking back along the streets, sort of familiar at eye level but every time I looked up to try and piece together which roof it had been I was struck with vertigo and immediately hunched over in pain. Throwing my guts out, hands clutching at the plastic wrapped daffodils harder and harder every time until all that was left was broken stems and scrunched up plastic.

I'd gotten lost and sat down in a park and swapped the daffodils for some grasses that hid the needles and the knives by the fence. Then I'd ditched the creased plastic, then I was a man with vomit all over my jeans holding grasses lost in London. All at sea.

And all I'd wanted to do was say sorry then, as I'd said sorry a million times all those years later. As I'm trying now.

-

In the opinion of Bruce & Elle I was done with India. But as is so often the case in these stories India wasn't to be done with me. At least my journey out of Varanasi to get my flight would turn out to be another scramble.

Bruce and Elle in their kindness had bought me a ticket out of Varanasi for Calcutta. Except they hadn't: they'd bought me a ticket from Mughal Sarai to Calcutta via Gaya. I didn't question it at first, I could get a rickshaw to the station same as I could to Varanasi station, so what was the problem.

It started with the hostel owner insisting he organise the rickshaw ' so I didn't get ripped off' – and the truth was he probably did save me a lot.

I walked with him to the rickshaw driver but not before I'd given him 2000 rupees. We walked up the bank away from the hostel, through the backstreets heading west along the river until the roads opened up. There, waiting for me like an Italian teenager, revving a Piaggio was the first driver. I get in the back. The hostel owner gives the driver 1500 rupees and we set off...

...Five hundred metres up the road we pull over at a rank of rickshaws where my taxi driver screams at a man to take me to Mughal Sarai for 1000 rupees. For some reason the man accepts. Confused, I switch cabs and we are away.

-

"Bad place." This final rickshaw driver warns me. And as we switchback and drive through the entirety of Varanasi's smokey fog, shit and chaos and up over the bridge I realise we've always been wrong about the styx. In real-life the boatman rides a rickshaw and you don't get to cross his palm – a hawker does that for you. And we go up, up over the river on an impossible span-bridge.

It is then that I'm told Varanasi is 30minutes in a bicycle taxi. Mughal Sarai is 2 hours in a rickshaw. But that we should make the train just in time...

And I settle back in the seat with my little backpack as a cushion.

Slowly, crossing by crossing the lights grow fewer and fewer until only the light of cars and roadside stalls illuminates the one long road to Mughal Sarai.

And then it grows darker still. There's something happening in the dark all around me but I cannot see or understand what it is.

"Bad place" the driver reminds me.

Sure enough we are flagged down a kilometre down the road.

Two men in a four by four are taking money for people to drive unhindered down the road, in return you get a white floral garland to hang – so people know not to throw rocks at your rickshaw.

"Bad place, I shouldn't be here, I'm a Varanasi driver, there people know me, here is Mughal Sarai, no one knows me, other drivers afraid I take their business. Not a good station, many pickpockets, many druggings." He starts.

I hand him some replacement rupees for those he's just lost getting us past the checkpoint.

"If anyone offers you food, don't eat it, water, don't drink it, coca cola, say no thank you – all drugged, they watch, you go to sleep and then you wake up with nothing or you don't wake up, this is Mughal Sarai."

The cab fills with dust as we hit a pothole the size of the rickshaw, the driver pulls his scarf over his face like a cowboy, I pull my jumper over my nose and mouth. It seems like its ashes we are driving through, can't figure it out. The dust starts to deposit itself inside the cab. Only the white flowers dangling from the rear view mirror escape the dust.

There's a commotion as a group of motorbikes drive away from a building in the gloom to our right, I've never heard gunshots outside of a shooting range but think the bangs and flashes aren't fireworks. Or maybe they are and I am still just a scared white kid in a foreign land.

The bikers pull alongside the rickshaw. They all wear neckerchiefs over their faces and designer ripped jeans, faux-plaid shirts. They smile. I can't see a gun. The driver touches the garland.

"Okay! Okay!" He shouts at them with a tired restless anger. He slows a little and the bikers laugh and pull back off the road and into the dirt and beyond.

"This road is bad, never coming back" he says.

I have nothing to say but "Thank you, it's a long way".

"Not long – dangerous" he says through his spittly teeth

as he wipes away the grit from his mouth.

This shouldn't be a journey, it should be a taxi ride to the station.

-

A few kilometres on and there in front of us is a giddying and over lit scene – done up like Las Vegas: Mughal Sarai station approach. Hotels, dosa stalls, amusement rides, cars, bikes, trucks all covered in LED lights.

Its cold but the driver is sweating. "I shouldn't be here." He reminds me. He pulls in to the station and into the car park. Shouting and waving at other rickshaw drivers he finally stops out the back. "I can't get you any closer – I shouldn't be here." I tip him the missing 1500 rupees and grab my rucksack and run for the train.

-

Delayed.

19hours late.

I walk back to the taxi rank and find my driver eating a pouri, he's about to go and he smiles at me. "You recognise me?" he says off-putting but I think I understand what he's saying. "Welcome back." We are both a little confused I think.

"No train" I say.

"Varanasi?" he suggests and points back at the darkness at the edge of town.

I point across and down the road at one of the bauble-lit hotels.

"Okay, bad place but I take you"

-

The first hotel had rejected me – for Indian Businessmen only. I'd found another a few hundred metres down from it. Spent a warm night in someone else's sheets and gone back to the station the next morning. There'd been another four hour delay meaning I'd almost got on tomorrow's train. I'd lost a day and a couple of thousand rupees for the hotel and further tip to the driver, but other than that I was good, ready to go.

The train started after lunchtime and I'd eaten at the station – noodles and ketchup – classic Indian railway fare. By the evening I'd gotten through three teas and some samosas too. It was cold, maybe it was the fog, the wind coming through the slats in the SL class carriage or that fact that unlike everyone around me I had no blanket, no sleeping bag and no warm coat. I pulled my arms inside the jumper and used Slocum's still unread tome as a pillow.

The morning began as normal with men and women rushing back and forth to the toilets and sinks, water everywhere. And the train just keeps going, people jumping on and off and on again. There's a guy selling toothbrushes, which I have, and phone chargers, which I don't have. I go to get out my stolen smartphone and show him the bottom of it, but he reaches past it into my bag and takes out Jay's phone. He's going to do me a deal, 2 for 1 full price he says.

Around me fellow passengers smile, I'm probably paying way over the odds but I accept, then they make way on the plugboard where there's already a half dozen adapters plugged in to one socket. Why the hell not join them I think and so in goes both plugs and both phones. Phones are kind of sacred on trains, they leave them plugged in and walk away as if there's some unwritten deal that you just don't touch another man's flip phone.

I sit back down and stomach growls, tea would do if there's a chai wallah, should be one soon. And then my phone starts beeping, except its not mine, its Jay's and there's some pictures on it, and they are from Johno, and this is when India isn't done with me. It's not the travelling to the station, the overnighting, those bits, that's not what's keeping me here.

Deep down I have unfinished work to be done. I'm here on someone else's money. I cremated Jay, I haven't cremated Johno yet. Because Johno isn't dead yet...

The man hands me my phone and sees the preview of the message on the front of the screen.

"This place, very beautiful, you have been there?" He is inquiring about a picture I haven't even seen yet, but before I can look the phone goes between him, his friend, then two kids on the top bunks and then a businessman on the middle bunk above me.

"This place is Sick King". I look at him

"Sick king" he says again, but this isn't what he is trying to say and it's up to one of the others to join in

"Sikkim Sikkim, oh yes very beautiful place, I have never been there." I take the phone and look, it kind of looks like Scotland perhaps, a big bush with red fruit and a waterfall. It looks cold. It doesn't look like India.

"Sikkim?" I ask back.

"yes yes yes." I look through the other pictures – mountains, berries, trees. It could be the Alps.

"Sikkim?" I ask pointing at the picture.

"This one Darjeeling maybe?" says one man.

"No, that is Meghalaya" says another.

There's one way to find out. I call the number.

-

"Hello?"

"Johno?"

"Yes?"

"Jay, Jay is dead, he passed on."

"Who's this?"

"Johno?"

"Yeah? Who's this?"

"Johno – do you hear me, your friend, is dead, Jay, he died" and I start blubbing, "he's fucking dead man, and you, you ran." I don't know what I was accusing him of really, neither did he.

"Jay's what? Dead?" he said. And I'm starting to remember his voice, that plumminess of wealth in there.

"Jay's dead Johno."

"Who is this? Really? How do you know? How do you have his phone?" he asks.

"We cremated him three days ago. I'm sorry." I say.

"How? Are you from the hostel?"

"It's Matthew Johno, Matthew from school?" I stress my name.

"What?"

"I've been looking for you, I've come to take you home."

"Where are you? What happened to Jay?"

"Jay died, he was okay, I was there."

"I don't believe you. Matthew? The geeky kid from karate class?"

"I was your friend Johno."

"Why are you in India?"

"I'm looking for you Johno, your family wants me back, you back." I listen to myself make the mistake and correct it.

There's a pause on the line.

"I know where you are Johno."

"No you don't"

"I'm in a room with experts in geography, they know every tree this side of Tibet, we're coming to Sikkim" I say, looking around and the rag-tag helpers and detective that I'd found in this carriage.

"Sounds like you're in a train to me!" And he laughs hysterically.

"Come home." I plead.

"You're the guy that peed in karate class?"

"No. That was"

"It was, it was you..." He's laughing still.

And suddenly I hate the guy.

"I've come to take you back Johno, you've got responsibilities back home. I've been asked to bring you back"

He laughs again and hangs up. The Indians look at me. They know it went badly whatever I was doing.

The phone rings again, the Indians quieten.

"Hello?" I already know its him.

"Matthew?"

"Yeah?"

"Please don't come looking"

"Why?"

He pauses "I don't want to be found" and the way he said this spooked me, I shivered. I went to speak.

He hangs up.

-

I sit amongst the Indian men, they talk animatedly. I've just tried to explain the last few months to them, I'm not sure how much of it they really understood or believed. I'm waiting for their judgement.

With the low light pushing up through the windows of the sleeper carriage they are cast in a classical chiaroscuro, more made of their darkness and equally more of their light for they do exude a light. Amongst them, like jumping beans is a magnetic energy, a fusion of fissile excitement at helping a stranger. And this is something I will never tire of, the generosity of strangers on a train.

They turn back to me, all of them at once, they have reached a decision. One of them takes his spectacles from his locked briefcase and makes everyone wait as he puts them on. From his tip left pocket he takes out what must be a timetable but in script, numerals and English.

"We have decided that for you the very best idea is to change at Gaya and then head North to NJP."

"NJP?" I ask.

"EnJayPeeeee" He echoes.

"The end of the line" another man adds.

"The end of the line?" I ask, sounds ominous.

"NJP is the end of the line to the north, from there you will need a jeep."

"Oh?"

"Yes"

-

They wave me off at Gaya.

-

The train heads north now, there's nowhere else left. We are headed towards the very end of the earth, the Himalayas.

Without a sleeper ticket I'd slipped on to what would be a fourteen-hour train to NJP, gateway to the north.

I occupied myself with reading Slocum, with trying to send the pictures from Jay's phone to Diana & Isabel, and watching the world change again.

I tried to call him back every hour. Again the carriage grew anxious for me, wanted to know where I was going, had I lost a girlfriend, why was I travelling alone, am I a bachelor, am I a business man, how long have I been in India, do I like it very much, have I seen Harry Potter (I don't know if they meant in person).

And if the outside of the carriage remained largely misted plains, agricultural and indistinguishable; inside the carriage was a different matter. Because I knew nothing, because I'm ignorant and because I'd passed by thousands of Indians I had in some way put them in a box marked – looks Indian.

Here, in the last hours into NJP the carriage changed a lot. Nervous businessmen (always a feature of any carriage) seemed to evacuate en-masse and the faces changed. At first simply more chiselled as if perhaps hungrier or healthier than the middle classes who frequent the SL class carriages of middle India.

But these more sculpted faces were in fact the north Indians, the hills people. Faces more Asian than Indian, could be mistook for Nepalese, their voices, accents and dialects also changed. Many who got on would ask me in languages other than Hindi or English who I was and were I was going, and it was only again the goodness of my fellow travellers that provided translation. And so I explained, I was headed to the North to look for an old friend who had lost his way. And in telling the story through the various translators the story started to tell itself.

Those in the carriage that evening took it upon themselves to translate, add and better the truth and turn it on its head. Johno had killed Jay in the backstreets of Varanasi, his wife and son had been eaten by a tiger escaped in London Zoo and only Johno had survived – stricken with grief he'd come to India in search of tigers to kill so that he might take his revenge. I was a bounty hunter come to bring back a holy man from the mountains. I was a world-weary adventurer looking to climb Everest.

Once the story is out you cannot put it back. And so as they continued laughing and talking at, about and through me I prepared myself for a little sleep.

-

I had been asleep for a few hours when I woke. Frozen in the night. The shutters rattling, cockroaches under my bunk rushing into the mattress to get out of the cold air. There opposite me was a new face, one I had never seen before. I looked at him and then I asked. "Sikkim?" He stared at me and smiled, two black teeth, two gold teeth up top and one white down below. He nodded and said "Sikkim!". He then turned to the window and pointed. "New City." He added.

I looked out of the window. For as far as I could see in the darkness the world was on the move, all dirt and yellow. There were hundreds and hundreds of JCBs working the streets of a new city. Milling about the JCBs like fishing swimming alongside sharks were workers in tin hats. The whole scene was illuminated by thousands upon thousands of fluorescent tube lights strung on wooden poles in all directions.

I rushed to the other side of the carriage to get a better look. It was like some secret truth of the world, the true creation myth: that in the night men go and swarm in the dirt around giant mechanised diggers, illuminated by monstrous Dan Flavin style wooden structures aglow with neon, mercury and helium. And in the morning a new city would be born there, with new people, and new streets, new lives, new loves and ideas, dreams. All made at night, and only visible from the windows of this diesel engine.

-

It's ten in the morning when we make landfall.

NJP station. Definitely the end of the line. People had tried to explain it to me on the train – it's a place where you can get a jeep into the mountains, start of the Himalayas and so on. Not

217

all of what people say is true. It sounded more organised from the second hand accounts.

From outside it looked like a plane hanger, just a roof and a massive hall for people to sleep in whilst they wait for trains.

Outside it was wooden shacks and then a few hundred jeeps.

I have no idea what I'm doing. I carry my backpack up and down the lines a few times.

I shout "Sikkim?" again "Sikkim?"

A young boy in baseball cap, baseball vest, big Nikes and a bob kind of haircut grins at me from the top of a roof rack.

"Sikkim not possible today, you need to go to Darjeeling today, Darjeeling is best." He smiles, lights a match with his fingertips and starts on a cigarette. "One seat left, in the front, one thousand rupees."

Looking at the people getting in the jeep none of them give anything away if I'm paying too much. Then I look at the luggage and who's in the care and its clear why it's not too much, or too little. In this jeep built to carry eight people it seems like there are a dozen of us getting in.

"You sure? Darjeeling? Not Sikkim? I need to get to Sikkim?"

"Today not possible my friend, last seat, we leave now."

Sure.

-

The roads didn't wait until the hills to give out. Rough from the start. I was up front and all squeezed up in front by a large teenage girl who looked like she was about to explode with vomit. Incessantly cheerful Indian pop music purged any possible ill feelings in the jeep.

Behind me a young boy busied himself being sick out the window, his dad cheering him on. Next to them an older couple who picked their teeth in the rear view mirror. In the back two teenage boys, a man in a boiler suit carrying most of a motorcycle engine wrapped in clingfilm and then a businessman with a locking briefcase – always a business man.

-

On the way up through the hills I have time to think. I'm coming for you Johno, It may take me a while but I'll get there. You can't rush anything in India, he knows I'm coming. The fourteen-hour train ride, the four-hour jeep ride: there's nothing I can do about that.

But what will I do when I see him. What will I do when he doesn't want to come down. Or maybe he will, maybe he will see his old friend and rethink how he's spent the last year, instead of running away he'll be drawn back, go back to normal life. Walk up that driveway in the home counties and announce his return. I am Steppenwolf, back, to sit on the sofa and watch TV shows about cookery. Is that the life he wants? I doubt it, is that the life I want – no.

Do I want that life for him? I don't think of it that way. I think about doing the right thing for a family who don't understand how their nucleus exploded.

-

We stop at the side of the road.

I'm scared, is something wrong with the jeep. I don't speak up much, no one does on this ride, and it's not like a train. There's a more formal etiquette it seems. So why have we stopped. The young bobbed smoker guy gets out of the jeep and seems to fall off the edge of the world. I get out my side if only to let out the girl who is now stuck in the gear knob, I leave her to it.

I look at the jeep. 'Jones' is written on the front of it. Dangling from the rear view is a Buddha. Jones is a Buddhist I'm guessing. But where's he gone.

At the precipitous edge of the road is a small stone path
set into the hillside. All around us is greenery, it is quite
different to anything I have seen so far. I try to take it all in.
Put Darjeeling together with tea and it clicks, this greenery is
a cascade of tea bushes. Jones is waving from the bottom of
the steps. On the next level down, tucked into the hairpin is
a wooden house, a smoking chimney, dogs. It's the welsh hills,
this is border country, this is the dales. I feel at home here. The
Indians do to. As we all walk down the steps I take their faces
in one more time, they are all mixed, some Indian Indian and
some north Indian , but all Indian.

Inside the hut is warm, a mixture of sun and the stove that
burns in the corner.

The food is strange, I have no idea what it is.

I wonder how Johno survived with all these decisions, what
did he do when he got here, did he try everything, did he
reject things, taste things, does he have someone to share these
experiences with. Is there love in his life. Part of me hopes so.
A lot of me wishes that there was one other person, anyone
here who knew me from before I got on that plane in London
who could share this moment with me now. I want one other
person to look on at me as I sit down in this wooden hut at
the side of the hills, looking out over the tea and struggle once
again to understand where I am and where I am going.

There's talking, pointing, a lot of finger counting. I just order
a tea. But then the food arrives and I wish I'd ordered. I go to
use the bathroom but really to weep outside, I am homesick, I
miss the world that knows me, not for the people but because
I am starting to become unsure who I am, unsure what choices
I am making, what is real and what isn't real is becoming so
confusing.

As I rest my head in my hands, sit on the stone step and cry
a young girl looks up – she looks completely different to the
Indians of the plains, she's from the mountains, you can see

it in her eyes, her cheekbones, the way her hair falls across
her face. She can't be much older than six or seven, she rolls
pastry out on a red plastic cutting board as a dog rolls over in
the sunlight. The father from the jeep uses the hand basin by
a bathroom built underneath the house and he looks up at me.
"Toilet" and he smiles. They never stop trying to make me feel
at home here.

He goes back into the café. The girl carries the pastry inside.

Jones slurps at little pastries and a plate of egg rolls and a
cup of tea. Then the rest of the jeep sit down and eat eggs and
pastries too. "Momos" says the dad and holds one up – a neat
little pastry, kind of like a translucent miniature Cornish pasty.

Smile and finish the cup of tea. I go to pay at the glass and
wood counter, under the glass top are chocolate bars. I haven't
really eaten since the day before, the dishes are being cleared
away and the driver drops a few notes on the table. I buy some
big bars of what looks like Cadburys. Disappointed – I tell
myself I should always eat what everyone else is eating.

The rest of the journey is alarming.

A chip flies up in the windscreen and over the course of the
final ascent into Darjeeling the entire window cracks. We stop
frequently to let large Tata trucks pass, we're in a Tata, the
other jeeps are largely Tatas. The road is a queue of Tatas. I tell
myself to look into that later – who is Tata.

Kurseong is the first town we pass through. The streets is
awash with tourists, mostly older men, with large camcorders,
we pull over. Jones puts sticky tape on the windscreen. I watch
these elderly men filming in the street. There's a whistling
sound and the tourists thrash around on the iron rails in the
street in their easy trainers and beige slacks. Safari waistcoats,
baseball caps from Florida. Toot Toot – blasts the whistle.

The sight of a train rolling through this hill town is
extraordinary. I don't know what to make of it. Not being into
trains I can't get too excited but there's something bizarrely

heroic about whoever first manage to get the train up here. Even passing all the Tata's earlier they still don't have the bulk or finery of these old engines.

The train is paraded out into the street, people film, take photos, and pose. Tour parties follow one another into the old buildings. And they look exactly like the provincial Victorian stations of the suburbs of London. Straight out of Brief Encounter, except the romance here is all about the throb of steam and iron, no young love to be seen in Kurseong.

Jones is happy with the repairs. The family in the back are asleep. The businessman leaps out and shouts something then smiles and climbs up into Kurseong town. The girl stuck in the middle of the driver and me is now green-faced. Jones teetering on the edge of laughter as he has been this entire ride.

We get back in and push on.

I'm coming for you Johno, I'm close, I know it.

If you're going to hide up above the world this is where you'd do it. This place that takes forever and a day to get to.

-

Tea country maybe, but the Darjeeling they don't tell you about is one long traffic jam all the way through town in both directions. The diesel from the Tatas makes for impossible breathing and the sun bakes the terraces in the afternoon. Soot from the diesel and the steam train is hard fixed into the buildings and from street level the great Darjeeling of myth and fable, of colonial majesty and health is largely dead.

We are dumped outside a garage along with hundreds of others. I'm guessing this place is as popular with Indian tourists as it is westerners and for the first time in India both the plains Indians and the westerns stick out – for all around us are the hills people. There are stickers, signs, banners and graffiti hanging around the garage area – "Vote for Ghorkaland". That's really where I am. I'm not in Darjeeling at all, at least not the pretty little hill town the British thought they'd created all those years ago.

The buildings fall in a cascade from the top of the hill down into the tea plantations. Almost uniformly the colour of diesel fumes. Springing from the roofs and running down the alley is a mass of wiring and antennae also coloured the same grey. This cabling takes on an organic form as it twists around the buildings as though feeding off whatever is inside them. Below me there's a large wooden structure that looks like a market.

I want to get to Sikkim, but it looks like I'm here for the night.

-

I walk up and down the streets trying to find somewhere to stay. I have a few hundred pounds in the account still but don't know when I'll need it. I don't need a smart room so take a place without running water or hot water. I clean myself with the bucket and crap in a hole on the floor. I guess that's alright.

I call Johno again but get no reply. If he's smart he'll start moving. If I were him I'd hide back in the UK. No one would come looking for him back there.

-

Hiking up through the grimy streets it's already dark. The cars have slowed down to a trickle. Small wooden huts raised above the ground seat men and women preparing meat, vegetables, cigarettes, butcher, grocer, tobacconist. Further up there's a meshing of old Darjeeling, new Darjeeling, and tourist Darjeeling. There are coffee shops with people frothing milk being drunk by young Ghorkas, there are Pure Veg restaurants full of Indians from the valley below, and there's a cinema, there's a Domino pizzeria.

Too late for the view at the viewpoint on the highest terrace in Darjeeling. It is a large pedestrianised plateau.

A rock and roll band are playing in one corner for World Music Day. They are as punk as any London band. The female singer shouts out from underneath long black hair, her non-Indian Indianess stands out. A camouflage jacket whips around her as she struts up and down, the young Darjeeling Ghorkas surround the band and are entranced. The others in her band dressed all in black, tough looking, hair spiky. I think again – they are more punk than a London band.

Again I'm struck by homesickness. All around me in this square area are the faux or real English buildings. The truth is its impossible to tell what is real – a bookshop straight out of a Surrey town sells maps and photo books of Himalayan animals.

I'm hungry and follow the trail of hungry looking locals up the small road that heads up the hill from the square. There are more wooden shacks here, one after another after another. They all seem to sell the same three things. Egg Roll, Momos, Meat Roll. And all of them do tea.

It was cold that night, so I got hot tea and a warming fried egg roll. Behind me there was a stable with a sign advertising horse rides. The horses brayed behind me as I ate. They seemed to be telling me something. They seemed to be telling me to stop. To enjoy this moment, to drink my tea and to go home. I turned as one of the horses banged its head against the bars on the stable windows, steam erupting from its nostrils, it scraped its feet on the floor. It stared at me, I knew it was warning me, I can't tell what it is saying exactly. Or perhaps it just needs help.

I'm still hungry, I order the momos. A couple minutes later the woman dishes up the deep spicy dumplings. Warming, making everything okay.

As I pay and leave there's a commotion at the stables. The horse has gone crazy. Kicking at the floor and banging his head against the bars – the horse has cuts down it face, a man rushes inside to calm the horse. The man turns and stares at me as I hurry up my walk.

It's still early. So much I can't see here but you sense that between tea plantations and the tourists' square there's a whole world that you can't understand. Different, colder for a start, than the rest of India and with its own customs. Female porters clamber up steep flights of steps between the buildings whilst male Indians sport bow ties and waistcoats at hotel entrances. And there's more than one club that wouldn't allow me even if I had some decent clothes on me.

At the side of the street there's a place selling warm jumpers for 150 rupees and I buy one as well as some gloves and a hat. I couldn't remember if my room had heating, or windows and they'd be good for that, and perhaps I hadn't slept my last night on a train so I was now prepared.

I get down to the mall with the cinema and dominos. Its not even 9pm and I don't feel tired. There isn't the square with warm air and late night tea drinking from what I'd seen. I needed a place to sit and think that wasn't that bed with a deep drop crapper.

There's a Jason Statham film on at the cinema. There's deep pan and thin crisp pizzas at Dominos but I'll give them both a miss. I don't know what I'm looking for.

-

The pub has one other patron, the barkeep and then me. There's a fire, which isn't roaring, but it's hot. Inside it is like a chalet, all wooden pine panelling, small windows, benches. There's a TV playing Scorsese's The Last Waltz – I recognise is from my days as a student, The Night They Drove Ole Dixie Down is the tune, and the barkeep is whistling along. His hair is slicked back, he wears a black leather jacket and rests a cigarette between his lips. I go to order from the bar and see a few guitars back there. He gestures at me to sit down. The one other drinker in there turned and looked at me – white guy, in his 50s. He turned away and said: "I picked up my bag and I went lookin' for a place to hide"

The bartender puts a plate of crisps on my table and stokes the fire into a growl of embers. He brings me a beer and points at the TV.

"Now Scorsese knows how to direct a concert" he says in perfect English. He smiles, continues "So where you from?" The man at the bar turns. "London" I say. The man at the bar says "New York, well Brooklyn via Manhattan".

"Pleased to meet you" I say.

"Johnny" says the barman "As in be good, or cash"

I sip the beer. "Good to meet you" I say to the both of them and get down to drinking.

Moments later a couple walk in. For a few brief seconds I think they are Fani & Archer, they sit at the bar, she leans over and kisses Johnny on both cheeks and they order whiskies. The new Yorker is telling them about the new TV he's bought for his apartment here. The Band has restarted the concert and is playing through the tracks again.

I think of Fani, and Archer, and where they are now. When she'll accept that her true love is gone, when he'll get caught and moved on. I think about Archer's brother, and what the two of them had done for each other, patience and sacrifice. Lying and accepting. What about Johno & I, would he treat me as a brother, would I lie for him, would he accept me, would I sacrifice for him. For a friend, more than for a sibling it is difficult to know how you will react in extreme situations.

I'd been on his trail for months now and I had to admit that I'd grown hungry and tired. Even this seemed like a failure, far from the exoticism of colourful Rajasthan or the postcard version of Darjeeling even, I had chosen a pub over a movie or a sit-down faux Italian meal. It wasn't that I couldn't engage with my surroundings anymore but I didn't know what part to play.

I wasn't much of a detective, I'd done better at the start, followed my nose for much of those early weeks and got heavily distracted by Archer. I'd all but given up in Varanasi. What was there to prove, what could I achieve by all this, by maybe bringing him back and putting their family back together, I wasn't sure, but I felt that it needed to be done still, that it wasn't all in vain.

"So how long are you staying?" Asks Johnny as he collects my glass and brings me another without me asking.

"I'm going to Sikkim, tomorrow." I tell him.

The American starts "You got your visa?"

The couple with their whiskies are smiling, they remind me of a couple in a film, Dr Zhivago perhaps, it's the fur on her jacket, its his moustache and recent shave.

"Visa? Course!" But Johnny knows more than I do and helps the American out. "He means your Sikkim visa, its different up there, different people, wasn't always India, you need a pass to cross the river."

The couple are kissing. Her phone rings. She puts the whisky down. "We're out, at a café, having noodles, sorry" She's not in a café, she isn't eating noodles, she's having a whisky and enjoying it, she's in her forties or maybe even early fifties and she's lying to someone because she and her husband or boyfriend like a drink.

"A pass? Are you sure?" This is an unexpected holdup.

"How are you getting there?" asks the American

"Jeep I guess?" The American shakes his head.

"Then you'll need the visa, and you need to get it stamped here" and he fingers the bar top. "...in Darjeeling, and counter signed..."

The couple have been listening and suddenly all three of them in chorus say "by an attorney".

"Hahaha" I laugh, almost hysterically. This is the only alcohol I've had since the whisky at Khajurahao. I'm drunk, I pipe down. Johnny smiles. The couple finish their whiskies.

"Hey, it's okay, means you don't have to get up early" says the American, "the attorney wont open until after his lunch." And the band are singing.

"The night they drove ole Dixie down,

And the bells where ringing, ..."

-

Bill was the American's name, he and I had gotten slowly drunk alone on our sides of the pub. And over the next few hours I watched as the place filled up with people who'd travelled uphill, downhill or from overseas to come and drink Johnny's beer, to watch his music TV. First a compendium of every live band on 90s Letterman, then Bruce Springsteen in the 90's crooning about his 'Tunnel of Love'.

Bill came and sat beside me to make space at the bar. The couple had also started to fall about in amorous oblivion and I think he was done with being swung at as the man told the woman how much he really, really loved her. So Bill introduces himself, and he really looked out of place here, somehow his face would suit better a film of the 70s, he should've been up there on Johnny's TV playing guitar. He looked like he must've been someone. No one drinks alone up here for no reason I figured and Bill would tell me the whole sorry tale.

He ordered us two more beers and some more crisps. Then

he crunched his teeth. Snorted as if preparing his lungs for what was to come out. He strokes his white hair back on his head and scratched at a stain on his shirt's wrist. Then he told me what he'd only have told someone else. But I guess I was there. Born in Brooklyn fifty years before that was something my friends would've aspired to.

He sort of skips to the recent present, the last twenty years and what comes out is definitely aided by alcohol and embroidered with distance and time. A good looking guy in his youth he'd successfully ridden the wave surrounding IT after college and sold computers door to door, fair to fair, business to business. He reckoned he'd sold a machine to every small business in Manhattan, made a lot of money, met a woman at the first Apple Macintosh expo, got her pregnant, moved into the lower east side with her, gotten her pregnant by accident, gone along with her desire to keep the kid, and then bought into a can't-go-wrong land investment scheme buying Libyan desert for condos. Lost everything he'd earned, lost the girlfriend, owing her child support, lost his home, moved back to his mother's in Brooklyn, got a job in the rail yard, got a job as a train driver, travelled the east coast as a driver, got the trans-am route, moved to California, got into yoga, retrained as a yoga teacher, made some money, bought a Lexus in the 90s, had a car accident and couldn't teach, sold the car, couldn't get his old job back on the railways, mother died, moved back to Brooklyn, couldn't find work, sold his mother's house, met his son for the last time, gave him what money he had left save for enough for a plane ticket to India and arrived out here some ten years ago.

Got a job in a bar in Mumbai, dug oil wells in Uttarakhand, evaded bandits in Madhya Pradesh, ran a inflatable tyre rental business at a beach in Goa, relearnt yoga, got into drugs, sold cocaine to Goan hippies, sold weed to gap year students, made some money, bought a laptop, started an internet café, bought a license to provide wifi services for a Japanese telecommunications company, sold the company, got chased out of Goa by some old dealer rivals who had done time when it should have been Bill and he'd headed north. And north, and north again. And now he'd retired in Darjeeling, away from it all, with enough of a view downhill to the rest of India to see if anyone was coming.

It's been a long night and we are both about to go.

"My son, he'd be about you age now" Says Bill.

And he opens his wallet. And there's a picture of him with his kid and a woman, very beautiful, standing with the twin towers behind them, and they look happy, and bill is very handsome, and he has a watch that shines out of the pictures, and he looks every bit the American dream, and I am also thinking of Isabel, of Johno and the picture of them with little Jonathan, and I know that I have failed them, and that Johno failed her, and that Bill failed his family, because for every man that does right by the ones that they love there are those that slip through the cracks that can only do wrong...

-

I help Bill up the hill, provide a crutch for him. Drag him up a narrow flight of steps and wait with him as he tries to find his key inside his leather flight jacket. He pats himself down and says "Did you know I fought in the war, did I tell you that?"

I shake my head. "You'll have to tell me about that tomorrow."

"No tonight!" he barks. He grips my collar. "I'll tell you tonight" and he leans back into the doorway and starts to piss himself.

"Goodnight Bill" good to meet you.

-

I'm hungover and late getting out of the hostel. Already

Darjeeling is a grey traffic jam with only the colourful knock-off climbing gear clothing, seemingly worn by everyone on the road that morning, interrupting the drabness of diesel pollution. I hike up the hills and regret all the drinking.

What was it that lured the British up here a century ago, and what was it that brought Bill, Johno & I up here now. A cold beer on a hot day, the breeze at the top of the hill, an escape, or was it more than that: a Mount Olympus for Europeans lording it up over the mortals below. Scarring a railroad into the sides of mountains to escape the world beyond.

Whatever the plan was at the turn of the 20th century it didn't work, because the mob is here. And although its the rich and the westerners that might still have the run of the precious clubs and spa hotels it is the people that rule Darjeeling now, and in particular the drivers of the jeeps that really run things, for without them no one would be here, and that rickety museum piece train set left by the Victorians would sit and rust as tea plantations turned to forest and the red pandas returned to chew all.

-

At the tourist office I'm provided with forms to get countersigned by the magistrate. I hand over my passport and wait as it is photocopied and I'm given the first pieces of paper I need for the inner-line permit for Sikkim. Then more hiking down the steep northern road to the magistrate's office where it is countersigned for the first time. Then I'm directed further out of town to a third office.

Sat within a tall evergreen wood is a collection of pre-fab buildings from the early 20th century. Some buildings seem to contain only rubble, or deep-drop latrines filled some several feet over the brim with faeces. Others have cars parked in what once must have been offices.

Finally I find a building that still is being used. Its mint, cream and white painted with ornate chalet style gutters and welcoming boards. It's a village hall from the shires transplanted to the footsteps of the Himalayas but it kind of makes sense. I think about Johno, what he'd have thought of all this, we shared some kind of a past together, he must've seen some of this, thought similar things.

There's a handmade map to the building on the entrance made of dark wood with rooms painted on, a cluedo board of administrative and filing offices, the inside of a hard drive manifest in mahogany and paint. I see the foreign inner-line desk marked up and make my way there.

Each floorboard creaks as I step into the doorway. There's no one here. Although I want to get to Sikkim as soon as I can I still give myself a minute to look around the place. There's no one in the office to my left, just filing cabinets shut with large padlocks, handwritten signs in English and script on the front of every cabinet, Building Applications, Road Permits and so on, cabinet after cabinet after cabinet. There is the same in the next room, and the room after that and the room after that.

I get back to the start and make my way to the desk I'm supposed to be at. Heading up the stairs, they squeal with each movement, my footsteps trudge away the dust like an astronauts boot print on the moon. How could anyone else be here.

At the top of the stairs there are pictures of "British administrative heroes" from the "golden days". The pictures are equally troubling, quaint and bizarre. Beards, chops and bowler hats, three-piece suits, watch chains and bow ties. A celebration of organisation. Heroic filing. Legendary data collection. Masters of handwritten spreadsheets and bookkeeping from another era another world. Ghosts of an empirical past still here, the cleanest part of this building are these figures. There's still no one here. I keep going.

There's a single person in this part of the building. A man in his 50s, Indian not Ghorka, his hands manicured as he dips them in on a finger pad and quickly shuffles through my paper work, paper clips, rubber stamps and staples another half dozen pages and then asks again for my passport. There are forms to sign, more pages to stamp after I've signed and then he hands me back a single piece of paper. He smiles at me, says nothing.

"Can I leave"

He brushes his hand towards the door.

-

Leaving the building I suddenly start sweating. I shake it off thinking that it's the booze. I leave the phantoms of British office workers behind and set off for Darjeeling when suddenly I'm struck by an incredible pain in my stomach.

I run to the latrine building and look at the giant pile of shit in front of me. I turn and drop my trousers and put my passport and papers into my mouth. It is only then that I see that the door is missing from the building. It's an empty doorway, four once-white tiled walls and two pits in the floor overflowing with drying shit. The buzz of bugs is the only sound here. I decide to just crap on top of the pile, same as everyone else. It's an explosive shit. A warning shot from my insides that I cant drink heavy and eat 'weird' anymore.

There's no water cup, no tap, no bucket, no paper. I'm in my one pair of trousers, my backpack is at the doorway and I don't trust myself to shuffle there. There's one solution. I take the inner-line permit paper from my mouth and wipe my ass with the carefully stamped, signed and counter-signed a4 sheet, flip it to finish and then drop it on the actually steaming soup of slurry that I'd shot out.

I pull my trousers up when I think its safe and I walk out of the doorway.

Straight back up the creaking stairs, straight into the office of the silent administrator. I point to the window.

"The wind blew away my permit" I say then make a begging sign with my hands. He understands, maybe it's the smell of shit around me, but he knows I need help. He shakes his head. But then brings out a copy he'd made for the file, photocopies it again and hands it over to me.

CHAPTER TWENTY-TWO - THE CLOUD PALACE

Sikkim,

A tranche of land half fought over for time memoriam. Dust, tea, forests and waterfalls all the way. I had picked a Buddhist Jeep to take me into Sikkim and it put me at ease with the possibility of falling off the edge of the world. For if Darjeeling seemed like a Valhalla for those done with India, Sikkim was a Cloud Palace one step beyond.

I hadn't heard of it before Varanasi. Certainly not mentioned before India. Now I knew why. The slice of land is accessible by only two roads from Darjeeling and one of them, the short one, is barred for foreigners. So we take the long route, the dusty route on the part made highway that they are hoping will link Sikkim to Darjeeling if not to India.

Women work the roadside, all Ghorka or Sikkimese. There faces wrapped against the dust in flower patterned handmade masks. Each equipped with fluorescent vests and gloves for a uniform. The women dig, direct traffic, wave in giant crane arms carrying pipes, and lug pneumatic equipment up the small paths that shortcut the hairpins bends.

There's the constant rush of water in the background, through more evergreens and lush floor vegetation a fierce and cold looking river flows. These are of course many rivers that congregate here and form the natural border of Sikkim and India. The Rangeet – a cold blooded killer of a river that starts in the Himalayas and forces its way across land separating this kingdom but also providing it with power for there, far below and glimpsed from the jeep as we kick up dust through another roadwork chicane is a massive hydro electric plant, austere concrete walls and terraces that hint that somewhere amongst all this greenery, water and rocks is a people that need a lot of power.

-

There are some formalities at the border, and I sign in to the tourist's visitor's book, fill out the forms and hand over my photocopy and passport from Darjeeling. The border guard takes my papers away and leaves me sat down. Another administrator's paradise. Its quiet here, and he's already gone a few minutes so I stand and look at the book in front of me. Above me a south African or German sounding name "Stollenwell" – I remember it because it sounded like bread. I flick back a page, more names, all nationalities. Wrights, Jones's, Silvers, Berthoud, De Gasconne, Lopez, Callas, Brightstone, Diego, Buscha, Barry, Ilich, Sipowitz, Phang, Yi, Caulder, Winrose and so on. They all leap off the page, all seem funny to me, like a school register of travellers who've made it this far only to have to sign in again.

Then I see his name, his signature a few pages and many hundreds of names back, but it stands out because I know him, because I'm looking for him, because we learned to write together and practice our joined-up writing together, developing cool signatures repeated on the back of pencil cases, text books and worksheets in case we'd ever get our own chequebook, because maybe as a twelve year old a girl might be attracted to someone with calligraphic nous. He'd practiced his more than others, making the most out of the J. He was Johno in his signature before he was Johno in real life, losing the – athan. The height of cool: his early adoption of a new name, a new life for himself as a pre-pubsecent. Johno – a big loopy J, staccato H and N and a O with a mark to the right of it, as if the signature was just the start.

I hear footsteps behind me before I think to look at the date, and I rustle the pages back as quietly as I can before the guard walks in.

There's no time to ask to look in the book as the jeep I'm riding in beeps me outside. The Indians and Sikkimese I'm riding with have been patient enough. I take my place in the back again, realise I've lost a couple more inches room through my stop and we are off again.

I'm just behind you Johno. I don't know where you are in all of this but I'll find you.

-

I get a room for the night in what seems like a popular travellers place. And sure enough they remember Johno when I describe him but he'd signed in as Jonathan but it was him. I couldn't really explain to these people what I wanted or why I was late meeting my friend and instead they cooked me some thukpa noodle soup and give me a thermos of hot tea and leave me to sit around a stove.

It wasn't warm in Darjeeling, but its very cold here. There's a sign on the wall in English warning about bears seen on the road. This hostel is run by teenage Sikkimese boys, cool haircuts, surfwear hoodies, big Nike and Reebok trainers, confidence, but like everyone I met so far they care about strangers, I'm in their land and they don't want me to get eaten by a bear.

"Be careful on the road" says Gus, though that's another name I've misheard I guess. "bears spotted in the road between here and Yuksom, very popular route with hikers, are you a hiker" he says to me and lifts my pack up to show of his strength "ah lightweight hiker, much better, very good on the mountains, you move faster, like Spiderman, cha cha cha" he finishes and then mimes clambering up the hillside. "But if you do see a bear make a big noise, and then run towards it, that's your only chance."

I hadn't bet on bears in India, snakes, rats and roaches maybe, but not bears. But my room was in the basement of this restaurant cum inn, and it looked like a log cabin complete with wood burner stove straight out of one of those westerns where the cowboys hold up in the snowy mountains over winter and have to overcome nature AND the posse to survive. But I was the posse here, but I was now cold to my bones and stretched out over the stove.

There was no heating in the rooms so you had to rely on sunlight, stoves and thukpa for warmth, but that was alright by me, I liked all three.

I turn the phone on and tried calling Johno. Maybe he's staying in the hotel down the road and wants to meet me here for a glass of beer or a Sikkim whisky or Irish coffee, maybe he just wants a chat which is why he brought me here and that's fine by me.

Gus sees me stretched out over the stove and goes into the kitchen. Moments later he comes back with a hot water bottle. My smile must've been huge as he handed it over as he smiled back. "In England it is also cold isn't it?" I nod.

"Thank you" I say to him.

Then I lift the phone up and show him the pictures Johno sent. He studies them. If you show one Indian street to a man

in London it might look like any other Indian street, busy, full
of stalls, cattle, hawkers, tuk-tuks, bikes, but you show a person
who's familiar with India and they will know not only the state,
the city, the street, which corner, which time of day but also
the season. Show a Sikkimese a picture of a cardamom tree I
learnt and you'd know which valley. My journey was just made
days shorter by showing a tree to a teenager. No teenagers back
in London would know this, maybe shops, maybe which street
corner, maybe which chicken shop, I guess it's the same just less
romantic, but this bush was apparently a couple of valleys away,
under a mountain, the second highest in the world, and one I'd
never heard of. My level of ignorance continued to surprise me.

Gus takes my arm and leads me out onto the balcony. The
sun is mostly set now. All around us the hills tumble down into
a deep valley below and it is too steep and now too dark to see
the bottom. But up above all that and to the other side I just see
the outlines of mountaintops in the low pink last of the day.

The view crassly reminiscent of the default desktop picture
on the laptop of Rossie and Russell that I broke. But this one
is more perfect, more impossibly exquisite. Gus takes my
finger and points it up at one mountain now almost entirely
disappeared from view. "Catch Cheng Chung Ga" he says
slowly for me. And I repeat it back to him slowly too. "Cat Ten
Chun Ya".

"Almost" he says back to me.

"This is where it is from?" I ask. Gus nods. The mountain is
enveloped in darkness. The light sucked from it by night.

"You go to Yuksom valley, which is at the end of the
end of the road, then you take a smaller road, and go to the
end of that road, then that road turns into a path, and you walk
to the end of that path, and that path turns into a track, and
when you get there Mr Matthew, that's when your journey
to Kachenjunga will start." And he picks up my empty thukpa

bowl and walks away into the kitchen. I stare at the landscape. There is snow on the hills as there probably always is. This is the end of the world and my journey has only just started.

-

You'd think that the towns up here might all be the same but they aren't. In fact below the surface they are so wildly different that although simple looking from first arrival I soon discovered that in these hills and mountains each hamlet, village or town took on an identity all of its own.

So when I arrived in Yuksom by shared Jeep and looked around me I was disappointed in some way. If this was where he was, if this was the end of the line it wasn't the magnificent Emerald City or Lost City of Z rising up out of the jungle, nor was it a secret camp high in the hilltops from where Johno was conducting some kind of heinous experiment.

What I found was a single road that turned into a single gravel road. Two cafes. A couple of sweet shops on stilts and an off licence discreetly tucked behind a what looks at first like a garden shed. There's a couple of empty looking concrete hostels at the beginning of town that I walk straight past. Can't work out who would've built them or who would stay in them. I order momos and tea at one of the two cafes and take a seat outside. I hear the jangle of bells in the far away distance, there's also a river, and birds, and when the one jeep on the road parks up it is an entirely peaceful place.

It's late afternoon when I check in to a hostel, its someone's home, a family of Sikkimese, beautiful home, little English. They take me out to their back garden which turns into a giant vegetable patch of squash, some kind of tomato that grows on large trees and further beyond is a broken down fish farm where they point out the root vegetables and prickly courgette that are growing in the rich beds below.

I show the father of the house, Mr Lim, the photos on my phone. I ask him about Johno and he nods, I think he understands, he asks to take the phone away. Mrs Lim appears with a thermos flask of tea for me and tells me in broken English that. "This village is very cold at night, and very dark, many people have fallen down at night, we don't find them for many days." I nod and reassure her that I won't be out late.

I sit in bed drinking tea. Mr Lim still hasn't returned with the phone. All I have left is the Slocum book ,a notepad with a few notes from the trip so far, and a few things I'd managed to collect on my way here.

I settle into the Slocum book, and after reading a dozen pages of him preparing for the first leg it strikes me that I've read these same pages again and again over the course of this trip, never making it past these early passages full of expectation and heady enthusiasm for a journey still to be undertaken. So with a reader's sense of Déjà vu I absentmindedly start flicking through the photographs bound in the middle of the book, seemingly a later addition to add some wow-factor to the reissued paperback. I'm struck by one of the notes underneath the picture. In it Joshua stands proudly against the boat Spray.

The caption reads "In 1909 Joshua set sail for the West Indies again in his favoured boat Spray, he was never seen of again. Some believe he disappeared in the infamous Bermuda Triangle. Others thought he had gambling debts he could not pay and so chose to life out his years in the sun some place unknown."

I wondered if this is what had drawn Johno to the book, not the voyage, but the character, not the life at sea but the disappearance, not the majestic ocean waves but the anonymity of stepping out into a world where no one can find you.

Johno hadn't faked his own death, but he might as well have.

And I still didn't know why. Jay had hinted at something going on, something that he and Johno had known of. Some kind of secret. And with that I head back to the centre of town in search of a internet café and Mr Lim.

Men in jeeps pull over at the off licence and buy whisky before roaring off. But to where; from the one street it doesn't seem like this place could support many more people, where are the roads, where are the houses, where is the infrastructure. The rest of India made sense, it was plain to see: food in the markets, cooking in the streets, wires and engines and fires everywhere, open sewers, and the constant thrum of a 125 Honda. Up here it is another world, and one I don't understand yet.

-

In the back of one of the cafes is a guided climb operation. They are the only people in town who have a computer I can use and its dial up. I offer them rupees but they wont take them, just ask for a cup of tea from the café, which I oblige. There's a group of climbers from Darjeeling sat around packing their gear for a tour. The leader of the group is a redhead, pale white skin, but Indian, like an albino. But his fairness, hair and stubble reminds me so very much of Johno that I go to talk to him. And then stop, he can only think I am commenting on his albinoness. But unlike me he isn't scared of conversation.

"Are you here for the hiking" he asks in perfect English?

"Yes, sort of, yes." I reply. He looks me up and down and I realise that ever since leaving Archer's I've worn a strange mix of hostel hand me downs and market purchases. I must look somewhere between a slogan strewn teenager and a geologist with a penchant for synthetic fabrics.

"Well okay" he says, shakes his head and carries on packing.

I log in to my emails, I have 200 unread, they seem to be
mostly junk. There's some from Rossie and Russell asking if
I could freelance for them tomorrow but its dated 5 days ago.
There's one from my dad "Haven't heard from you for a while?"
is all it says. Then there's a dozen from Dian asking for updates,
each email getting more and more angry with me. The last
one finishes "Are you giving up on us just like Johno did?" I
reply saying that I'm in Sikkim, that I've heard Johno passed
through here but like the rest of my trip information is vague,
the timeline is uncertain. I leave out as many facts that might
no longer make sense to her. Or that would hurt later down the
line.

Looking out of the window at the hills around me I sense
that Johno could be just over a peak, just around a hairpin; he's
close, I believe that, but I cant say that to someone 800 miles
away and have them not be devastated if I route around in the
rhododendron bushes and come up with nothing.

-

The mountains turn the lights out early up here. And so it
is dark when I walk back to the hostel. I buy a couple of large
beers from the off license and the young woman serving me
smiles, and she mimes drinking from her thumb, tipping her
head back and wobbles her body, then she laughs.
   "You're right" I say "I am going to get drunk tonight." I pay her
a few hundred rupees, more money than food, and I take the
brown paper wrapped bottles away up the road.

-

My room is colder than ever, someone has put a hot water
bottle on my bed but it's too early to sleep. I take the bottles of

beer with me outside to drink in the moonlight. I open the first one and someone taps me on the shoulder, worried I shouldn't be drinking here I hide the beer under my jumper.

"No worries geezer." Says the figure and he steps into the light. "Mr Lim's got a rager on" says the man, ponytail, hat, glasses on string, West Ham football shirt on under several open jackets. "You alright?" he continues. "The name's Liam" I smile at him. Then I say "Matthew, pleased to meet you."
"Likewise" he says.

-

We are sat around a small fire in the vegetable patch. Hardly a rager, nor is it raging. But the fire does offer more warmth than the house. Liam drinks from a water bottle that I'm fairly certain is reinforced with Sikkimese scotch. Mr Lim sits showing Liam the photos on my phone.
"Perhaps you know this?" He shows the photos on my phone, then he flicks to the next "Or this" he continues. Liam looks at them, he zooms in on the pictures, seeing things that I hadn't seen, that no one had seen. Mr Lim smiles. Mr Lim knows what no one so far who'd seen those pictures knows. That within them, eating the berries, hovering, or bathing in the back of them are birds. And birds, more than bushes are particular about where they live. Mr Lim also knows that although he has local knowledge it is Liam who has the special knowledge.
"Yeah boss, I'm a twitcher, you know, normally in Ladakh this time of year but I'm hoping to meet a fella down this way to get a flight down south so I'm stuck here a bit longer than usual you know? Anyways, yeah I know this bird. It's in this valley, for sure. You know where this is?" He asks Mr Lim and takes out his own camera and shows him a photograph of another

bird. "That is where this is, it's up the trail I think."

Mr Lim studies the picture. He prods the fire and searches his memory for this particular path, the bush. He nods. "This is below the monastery, off the trail." Liam nods in agreement.

"Sounds about right to me." He nods and passes back the phone to me. "All this is up there" he points up the hill. These birds, sure you get them all over these hills but not like this, not in these groupings, and not out in the open like this. You see, these birds, they've been hunted all their life, haven't they Mr Lim?" Liam smiles at Mr Lim who says "I know, my people shouldn't eat these birds…" Liam cuts him off "But they do, so here they go a little higher, but then there's no threat up there, and around the monastery, although some of the young monks have catapults, the older monks tend to keep an eye on things like hunting, not very Buddhist is it?"

I look up at the sky, the peaks creating dark triangles against the stars. I point at random. "Up there?" I ask. Mr Lim and Liam nod in unison. "Look, I'll take you tomorrow to where that trail starts. Sound good?" I nod. We'll be leaving early mind, early worm catches the bird" and adds a wink. I smile. He reaches towards me, "let's have another look at that bird" and I open the photos. He stares at the birds in the foliage, heavily pixilation caused by the zooming. "I've seen this one, or one like it." And again he takes out his camera, shuffles through pictures and shows me. Sure enough there it is: a dull looking bird, sort of head like a kingfisher, drab colouring of grey and brown. "Babbler?" says Mr Lim. Liam nods. "Very rare" says Liam "a beautiful bird."

-

I sit down outside the hut. It's much like any mountain hut in England, simple, sleeping area raised above the floor, a log fire, deep drop toilet area outback, old climbing equipment left for those in need. A map on the wall from the 70s with a picture of Hilary and Tenzing Norgay shaking hands. There's a party of three girls, two from Germany and one from Scotland, then their guide a two sherpas. Johno and I sit in near silence opposite one another. The guide looks suspicious and the girls move away from us. The two sherpas look us up and down and shake their heads, I can see that they think we are two stupid westerners for being up here without any gear, shivering, and the truth is that when they found us I wasn't sure I could keep going. The girls are the first to go to bed and the guide sets up his sleep pad outside the women's tent. The horrid realisation you're the only danger to these people out here is horrid. I look at Johno, but I don't think he's thinking like that anymore. He's sniffing, as if keeping his tears inside, emotions worn on the outside of his fleece and eared hat.

-

The others have gone to bed, and so should we except neither of us know what will happen next. If I went to sleep he surely would have taken off, but where to? So we sit and stare at each other. No one says anything for a while. He looks pretty beat up, very skinny, cold, his cheekbones stick out the side of his face, his fingers are cracked, his teeth black. Eventually he asks.
"So how's my boy?" And starts crying.
"He's okay" I say. "He misses you, they both miss you. Diana – she also wants you back Johno."
He wipes his eyes. "I can't go home, there's some things you can just walk back into, like, you know places you can go, and feel okay again, but not anymore, there's no home for me,

nothing." And he sobs again.

"What happened Johno?" I ask him, "you can tell me."

He looks at me, eyes red, nose dripping, not a monster, a very sad man. He gulps. "What happened with Jay?" He shakes his head, he drinks from his flask. He lights a cigarette, his nose running down onto the filter, he wipes his nose on his hand.

"You came out here to take me back home. Well, I came out here to make sure Jay never could go back home." He stares at me. "You see, I'm not a good man Johno. I done bad things, stuff I can't get past. You have anything like that?" I nod. Then his expression changes, he stares at me. "No you don't" he says angrily. "What you pissed yourself once? Is that it, fucking idiot, you wouldn't understand, want to know why, because you haven't lived like I have, always too scared, well sometimes stuff gets you into trouble."

I stare him down, and he lowers his head and stares at the floor.

"I stopped off in India to find Jay, to make sure he could never tell nobody what he knew, but he ran, and it took a while, but I found him, because Jay was a piece of shit, a piece of shit junkie that no one should or would believe anyway I needn't have worried, and when I caught up with him I knew what he didn't. That he was on his way out." Johno smiles, a big grin, he smirks. "He was on his way out, and high, and no one in the world cared for him anymore, only person that cared that he was alive was the hostel owner so he'd keep making his 500 rupees a night. But that's it Matthew. No one cared, no one would listen to him, to be honest, in the last days I saw him I don't even think he could remember why he was out here either." He laughs to himself, smokes a little more.

"What did you do Johno?" I ask. Johno starts nodding to himself, nodding like he can't stop, like there's some kind of beat in his head that he can only here, and if he just keeps nodding along to it maybe he won't have to tell me. I reach over to his shoulder to get him to listen, he strikes me hard with his arm pushing my arm away.

He grips the side of my head and quietly spits out "I'm not going to tell you Matthew. So you can just go home now. That's what's best for you, just turn around and go home." One of the sherpas starts snoring, the yaks are snoozing, the trail team shuffle. I shake my head. "You got to go home, whatever's happened Johno your family need you." He blows smoke out through his nostrils, and takes a few deep breaths. He stands up, takes his pack, turns his torch on and starts walking.

I watch him go. I don't know what to do. A couple of hundred metres later he stops. The torch is flashing. He is talking to it. It goes out. He keeps walking in darkness. Then I hear him curse to himself and stop. I hear the pack go down. I move a little closer to the sherpas and the yaks and wait until I'm sure he's stopped. Without knowing I'm suddenly asleep…

-

At first light the sun warms the ground and as if some kind of god is breathing on me I'm stirred into life. I see him still at his makeshift campsite a few hundred metres away but I cant move yet. Crinkling sounds as I push away the foil blanket and sit up in the sleeping bag. I could rush him now, if I could only move.

The sherpas and tour group has gone. There's just us now. Frodo and Sam and Mount Doom.

The flat vast emptiness between me and him has a few drifts of snow, rocks, scrubby bushes struggling for life, a few yak pats and some straw left behind by the tour group. That's it, I'm so close. I lean forwards in the sleeping bag and test my toes. I pull my bag out from the bottom of the sleeping bag and take out some fresh socks but then think 'what's the point'. My trainers are damp with dew and frosty in the toes. Pulling them closer towards me I'm aware of my own smell, deathy, like nothing works anymore, like my pores are releasing the last of my life-force through them, dribbling out, garlic and blood and urine. I stuff the shoes under my jumper to try and warm them up.

He's stood before I am stood, he is packed before I am packed, but I'm faster than him. I know that. So I wait until the last minute and stuff my sleeping bag into my backpack and pull on my trainers.

He trips as he leaves his camp and I gain a few metres before we've even started the day. He turns and looks at me and hurriedly picks himself off the floor, he swears at me with his hands that look to be black with dirt. He picks up whatever it is he tripped on and throws it a few metres towards me. On his back is his pack – much larger than mine and better prepared.

I keep walking. I'm not fearful of him or of anything. Up here in this arena of nature I have no say over what happens and nor does he. Back down on earth perhaps we could've had it out in a pub car park, pushed each other around in an office bathroom or bumped cars outside a supermarket and had a pithy shouting match. But up here, amongst the crevasses, spires of rock, snowfields, freezing rapids and ice falls we have no say in our fates. It isn't that they are decided, but the opposite, there is no choice up here, no fate, it is the unpredictable world and we two men are not built for this. If I was a young Sikkimese I'd have some say up here, I could call to the mountains or to my mountain gods for strength, ask Buddha for guidance or ask that Vishnu give me protection in this tough time. An

Englishman up a mountain in pursuit of another Englishman
up a mountain, hungry and tired and at the end of a long road.

-

A patch of loose grey scree falls down and across the path,
there ahead is a turn in the path and then a wooden beam
stretched out across a river. Johno is the other side of the river
trying to dislodge the beam. It looks sturdy, but if it gives way
there is no way I can cross. My backpack clunks to the ground
as I throw it from my back, if I catch him I'll come back for it, if
I don't catch him I'll come back for it.

I run as fast as I can, falling and floundering as I lose my
footing, but on the steep slope down to the river I catch my
step and I'm gaining ground on Johno. Just as he moves away
the beam I take a leap of faith and step onto it.

On his face the horror as he realises in his effort to pull away
the bridge he's dragging me closer towards him. He gives up
and starts running into the snowfield ahead. A few quick steps
and I land off the beam bridge and onto wet land. He's ahead
of my by just fifty metres now, and there's no where for him
to go, he also drops his backpack on the ground and is now
sprinting for all he is worth into the snowfield, but he is slowed
down by the snow, and has already made a track for me to run
in. So I am faster than him, I am fitter than him, I am stronger
than him now. But I don't want to be, I don't want to be, I
don't want to... to catch him up because I don't know what
will happen up here, in this cloud palace, in this world without
rules.

He's fallen again as the snow gets deeper, behind him
Kachenjunga shows itself glorious, the peak in light but this

side of the mountain now shadowed already as the sun moves around it low in the heavens.

I am almost upon him now and I slow down and I catch my breath. He spins on the spot and stares at me.

He is crying, tears pour down his face, he holds his hand across his eyes like a face mask and his nose starts to drip mucus, this he wipes away and stares at me. And he knows before I do what I am come here to do. Because we both know that he isn't coming home.

I stand there unable to move, I don't know what to do, I can't carry him home, what am I hoping to do here. I step towards him, arms at my side.

"Johno, I've come to take you home mate." He turns and starts walking deeper into the snow.
"C'mon mate, let's go home" I say.

He keeps walking, deeper and deeper, until he's pushing it aside just to keep moving. He's still crying. So I start crying too. He turns again.

"Come on Matthew, you piece of shit, what are you going to do, what are you going to do? You don't know do you? You never had a plan, never thought you'd get this far? Did you? You didn't? You took my mother's money, and went on holiday, and now you're here, you got me, but you don't know what's next do you? You don't know how this ends? There isn't an ending, it just goes on and on, until we get up there." He points up to the mountain.

Whilst he's staring at it I feel an angst rise up inside me, and

251

I want to vomit. I rush towards him and tackle him to the ground. Force him over in the snow. We both are quick to stand. He rushes back at me and pushes me over in the snow, I look up at him and he shakes his head and starts walking back towards the bridge.

My foot has come out of one of my trainers, I dig around for it in the snow and see the red plastic shape. Putting it back on I start after him again.

"You have to go back Jonathan, it isn't too late, to, to, …to make things okay again." He keeps walking. And I know that he knows that it can't ever be okay.
"So where are you going then?" I shout after him. And he starts crying again and just keeps walking. And I have to run to start catching up again but the air seems thin and I'm losing my breath.
"Come on then, where are you going, if you aren't going up, and you aren't going down, tell me, I've come a long way to take you home, to your kid, to your wife, and they both love you, they both love you still."
He turns, his eyes already red from crying, he wipes the tears down into his beard.

"Do they love me?"

I nod to him, I have to gulp to keep from crying myself.

"I think they do" I say.

He starts walking again towards the bridge and straight past his pack. I stop and pick it up. "You need your bag mate." To which he just waved his hand in the air and keeps walking. Walking back towards the bridge. I run to keep up, I don't want to be left up here, cut off from the world because of a bridge. I get a bit of pace on and so he starts running too. His boots are better than my trainers over the rocks that lead between snowline, scree and the river where the bridge sits. He makes better time but he stops, turns and he points at me.

"Stop, stop following me." he says and starts onto the bridge. It creaks under his weight, as if perhaps his twisting it before had damaged it. I slow my pace.

The only sound is the water rushing under the bridge, the river banks are dressed with rocks made smooth from years of melt water, and I slip a little the closer I get. He's halfway across the bridge, when he stops, he purposefully puts all his weight on the centre of the wooden beam. There's a creaking sound as the ties that bind the beam to the other beams twist under his weight.

He is smiling at me, because I've stopped moving. Because he knows I'm scared of the bridge. He bounces on it now, cocky, it creaks a little more, the ropes seem to twist in on themselves a little more.

"You can't stop, can you?."

I shake my head. He adds, "You want to know what you're doing here don't you?"

Again, I shake my head. But perhaps I'm not very believable, or perhaps it's because I'm human. Now I'm here, having followed him across the continent, and him having followed Jay too, I feel that, as much as I want to know, he also wants to tell me, needs to.

Johno sits down on the bridge. The water rages just a few feet below him , frothy, white, pure, it's fast flowing, and ends in a waterfall that drops down onto the next plateau below. But he doesn't seem to care. He takes out his cigarettes and struggles with the lighter, then finds a box of matches and starts to smoke.

I step closer to the bridge. "Here is okay!" I shout at him. He shakes his head. He taps the wooden beam of the bridge and says back to me "HERE is okay!" I want to know, so I step on the bridge, it sways under my weight, meant for crossing one at a time. Johno doesn't seem to care.

Waving his legs above the torrent. His knackered jeans ripped all over, his boot laces dangle, hands all cut up under the fingerless gloves popular amongst the market traders in Darjeeling.

He wipes his face on his jacket. Looks at me.

"So what did you think?" he asks me. And gestures out at the river running away from us.
        "of what?" I ask.
"India?" he takes another drag on his cigarette. "Your first time?" he adds.

I smile. And start to tear up myself. "It's been a trip for sure." I look at him. He breathes deep, shakes his head at me, and grins with his plaquey teeth. "I couldn't think of anyone less suited to life out here, what were they thinking?"
        "No one else would come." I say.
He nods. He knows that's the truth.

"Jay and I were friends at university. He was the first person I met on the first evening at halls. Standing in front of me in the line in the canteen, dreadlocks down to his waist. Sun faded t-shirt and shorts, he didn't even have shoes on. He was there to study economics, talked a lot about smashing the system in those first months as we stayed up talking philosophy, talking politics, interested in everything, there was a small gang of us on the corridor, and whilst others went out to clubs we'd stay in drinking red wine and smoking weed." He gestures with his cigarette. "Jay was the hero of the group, he'd lived, already been to morocco to smoke opium in the Atlas, drank coffee with ex-spies on the Beirut waterfront, prayed at the wailing wall, and also he'd been to India three times by the time he was nineteen – turns out his mother was an ex hippie turned interiors manufacturer who got all her curtains done out there still, he'd come back after half term break with tales of visiting her factory out here – we'd all been inspired, the guy's tales spread and he became a bit of a legend amongst other corridors, then other floors – there was no one he didn't get on with. Then slowly our little group started to disband, to find sex, drugs and rock and roll. Jay got into clubbing, got a girlfriend and started putting on a regular club night, they played trance music, some of the worst dancing but the most fun at those nights. And he was happy."

He's finished the second cigarette and lights a third, he only has two more left in the pack. There is no one else out here, when he stops talking only the sound of the water, and it grows ever louder.

"In our second year Jay and I, although we'd started growing apart, decided to move into a house together and out of the halls. We both were earning a little money on the side and neither of us wanted for much anyway, for all our talk of realpolitik Jay's mum and Diana and my dad kept us in fags and drink if we needed. Anyway with Jay's club night and my selling a little weed to the first years we could get what seemed like a palace. And the first thing we did was throw a party there. The first party was great, he knew a lot of people and I knew how to keep the kids dancing. The party paid for itself as I dealt out ketamine and ecstasy, you know mild stuff. I won and lost the prettiest girl at that party, although I wasn't outgoing like Jay she came to like me, and by that time I was also on the fencing team and I think she was a bit of a kink because she'd make me dress up in the mask. She came and went, the house stayed full for the term, after parties, move nights, same old shit you know?"

I nodded. Although it was still the middle of the day it had grown colder us sitting here. And to be honest my work was largely done, I had found the guy. I just needed to get him off the mountain. I took out my phone. There was signal all over India, but there was no signal here. Still I punched in a text message to Diana and hit send. Nothing happened. Johno grabs at the phone and in swapping his hands over drops it into the water below. He spits a tobaccoey string of phlegm into the water after it.

"Then one Christmas I returned from home early, there'd been a mighty row on Christmas eve between my mum and dad, it had spilled over into Christmas day with mum being drunk in the church pew and us having to leave, then fighting into boxing day, which is when I left. I got back to the flat and although no one was in I got the sense that I wasn't alone. The next day a smell started to come from Jay's room. That's when I first found him like that, he'd started using after parties, to bring himself back down after all that fun. He smelt awful, I helped him clean himself up, and I promised to never tell anyone if he'd sort himself out. Term began and things largely went back to normal, I think things were going well for us both, we had just a year and a half left, broken the back of it. IN quiet moments Jay would take me aside and thank me for finding him, thank me for intervening, and he reassured me that he was clean. We got to the summer of the second year, Jay split up with his new girl, I was single and had been dropped by the fencing team for poor attendance, but courses were good, I think Jay didn't ever have to work, he was one of those guys, handwrites his essay in the morning on the bus you know? Anyway, we decided to have one last party in that house coz Jay wanted to on.

"We'd planned the perfect party. Everyone wanted in. One last hurrah before real adulthood. We had Jay's DJ friends come a rig a sound system in the living room – we bought cheap fairy lights and Jay dug up a smoke machine from somewhere, bought in a load of cheap booze, warned the neighbours, moved the furniture out. Same old, same old. And then people started to arrive. And there was a strange feeling I had, a feeling that things might go wrong, but I couldn't work out how. I knew it, in my gut that this was too much. First there were just a few of us, then more and more people started to arrive. It was filling up fast, Jay and I made sure no one went without drink. The music switched early from the Cure's "Love Cats" to house. Guys in worn out jeans and skate trainers, girls in skinny jeans and band t-shirts. Bodies on bodies on bodies moving in time as the music got louder and louder. The usual arrive early leave early brigade ate Pringles and humus and talked politics in the kitchen, they'd brought with them a girl from the first year, and American, she was talking about Delillo, Virilio, Baudrillard, the humus crunchers jaws opened stood and stared, she was articulate and also very beautiful. Not for her the top-shop repro of a nirvana tee or look-at-me bangles and beads of Jay's gang. Dressed all in black with glasses she carried herself in ways beyond her years. Suddenly we all had to grow up a little around this stranger as she talked about Tony Blair, the Iraqi war, the internet. Following her was almost impossible but we all took time away from the last days of Rome in the room next door to listen to this young woman tell us all where we went wrong.

"I tried to get some chat in but there was already a guy from PPE who started down a route linking Bush to Libya and the last great American novel so I went back to dancing.

"About midnight I saw the girl leaving again. One of the philosophy guys had sick down his front and she and this irritating guy we called Christian Gary was helping get the drunk guy out the front door. Jay and I had worked out there were about a hundred people at that point in the house – it took me a couple of minutes to get outside to talk to her before she left.

The philosophy sick bucket was just being refused his first cab. Christian Gary did the good thing and was offering to take him home. The girl was going to leave – I took my chance to introduce myself.

"He'll be alright – he always does this. I'm Johno by the way - this is my party" She looked at me then like she knew what I wanted. I handed her a beer and she took it.

"I'm Alice" she said, sipped the beer and then "You sure he'll be okay?" Christian Gary looked over at me and at her and tutted at the drunk in his arms. I remember putting my arm around her then, already drunk as if that's an excuse, but she moved away from me. I apologised and she seemed okay. We went back into the party." Johno pauses in his telling. His face started to quiver, more tears were coming. I thought I knew what was coming next. I didn't need to hear it to know.

He started again, "The following morning I woke next to her, she didn't move." He is crying again, he looks at me, as if I could help, as if I could make it better, take this testimony, receive his confession. "She didn't move" and he snorts and cries and again his nose starts to flood with snot. "I pulled the sheets back, and looked at her body, bruised from where I'd forced her. I hadn't know what to do, what to say, nothing would make it right. I thought for a long while that she was dead. I sat there that morning and cried. Jay hammering on my door to get up and help with the clear up. I couldn't move."

"About midday he forced his way into the room. In the night our front windows had been smashed in. Someone had called the police and the TV had been stolen. It had taken him a few moments to realise I was hiding something under the covers. I still remember that proud smile on his face before he snatched away the duvet to see Alice's body. He started screaming. Some life found its way back into her body and she suddenly sat upright, she vomited a thick black mess over herself and the bed. Then she stared at me and started screaming. I put my hand over her mouth. The black vomit forcing its way through my fingers. Jay had pulled me away from Alice. I had hit back at him hard and he'd fallen against the shelves. Alice passed out again and Jay stared at me, he wouldn't leave me alone with her in the room. Late in the afternoon she woke again. Jay and I were downstairs. She had washed herself and found her clothes. She was crying as she tried to tip toe passed us trying to put everything in bin bags before the landlord check. It all seemed so normal, but in her gone was the confidence, the bright clear eyes, the surety, I had taken that from her, forced myself on her, taken to her, because I...I wanted her to fancy me. As she got to the front door I went after her. I said to her "Please don't go to the police." And she cried and walked away. After that day only Jay and me knew what had happened, but we were never friends again after that, but the switch had gone off in him, and soon enough I found out he was back using."

"He had run out of money in the summer, that's when the first email had arrived. He needed money, and I had money. But though Jay was a burden he was also my only confidant of what had taken place that evening. So when I got a message from Alice a few months after the fact saying she'd moved back to the states but had the kid I knew of no one else to talk to but Jay. And so Jay became this rope around my neck, he knew the very worst truths about my life, and I paid him every month not to tell. Which was fine. In that final year I met Isabel. She thought my fragility was sweet and there was no way at that point that I wasn't broken, no way I could warn her about myself. She thought I was cute, at that point I'd already grown a beard to try and change who I was, so people wouldn't recognise me in the hallways. I wanted out, but Isabel had given me reason to live again. And I promised to myself that one day, before things got too serious that I would tell her. I think I saw you about that time, at a party maybe?"

I look Johno up and down, I think about Isabel, about Jonathan the baby he left behind, about Diana, time changes everything, but still, would they want him back. Was Johno a monster? What was I to do? He lights another cigarette. He keeps talking.

"Anyway, I promised that. I would tell her that I had a child somewhere I could never see. But I'm a coward so of course I never did. University ended and we moved in together. I got a good job and as I earned more and more money Jay asked for more and more. And I came to realise that Jay the junkie was better than Jay the sober thinking man. Jay the junkie didn't think to tell anyone, he never turned up to my wedding, nor any university gatherings, parties or nothing."

"But one day he showed up, hand out, he was sick, he couldn't have weighed more than five or six stone, his ankle scarred and weeping. I gave him what I could and told him to leave. He said he blamed me for the years he had already lost. Said he was going to tell all. He'd made himself homeless, had moved back in with his parents or something, I took him to the bank and took out some cash for him. I told him he needed to go away. A week later I'd arranged for him to go to India, paid for everything. Didn't hear from him again, until a postcard arrived from Delhi, addressed to me and Isabel from Jay , Jay who she'd never met, she started asking questions, but then another postcard arrived, until we were getting one everyday, rambling craziness. So, on my way back from work I decided to stop over in Delhi to find him, to ask him to stop, but he wasn't there…he'd given all his money to a man…."

"Archer?" I mumble, Johno nods.

I look at Johno. His sad face, nothing left in him. He has nothing more to say.

"What happened to Alice, and the kid?" I ask. Johno shrugs. "I send her money, not much, but a little." He breaks down completely, he is bent in half, and he starts heaving with tears. I wonder if she ever got to cry like he is now.

"Let's go home." I stand on the bridge, and offer him my hand. Johno keeps smoking, lights a second cigarette from the butt of the first. "I think I'm going to wait here a moment. I'll catch you up." So I put one tired out old trainer in front of the other and walk away from him. Who am I to judge, sure I can take the confession but I can't tell him what to do.

"Aren't you going to say something?" he asks. And I keep walking.

"Come on Johno, let's go, it's okay." I say and keep stepping across the bridge.

"You always were weak" he calls after me. "You always were one of the weaker ones Matthew." I don't turn back, I just keep going. I hear the bridge creak as he steps up, turning back he is moving quickly across it.

"You, you aren't saying anything, nothing? Nothing at all?" He taps me on the back of the shoulder as I get to the edge of the bridge and lower myself down the three rocky steps that lead up onto it. One, two, … I don't get to three. A sharp push in my back sends me falling onto the ground. I feel a massive pain in my hand and look at my right hand, the index finger bent all the way back on itself.

Johno steps down off bridge, stands over me, I shuffle back, pain also in my wrist as I scurry and stand up.

"Well come on then!" He pushes me like a Friday night pub drunk and he's crying like one too. But the pain in my hand is real. I am such a long way from home. I push him back and start again towards the trail. But if Diana's desire was that I bring him back Johno's was that I not let him. He pushes me again.

"Come on then..." he says.

"Come on what?" I reply, "What do you want me to do Johno?" He starts walking away from me towards the river, the rocks crack under his feet as if he's stepping on glass. "Don't be stupid!" I shout at him. I drop my bag and start towards him. He is starting to wade into the river. I run to keep up, I don't know how I'll get him out of the water. Already amongst the peaks of the Himalayas the day is drawing to a close.

"Johno, get out of there" I shout from the side of the stream. But he starts walking deeper and deeper. I throw off my jacket and run into the river. I quickly catch up to him and he turns. His eyes now two red sockets of pain.

"Coward" he says to me. And I take his arm and try to drag him to the shore. But instead he grabs me and starts to drag me towards the fast flowing deep part of the river. The bridge is just upstream from us, which means below is the waterfall, and I can't keep my footing.

I try again to pull him towards the bank but this time he snatches back his hands and pushes down on my head, holding my neck and hair to his stomach and pulling me down, down, underneath the cold iced water. I scratch at him to get free. I surface for a moment and catch my breath before he pulls me under again. Biting down on his hand I feel my teeth snip through skin and taste blood, he releases me for a moment and desperately my legs move me towards the shallows. The cold water anaesthetises my broken finger but also the rest of my body, I am so very cold. But he isn't done. He grabs me and pulls me under again, this time my face scrapes along the rocks on the bottom of the riverbed. We twist and turn, I feel I haven't much left to give. I move my hands around his throat, he kicks hard against me, his heavy boots hurt but not like my hands around his neck, he still won't let go of me, he holds on to me, clutches at me, clings to me underwater, still I force my hands against him, hoping that he will let go. I have nothing left to give, one of my trainers gets ripped off my foot, the water now is tumbling us downriver. Still Johno won't let go. I look at him, through the bubbles. He kicks again at me, but how can I know if I release him that he will release me. I feel like my head is about to explode. As if being in a nightmare when you might awake suddenly, gasping for air as if bursting through water's surface. He looks at me. And in that moment, he smiles. He smiles as I pull my hands away from his throat, and he smiles as his body gets taken by the current, he smiles as his head bleeds as it gets scraped over the rocks, dragged between two rocks and away. Gasping for breath I vomit as I surface, and I pull myself out of the river. With one foot shoeless I run down stream to catch him, but there is no point. He is gone. The river has taken his body, and I had never felt so alone.

-

I hadn't wanted to come down off the mountain. It had taken me a couple of days to move beyond the river. I spent that first evening in denial, sat shivering by the water's edge waiting for his body to lift him out of the shallows and into my arms. I cried for Johno, for Diana, Isabel, Jonathan, and then I cried for the girl Alice and her baby who would never know his father. For myself I sobbed a great deal, all that I had hoped for was gone. India had killed Jay, but I had killed Johno – he had wanted me to, hadn't he? He would've killed me – wouldn't he?

Whatever it is that keeps you putting one foot in front of the other, taking that next breath made me search for matches to light a fire. I found Johno's lighter by the bridge approach. That fire saved me the first night, without its heat I feel sure that the cold would've taken me.

-

I woke in the arms of a child. A young bald-headed boy looking down at me. Precious mana from a sunlit window filled my body with warmth. He put a small rock in my hand and closed my fingers around it, he giggled and ran out of the room. I looked at the rock, a small dried cardamom pod. Another young bald boy peers in from a doorway. He walks towards me and snaps open the cardamom and puts the seeds in my mouth. He waves his hand by his nose. He too giggles and walks out the door. I crunch the cardamom seeds -deeply minty, like the strongest of chewing gum, and I smell my own breath – truly the smell of death. In the mirrored window's reflection I see my face, scraped bloodily all across as though brushed with beetroot. Beyond, through the window the young bald monks run through a field of white prayer flags, clutching their books they make their way down to a building down the hillside where a bell sounds the start of lessons.

-

We eat noodles and drink tea in silence. The young monks occasionally stare at me but I get the feeling they've been told to treat this guest with respect. After we finish our lunch an older monk takes me aside and points down the hillside. There, hiking up a spindly trail is a man in a khaki uniform and a couple of men in white shirts, all three carry their jackets over their arms. All three look to be struggling with the climb.

Outside in the quad between dormitory and schoolhouse cum canteen the prayer flags continue to flutter. The older monk leads me away from this and to another doorway onto what looks like a store or toilet block. He pauses at the door and looks at me. He doesn't speak, maybe he doesn't speak English, or maybe it is simply his way. He looks at me and he must've decided I needed to see it, he must've known I was also ready to see it.

Inside on a trestle table is Johno's body, wrapped in a white sheet and covered in a red robe embroidered with gold thread. On the floor is my backpack, the monk lifts this up and passes it to me, but I don't take it. Instead I walk closer to the body. The men in uniform will be here in a moment to take me away. I want to make peace, I want to say goodbye to my old friend.

The monk moves the cloth away from Johno's face, his eyes are all puffed out, his cheeks swollen, his neck though shows no sign of the struggle, but his shirt has been ripped from him, his chest is cut deep to the ribs in places and his left ear hangs off at a funny angle.

I start to cry and the monk moves the sheet back over his face. He makes the prayer sign with his hands and I copy him. I do not know what will happen next. I join the monk in silent prayer around the body. I pray for Johno, and I pray for myself. In this most tragic of moments I still think of me. I never asked for any of this, this is not my life, he chose this for himself.

There is a knocking on the door and the three men let themselves in. The first, in his uniform is a policeman, he wears a moustache in a sling and a turban, a Sikh, the next is a Ghorka, around his neck is a lanyard, he is also police, the third is an Indian, he prays as he enters the room, he carries a small bag in his hand, a camera bag. The Ghorka speaks to the priest who then lifts the sheet from Johno's face. The Sikh lifts the sheet from Johno's legs to reveal a mess of fabric, swollen bruised blue skin and bone. The Indian starts lining up a shot.

"You are a very brave man" says the Sikh.

I am dumfounded.

"Has he spoken yet?" asks the Sikh to the Ghorka policeman who translates for the monk who smiles and then mimes with his hands the international slurping noodle gesture.

"You've eaten?" asks the Sikh.

"Yes."

"Was anyone else with you on the mountain?"

I shake my head.

"We've a lot of questions to ask, but the most important thing for me, right now is that you are okay in yourself." He strokes the sling around his moustache.

I nod. "I'm okay." I say.

"Poor poor man." Says the Sikh.

The Indian photographer switches on the lights to the room, suddenly the outhouse becomes an over lit morgue. The photographer fiddles with a flash gun and I'm marched into a line with the two policeman. The monk leaves the room – the only man with dignity in here.

"English?" asks the photographer.

"Yes." I reply.

"Picadilly circus?" he asks.

"Picadilly circus." I say.

PART THREE - BELOW

CHAPTER TWENTY-THREE - THE DARJEELING TIMES

I was in the Darjeeling Times on page seven – a trek gone wrong, two old school friends on a hike, we should've had a guide, we fell off a bridge, the same bridge where two yaks died earlier that year. Little else was said. On page three was a picture of Archer, he'd been caught, his business shut down, he'd broken out of jail and made a run for it to Pakistan. At the bottom of the article: Fani in cuffs, she'd never left him.

I was reading the paper in Darjeeling. I was putting off calling Diana. Although they'd been informed by the British Consulate already. I felt I had to call her, to tell her, to try and explain those last moments, but the truth would hurt her, and I couldn't work out what to say.

So I said nothing. I took a jeep down the hills back to NJP. From there to Calcutta.

-

I hadn't counted on hating Calcutta as much as I did. It wasn't that the people weren't kind to me, that the tuk-tuk drivers weren't gracious, or that the food wasn't warm and filling, but something in me had changed, and I couldn't be here anymore. I didn't want to see the monuments, or the museums, though on the first day I dragged myself around the sad Museum of India. I no longer felt the need to see where we'd once played polo whilst quashing rebellions, no part of me felt like a visit to the luxury malls where security guards keep the poor at thirty metres.

In fact, all I could bring myself to do was buy doughy egg rolls from the corner near my hotel and then decamp to the bar.

-

Not wanting to be anywhere anymore I found, for a few hours a certain peace in the comfortable garden bar off the hostel strip that makes up Sudder street. More egg rolls, eggs on toast, mild masala dosas with chips and jugs of German lager. What was I to do, where was I to go?

After lunch the garden started to fill up. On the table next to me two young blonde women from England entertained a Dutch investor and his son who was the same age as the girls. Through my foggy stupor I listened to the father flirt with the charity workers, bragging about how much he'd given towards their school for girls, offering them a night away from their school dorms in his hotel suite. Coming on to them hard, encouraging his son to do the same.

I moved tables, was asked to settle up my bills. I'd spend a hundred pounds in the few hours I'd spent sat here. It was growing dark. I could go back to my room - a simple single room with a shower and sit there, but I didn't feel I could sleep.

Off of Sudder street there's an internet café. I logged in and wrote three emails. One to Diana saying how sorry I was, that I'd done all I could to bring him back and that Johno was coming home with me when I slipped on the bridge and he had tried to save me. The second email was to Nico – I asked him to clear out my stuff, he could keep anything he wanted, could he find a new flatmate, I wouldn't be returning anytime soon. The third email was to my father. This was the hardest to write. I wrote to him of the landscapes I had travelled through, of the people I had met, of the food, culture and sounds I had tried to soak up. I wrote how I was out there to help someone who needed to go back to England, how I had found them, and how we had argued. My father should know the truth I had decided, and so I told him what had happened.

In my inbox I had an email from you, there was a picture in it of your nephew, you held him on the banister of the millennium bridge, the big wheel in the background. You wished me well, asked if I'd like to see the new installation at the Tate. I didn't reply.

Searching for a flight, for a destination, for some kind of future to offer itself to me. Could I head to Thailand, Cambodia, Laos? Those all are popular, I could disappear amongst the expats, the travellers and the beach bums perhaps. There's a flight in the morning to Myanmar – I've never heard of it. I look it up – Burma. I had always believed Burma to be a sort of North Korea with monks. It looked remote. I booked the flight.

Checking my mail Diana has replied, she has sent me a few thousand pounds she says, she wants me to be okay, to get back as soon as possible. There's a ceremony for Johno next week, would I make it she asks.

-

Up in those hills, after the photographer and the policeman had left, I waited a day at the monastery for a representative of the British Consulate to contact me. Three days had passed before their man in India "Brian" had arrived from Delhi in time to hear the long horns playing. There was no mention of

271

their failing to find Johno in the past, nor did they seek to ask me questions about the present.

The older monks and I stood around the body waiting for something to happen. Perhaps Johno's soul would ascend. Perhaps with all the incense and the drone of the horn and the chattering of shuffled beads and chanting his crime might have been washed away. But if the river couldn't clear him of what he'd done this ritual certainly couldn't.

-

Brian was one of those guys that has somehow coasted his way through his whole life, a civil servant with a bulletproof pension retiring in the balmy heat of India where his salary goes a lot further and no one is looking over his shoulder at how he spends his evenings. But here, in the tough-pretty Kingdom of Sikkim he was very much out of his depth. Struggling to adjust, from what I can only guess was a car-to-door-to-car lifestyle of a sub-diplomat doing his Queens duty, to dirt and flint roads and yaks not cows, he seemed distraught, consumed by fear, as if the whole of the Himalayas might chomp him up to and leave him to be buried with Johno. I watched as he paid way too much to local farmers to ferry the body down in a pickup to where he'd arranged another vehicle to take it to Gangtok airport for repatriation. It wasn't Johno in that pickup, it was a bloated deadweight. What was left of Johno after that fateful night at university had slowly, invisibly been eaten away by the guilt, until he had become the man who tumbled me into the water. It wasn't Johno. It just wasn't. They were carrying a corpse alright, but it wasn't Johno. It hadn't been him for a long time. It wasn't, it wasn't, it wasn't.

Brian offered me a lift in the pickup with him. I refused. I watched as he drove away. The body bag kicking up with every bump in the road.

EPILOGUE - BURMESE DAYS

CHAPTER TWENTY-FOUR - BAGAN

I was lost in the backstreets of Nyaung U. The bike no longer had any purchase in the soft sand and I slipped and sled all over the road until I gave up. A woman stopped in the street, her face as worn and beautiful as any temple here. She smiled a big and toothless smile and spat a brilliant French ultramarine jet of paan spit lit in the end of daylight.

I got off the bike and started pushing it through the sand. I couldn't find the main road. Rounding a corner into an alleyway it grew darker, the walls here guiding me somewhere, Like a hedge maze these low concrete walls or fences of briars were hard to navigate. I had torn my long beach shorts earlier in the day so the surfboard on the knee looked cracked in two. This wasn't were I was supposed to be. There were thousands of temples here but I couldn't see any, just the sound of guard dogs, unfinished buildings, the acrid smell of burning plastics and that feeling that not all the Burmese had forgiven us for the past.

I was scared for the first time since I'd come off the mountain. Some travellers had been mugged and had their bikes taken at knifepoint just two nights earlier and I didn't want to be here at dark. I continued pushing the bike and the sand got deeper and the road narrower, the trees more enclosing.

Light ahead and the road moved downwards, I got back on the bike and coasted down the soft sand which turned hard as I got closer to wherever this path was taking me. Stepping off the bike I looked at the river and knew that this is the river they sing of when they sing of the river in Burma, this is the Burmese Nile, Bagan's Thames, Nyang U's Mother Ganges: the Irrawady.

There, backlit by the light on the flickering surface of the river, picked out by the sun as if delivered by forces solar was a woman, her longi falling low on her breasts as she washed herself, open sachets of shampoo on a piece of wood jutted out from the bank. She started to lather her hair, then she saw me, and stared at me. Her hair thick black and oily and her face painted beige with thanaka paste. Her skin was olive, her lips pursed. She seemed not to care that I stood there and stared, I felt that I should leave but where to. Further up the shoreline I could see what looked like a concrete slipway that perhaps might lead out of here, but between me and that was this woman. She turned away from me and let the longi fall down her back to the cleft; and she dipped herself under the water. I was immediately taken back to that apartment, to the sound of bath water on skin. And as this woman surfaced her long her fell about her shoulders and she turned to face me, to confront me and the longi was now all about her waist, and she seemed not to care. Her body was slender, very beautiful, her face rendered by some ancient skilled architect. And in her face I saw every temple carving, every mural, fresco and icon of my travels, and more importantly in her face I saw hope. Hope that I might fall in love again. She pulled her hair taught and squeezed the lather out of it.

I could see another jetty further along with a scooter parked on it, but I'd need to pass by this woman first. I think in that instant what was left of the sunlight for that day glint hard off the surface of the Irrawady and into my heart. It lifted me up.

"Can you pass my sandals" impossibly, in a perfect American accent. I dropped the bike on the floor. I walked her to her scooter. I told her where I was staying. She looked at my bike and told me to come by her cousins' shop the next day and pickup a new bike, an electric one.

"You must be the only person in Burma still on a push bike" she said and giggled.

"Where did you learn.."

"English. Where did you learn English?" she says right back at me.

"School"

"Right."

"See you later"

"See you later."

-

Her name was Pya. Or at least that's how she wrote it. Her dad was ex-military, she'd been educated in Yangon, taught English as a kid. Now she was visiting Bagan, a tourist like me. She was smart, beautiful, so beautiful.

I met her at her cousin's scooter hire shop in Old Bagan, picked up a hot pink scooter that you plugged into a wall socket. Baba would not have approved I thought to myself. This thing was a long way from a Honda.

She let me give her a lift back to the fancy hotel she was staying in outside of town. One of those spa hotels that catered for retired westerners and ex-military Burmese.

Pya asked me to wait outside the front of the building, she came back with a book. It was by Orwell, Burmese Days. She showed me the front cover, an old photo from an era past – a Burmese woman and a British soldier.

"Is this who I am?" she asked.

"No" I said. "Would you like to, to" I didn't finish my sentence. She kissed me on the forehead. In the shadows, out of the light of the hotel frontage.

"I've travelled a lot." She said. Then a call from a child. A young boy runs out and Pya turns and picks him up.

"Shall we meet again tomorrow Matthew?" She asks.

"I'd like that very much." I say.

"Say hello to Matthew." And she holds the boy's hand up to high-five me.

"Hi there kid." I say. And he buries his face in his mums shoulder.

"He's shy." She says, and the two of them walk back into the hotel.

CHAPTER TWENTY-FIVE - DAWEI

A month later, I queue up at the post office to send the stack of postcards. All to one address. There are smiles and laughter from the teller. Everyone in the post office is in high spirits this day. They look the cards over and put them inside a parcel for me. Weigh it out. The teller writes down some Burmese script on the front of the parcel and shows it to me. I point to my head. A woman behind me with a parcel in a barrow leans over me.

"fifty dollars" says the woman and then raises her eyebrows.

"How much for the envelope" And I tug the parcel's paper. The teller holds up one finger. I pay him a dollar for it and take the postcards back out. The woman with the barrow watches me walk out into the tropical heat of the day. Walking from the new post office through the old town carrying the weight of the parcel I know that I need to get rid of it, 'I've met someone new' I had written on the final card, so you'd know that I'd moved on. Amongst the wooden homes, people sat in the shade watching TV. Only an Englishman would be out in this, carrying a parcel of postcards he was never to post.

Further along in the street a man is crouched over a metal dustpan and brush. Besides him is a small fire of plastics and palm fronds. I squat down next to him and point at the parcel and then at the fire. He nods.

The fire takes straight away to the parcel and quickly burns through the hundreds of postcards, impossibly beautiful palm trees, colonial Mandalay, temples of Bagan with enhanced colours of sunset, women in thanaka, fake fisherman on Inle Lake, reclining Buddha's, golden rocks, Yangon's downtown, rural pagodas, city pagodas, women dressed in 20's curls, beaches, mountains, villagers, ships made of gold, and lucky owl after lucky owl.

All of these cards burned up in the small fire. All the scrappy words to explain where I'd been turned to ash. The memories of people and places that I'd met made grey. The man with the dustpan spits a thick red streak of pan into the flames. Toothless he stares at the pictures rocking his head here and there to better see the sites he may never see. He prods at one as it burns – the old railway line of Yangon – rendered into a museum piece by the photographer – it too turns to cinders.

I stand, I'm done. That was my last link to my old life. And this man saved me fifty dollars and you the effort of reading it, or not. I feel lighter on my feet.

On my way back to Pya's house I stop at the bakery, they've cream puffs freshly anointed with squirty cream and chocolate, and big jam donuts. I buy six of each and skip back home.

She greets me with a kiss. "My father, he wants to talk to you, says he wants to understand you better, now that you are here." I kiss her again. I smile.

"Perfect" I say, and then I pass her the bag of pastries. Her eyes go large and she licks her lips at the

I wave goodbye to Pya and the boy, give him a hug, I tell her I'll bring back some water that we are low on and some watermelon for breakfast. I kiss her and she still tastes of the chewing gum. She opens her mouth and blows a bubble with it. I kiss her again.

The heat is more bearable now that the sun is low in the sky. Walk past the clapboard houses, moped repair shops and late night pastry cafes until we run out of town. There's just bugs in the air and the sea to the left, a partly finished boardwalk like the French Riviera continues north up the peninsula.

It takes another fifteen minutes of walking in the dying light and all the while he mumbles at me and smiles and I don't understand.

"I love her very much" I say, trying to make him understand. I smile, and he smiles back and he laughs a little. And I feel good, and although we don't understand each other we get on well, as well as could be expected anyway. I'm a little cold and turn back to look down the street.

"Cold" I say and mime shivering, he smiles, I point back towards the house and add "I want to go back and get a jacket".

He looks at me and smiles again, he points to some flashing lights not far away, he mimes fanning his face and grins, his black teeth ghoulish in the barely-there amber light from the street lamps that run only part of the way along this boardwalk and act mainly as a nursery for budding mosquitoes.

We get to the bar, it's the same as most of the others, gold and green of Myanmar breweries all around. There's more kpop on the television, but the mute sign is visible in the corner overlaid on the five-piece boy band singing their hearts out. Sting's

Fields of Barley is playing but a synthetic version, robotic, with Burmese or Korean over it, I still can't tell. A barbecue grill to the side, toilets out back, a small bar, white plastic garden furniture tables, green Myanmar brewery chairs. Men in leather jackets and sportswear drinking beer and whisky after a long day. Ex army and the repressed drinking alongside one another, but that tension, indefinable, is still here amongst men beyond their teens, they've lost or gained too much to lose now in this peacetime.

We sit at a table, the waitress nods at him, he's well known here. He says something to her and she looks me up and down and nods back to him. She brings peanuts and large litre bottles of beer and I get my roll of bills out and put them on the table and she takes them away bringing back a little change and taking a large and well deserved tip for herself.

Her dad tries to talk to me and I guess that he and I share a joke that neither of us understands. The men continue to try and raise the wrecked fishing boat from the shallows of the rocky sea front. The sun has set. Another bottle of whisky arrives at the table, we drink it with bottled water until our eyes turn red. All the while laughing at the joke. What is the joke. His friends appear, also former soldiers. One of them whistles at the waitress, another slaps her hard on the backside. She orders this friend out. I apologise in English but she rolls her eyes at me, she knows I'm not man enough to stop the guy doing it in the first place but I'll apologise after it. After all this time, all that distance I'm still the same person, still scared of the bigger boys, I'm still the young boy that Diana saw in me when she first asked me to leave for India. Maybe there's no running away from that.

We continue drinking, I order a six Myanmar beers to slow the pace of the whisky drinking. I keep expecting Pya to arrive any time soon, to pick me up, to take me away from all of this, where is she, is she late, what's happened. I'm now really drunk. The men order skewers and her dad drags his brewery-green plastic chair ever closer to me. His breath smells strongly of whisky masking a deeper waft of fish, he grins at me, laughs again. One of his men falls back in their chair pulling the table with him. The whisky bottle smashes and leaks onto the ground. I grab my beer before it also falls to the floor.

The man on the floor is laughing. Her dad is laughing. The waitress has had enough. We all get asked to leave. I pay up with the last of Diana's money. But it doesn't matter. The last money of the old life and the start of the new life.

We leave in a rush. Her dad's leather jacket is covered in leaked whisky. Three of the men carry beer bottles and neck them, throwing the empty bottles in the direction of the fishermen still working on the wreck in the dark - there are screams which must be swearing from the rocks and lumps of wood and massive stones land on the pavement and the men shout back and laugh and we move into the road to evade the stones and I'm almost hit by a moped heading towards town.

And all the while the laughter at the joke I didn't understand. Until, in the hysteria, with the rocks landing around us, mopeds lit and unlit dodging me in the dark, the smell of whisky, the drunkenness, the half-light of a slipper moon I understand.

I grab her father by the face, he breathes his fishy whisky breath all over me. I look at him in the eyes and he laughs. And then, for the first time he speaks in perfect English to me.

"She is gone, back to her husband. You, idiot."

And he looks at me and laughs. I watch him fall down the road with his friends. They throw stones back towards the fishermen and run away into Dawei.

I'm stunned, and cannot move, I don't know where to go, or what to do. I'm stood motionless. And I burst out crying. A figure comes towards me from the shoreline. The boat now raised on the rocks behind them.

And I think back to Varanasi, I also think of our trips together to the coast. And the figure is getting closer. His shorts and t-shirt once white are now black with engine oil and grease. He's seen my distress, he is come to comfort me, he takes me in his arms, and I hug this stranger back, and then I look at his face, a large cut on the side of his head from the glass bottle, his eyes red with drunkenness, his left hand sore with spending the day lifting the boat from the water and his right hand red, red with my blood. He looks at me in horror as he realises that I am not Burmese.

"English?" he demands "Englishman?"

I nod. "Yes" I say. And I hug him and I cry, but this time not for comfort but for support, because he has stabbed me in the side, and I'm having trouble thinking straight. I feel feint. I hold on to the man, I don't want to die alone, not like this. I won't let him go. The man shakes his head at me. He drops the knife to the ground and pulls away from me and then he runs away from me into the darkness leaving me to slump to the floor.

And I fall on my side, and the blood is pissing out of me, and it's sticky and it's warm like chai. I want to be sick. I think of you. I don't want to die alone. Please. And a scooter wheel stops by my head, and from the floor I can see a young boy sat on the front, his mother screams in Burmese, the father gets off the bike and holds my hand as I lie dying. I cry. And he puts his hand over my eyes so I can't see anymore. I cry again and he puts his other hand over my mouth so his son doesn't have to hear a dying man wailing.

I resist at first, but then his hands comfort me.

Drowsiness begins, cold and sleepy, us in bed with the windows open laughing. An afternoon siesta at the beach. The cooling breeze outside a pub in Highbury.

It gets harder to breathe. And the pain hits and I want to scream but his hands now stop me convulsing. He is helping me to die quietly. The stranger starts chanting softly. He is whispering the words to a song, or a poem, it is English and I hear it clearly as I let myself go....

By the ol• Moulmein Pago•a,
lookin' lazy at the sea,
There's a Burma girl a-settin',
an• I know she thinks o' me;
For the win• is in the palm-trees,
an• the temple-bells they say:
"Come you back, you British sol•ier;
come you back to Man•alay! "
Come you back to Man•alay,
Where the ol• Flotilla lay:
Can't you 'ear their pa••les chunkin'
from Rangoon to Man•alay ?
On the roa• to Man•alay,
Where the flyin'-fishes play,
An' the •awn comes up like thun•er
outer China 'crost the Bay!

Note:

In 1906 Joshua Slocum ha• been charge• with raping a 12 year ol•
girl. With frien•s in high places events were 'clarifie•' an• he was put
in jail for in•ecent exposure. Three years after his conviction he set
sail, never to return again.

Printed in Great Britain
by Amazon

53707790R00173